PRAISE FOR
Find Me in the Story

"Bookstore romances always draw me in. This one was no exception. This is perfect for book lovers, too, with interesting glimpses behind-the-scenes into the writing business that fit naturally into the story and add to its authenticity. I'm ready for my next visit to the Island already."

—SHARON, GOODREADS

"I was so excited to get back to Jonathon Island! I'll remember this book for the exploration of integrity. It's not a characteristic that's often discussed in literature and I'd love to see more of it!"

—THE LITERATE LEPRECHAUN, GOODREADS

"Get ready for the best festival of all on Jonathon Island—a book festival!!! You will want to grab all of your books and get them autographed while you are there! There might be some great surprises in store for you during the festival as well."

—KROOS READS AND REVIEWS, GOODREADS

"*Find Me in the Story* is about loss, grief, broken hearts, and healing. Oliver and Eliza make a great couple and complement each other. If you enjoy a contemporary romance read about workplace romance and a bookstore with faith woven into the story, you don't want to miss this one."

—ALLYSON, GOODREADS

"This wonderful romance is about being given a second chance at living, as well as finding refreshment and renewed faith while never forgetting the past, but also realizing it does not have to stymie future growth and/or living. The cherry on top of this story is the festival in this Jonathan Island book is a Book Festival. As a reader, I wanted to join in the festivities. Once again a Jonathan Island book has stolen my day, but I have no regrets for the time I spent devouring this book."

—Tammy, GOODREADS

Find Me in the Story

JONATHON ISLAND • SEASON 2

Find Me in the Story

LISA JORDAN

SUNRISE PUBLISHING

Find Me in the Story
Jonathon Island | Season 2 | Book 1

Published by Sunrise Media Group LLC
Copyright © 2026 Sunrise Media Group LLC

Print ISBN: 978-1-966463-31-3

This book is a work of fiction. Names, characters, places, and incidents are either products of the author's imagination or used fictitiously. Any similarity to actual people, organizations, and/or events is purely coincidental.

Scriptures taken from the Holy Bible, New International Version®, NIV®. Copyright © 1973, 1978, 1984, 2011 by Biblica, Inc.™ Used by permission of Zondervan. All rights reserved worldwide. www.zondervan.com The "NIV" and "New International Version" are trademarks registered in the United States Patent and Trademark Office by Biblica, Inc.™

For more information about Lisa Jordan please access the author's website at the following address: lisajordanbooks.com.

Published in the United States of America.
Cover Design: Sunrise Media Group LLC

In memory of Cheryl Snyder, my beautiful mom,
who instilled my love of reading and championed
my career with love and prayers.

Beautiful words stir my heart. I will recite a
lovely poem about the king, for my tongue is like
the pen of a skillful poet.

Psalm 45:1 NLT

Jonathon Island

JONATHON ISLAND
N
W E
S
Jonathon Family Home
Sullivan Pumpkin Farm
MacBride Resort
Lake Shore Drive
State Park
Sullivan Way
Airport
Jonathon Blvd
Quinn Ranch
Sunset Cove
Barrett House
Sugar Maple Ln
Blueberry Hills Neighborhood
LAKE HURON
Partridge Ln
Dahlia Dr
Lilac Ln
Zinnia Blvd
Poppy Place
Rose Rd
GRAND HOTEL
Blueberry Blvd
Pinnacle Dr
Blueberry Hills Park
MAIN STREET
Downtown
Marina Way
Marina

One

RETURNING TO JONATHON ISLAND HADN'T worked out as well as Eliza Quinn had hoped.

She'd come home two months ago from Pittsburgh to help with her mom's recovery from thyroid surgery, but saying goodbye to her family home was harder than expected, especially the stables where she'd spent much of her childhood.

Midafternoon sunshine warmed her chilled face as she dropped another box on the end of the dray wagon to be taken to her parents' new cottage on Rose Road.

Taking a breath, Eliza stepped inside the whitewashed building with a forest-green metal roof and inhaled the scents of hay, warm animals, and leather to imprint them into her memory.

Her breath puffed out in front of her as she drew her jacket tighter around her middle.

Even though spring had officially arrived yesterday, a mid-March storm had swept across Lake Huron last night and blanketed the northern Michigan island in a light snow.

Pegasus, one of the hard-working, dapple-gray Percherons that lived on island year-round, raised his head and looked at her with his dark eyes as he munched hay from his feeder.

She strode inside, reached over the aged wooden stall door, and rested a gloved hand on his muscled neck. "Hey, Gus. How's it going?"

He lifted his head and nuzzled her hand.

"Sorry, I didn't bring a treat with me."

"That's not like you. You always try to sneak treats to Gus and Ginger."

Eliza turned as Dad crossed behind her and dropped a hay bale on the cold concrete floor. She glanced at Ginger, the other Percheron, whose stall was next to Gus's.

"They work hard and deserve treats."

Dad laughed, the carved lines around his blue eyes deepening as he broke the bale apart and dropped a hay biscuit in each stall.

Tall and lean with more silver than dark brown in his short hair and weathered skin from years working outside, her father exuded a quiet strength she always found comforting. Dust and dirt clung to his faded jeans and knee-high boots he wore while mucking out the stalls.

She moved to him and wrapped her arms around his waist, the top of her head coming to his shoulder. Her cheek brushing against his soft flannel shirt, she breathed in the scents of his hard work. "I'm taking a break from helping Mom pack and heading into town to pick up takeout from Kelley's Bar & Grill. Need anything while I'm out?"

Dad's arms tightened around her as he rested his chin on top of her head. "Want me to hitch up the team and drive you?"

"Nah, I can use the walk after packing boxes."

"You planning to head to the cottage with us after dinner?"

Eliza pulled herself from her father's warm embrace and lifted a shoulder. "We'll see."

Dad studied her a moment. "The move's an adjustment for all of us, but your mom and I don't need such a big house and all of this property, but we still want to keep it in the family. Selling it to Asher and Sadie is the right decision. For all of us." He waved a hand toward the four-bedroom house with a stone exterior and wraparound porch nestled in a grove of leafless sugar maples and pines. "I'm sure you'll come to love the cottage too."

Blinking back tears, Eliza forced a smile. "Asher and Sadie will do great here. It's just hard to say goodbye to the only true home I've known most of my life. Mom's all healed now, so once you're moved into the cottage, I'll figure out what's next now that I'm no longer working as Aunt Sally's assistant. Her generous severance won't last forever."

"I hope you'll consider staying on island." Dad caught her chin and lifted it with the calloused knuckle of his index finger. "Your mom and I are winding down, considering retirement."

Eliza batted her father's chest. "You're not even sixty. I don't think you'll ever retire." She waved a hand toward the stable. "The horses, the stable and livery in town, and now the carriage tour business that Asher and you revived . . . well, it's in your blood."

"Sunshine, it could've been yours too, but you turned us down."

Eliza glanced down at the toe of her Dr. Martens leather ankle boot. "It's not the same without Jared. We talked about running the 3Q Ranch together, but . . ."

"But then he was killed."

"Yeah."

Even though she lost her brother over five years ago in a freak accident, there were days when the grief still felt raw.

She'd left the island and spent five years in Pittsburgh with her aunt while her parents clung to each other.

Eliza pressed a kiss to Dad's whiskered cheek. "Well, I'd better head into town and pick up the pizza and wings from Kelley's.

Then I'm meeting Sadie at the cottage to get the living room re-painted tonight like I promised."

"Thanks, El." Dad's words followed her as she walked out of the stable.

She fished her sunglasses out of her oversized purse and slid them on her nose as she headed down the gravel drive and cut onto Sugar Maple Lane.

She turned toward Henrietta Hudson's white storybook cottage and caught a glimpse of the thawing lake through the bare branches. Seagulls soared over the treetops and circled over the water, their caws echoing in the quietness of the island in its off-season.

The whistling wind picked up and sent a chill down the collar of her white puffer jacket. Her footsteps crunched in the snow as she hurried down Blueberry Boulevard and passed the post office, a small white clapboard building with trimmed hedges crowned with snow. She waved to Herb Easton, the local postmaster.

Ice slid off the roof of the brick and wood-sided police station that sat in front of the island's small firehouse.

Dr. Nova Lake exited the neighboring medical complex and waved to Eliza. Wearing a long gray wool coat and a light pink hat over her dark hair, she held a medical bag in a gloved hand and hurried across the back lot to the Blueberry Hill residential neighborhood down the slope from the businesses.

Feeling her toes turning numb, Eliza picked up her pace and hurried past Dahlia Drive, Lilac Lane, Zinnia Boulevard, and Poppy Place on her right. Her steps slowed as she reached the cute white clapboard cottage with blue trim and covered front porch on the corner of Rose Road and Blueberry Boulevard.

Her parents' new home. A cottage for two. Not three.

Dad loved that it wasn't far from the livery and stables next to the Island House Inn. Mom loved the large lilac in the backyard trimmed with a hedge border, the weathered picket fence, and the promise of wildflower gardens when summer returned.

Blowing out a breath, she headed for Main Street where sunshine glazed the snow-covered cobblestone streets running in front of the Victorian-style businesses.

Thanks to Dani Sullivan's island revitalization project last year, the buildings had been repainted in pastel colors with new striped awnings. Soon, the empty flower boxes would be filled with a kaleidoscope of color.

A cyclist buzzed past as her phone vibrated in her back pocket. She dug it out, bit off her mitten, and thumbed open a text from her aunt.

Aunt Sally
____

Just learned Candace is retiring.
Call me. 😭 😭 😭

Eliza tapped on her aunt's number and held the phone to her ear.

"El, hey. You got my text." Her aunt's voice sounded in her ear along with the sound of papers rustling.

"Hey, Aunt Sally. Sorry to hear about Candace."

"After thirty years together, I have to find a new agent in the next two months since Candace will be done in June." Her aunt's subdued tone stopped Eliza in the middle of the sidewalk. "Would you do some research and see who could be a good fit? I need someone who will put up with me, you know."

"Yes, you are a handful." Even though Eliza laughed, there was some truth to her words. "You do remember I don't work for you anymore, right?"

"Sorry. Old habits." Her aunt's deep sigh caused Eliza to jerk the phone away from her ear. "Kimberly's doing well, but she's not you."

"Auntie, she's your daughter—she'll pick up being your assistant in no time. You're the one who didn't want me working remotely, remember?"

"I know. I know. But you were the best assistant I had." Her aunt's voice resonated in her ear. "I've become spoiled and need someone closer to me."

"Someone to be at your beck and call."

"Exactly. You know me—I like things a certain way. Find a job yet?"

"Still looking and figuring out what's next. Being an author assistant to the multi-published, bestselling Sally Jo Wilson will look good on my résumé." Eliza's eyes watered, but she blamed it on the wind blowing across the lake and biting her cheeks.

Her aunt laughed. "I will give you the highest recommendation."

Eliza perched on the edge of a snowy bench lining the sidewalk in front of Blueberry Hill Park and inhaled the scents of yeast and sugar drifting down Main Street from Good Day Coffee—the best coffee shop on the island—along with grilled burgers from Kelley's Bar & Grill.

Her stomach protested the lack of food as an idea took root. She tightened her fingers around the phone. "What if I became your agent?"

"Girl, what are you talking about? You're not an agent."

"No, but I could be. Since Candace lives on island, I could shadow her and learn how to become one." Eliza shifted on the bench and glanced toward the upscale Driftwood Hills neighborhood along the southwestern shores. Candace Bishop of Bishop Literary Management ran her agency from the comforts of her on-island home. "I have connections with publishers and industry professionals after working for you and attending conferences for the past six years."

"Oh, honey, but is that what you truly want?" Eliza pictured her aunt pacing in front of her standing desk—something she did often when trying to talk someone out of something.

Problem was, Eliza didn't know what she did want.

Eliza blew out a breath that clouded in front of her face. As the chill from the metal bench seeped through her jeans, she stood and crossed the street to Main. "I don't know what I want. Maybe this is it?"

"Are you asking me or telling me?"

She lifted a shoulder, then let it fall as she passed the newly reopened Island Bookstore. A red-and-black Help Wanted sign was taped to the glass.

"I don't know. Until I figure out a new career path, I figured I could take on a couple more authors and become their virtual assistants or something."

"Now, see—to me, that's closer to where your heart lies. You get more excited giving authors the exposure they need rather than learning how to broker book deals."

She sidestepped a sandwich board in front of Doug's Market advertising the daily specials, then turned back toward the bookstore. She stopped in front of the door and inspected the sign.

Part-time work available. Inquire within.

The pizza and wings take-out order could wait another few minutes.

"Aunt Sally, I'll call you back." Without waiting for a response, she ended the call, shoved her phone in her back pocket, then pulled the sign off the glass door. Turning the handle, she stepped inside. Bells jangled against the glass.

The warmth of the room that smelled of paper and something she couldn't quite place blanketed her face. She wiped her boots on the black-and-white patterned runner that stretched across the dark wooden floor to the checkout counter. Soft jazz played through a hidden sound system.

Gray curtains covered the lower half of the storefront windows, allowing light to stream through only the upper half. Pendant lights hanging from the tiled ceiling cast a warm glow over the white brick walls, wraparound wall racks, and multiple rows of chin-high shelves arranged behind a cozy sitting area in front of a lit electric fireplace.

Oliver Sullivan, her friend Dani's older brother, looked up from the register, where he added something to the drawer and closed it. He folded his arms over his chest. "Eliza Quinn. Dani mentioned you were back on island. I haven't seen you in what—ten or eleven years?"

She took in his short, dark-brown wavy hair, sharp, well-defined jawline, high cheekbones lined with dark scruff, and those striking blue eyes. Shouldn't he be wearing a stuffy cardigan or something instead of the black polo shirt tucked into black chinos that emphasized his broad shoulders and flat abs?

She'd always admired her friend's older brother who was going to take the literary world by storm. But he was five years older and definitely off-limits. He probably never saw her as more than Dani's pesky friend.

The Ollie she remembered, though—the one with the windblown hair, easy smile, and quick comebacks—wasn't the one who stood stoically behind the counter and watched her with eyes that had lost their spark.

"Hey, Ollie." She flashed him a wide smile. "The last time I saw you was the summer that the . . . uh . . . you were living on a houseboat—the *Molly Brown*, was it?—with Kyle Munson, your brother Ty, Waylen Barrett, and who was the other guy?"

"Brandon Kelley."

"Right." She fought the cringe that wanted to scrunch up her face and mentally kicked herself for referencing the summer that changed the island forever—the summer the Grand burned.

She waved a hand over the room. "Congrats on the new store.

Heard you and Jonah White took it over once Bob and Lucinda Johnson finally decided to sell."

"Only took 'em fifty years." Hands tucked under his arms, he lifted his chin. "What are you doing with my sign? I just hung that up."

Eliza slapped it on the counter. "I'm the answer to your prayers."

She hadn't expected to stay on island once her parents were settled in their cottage, but seeing that Help Wanted sign stirred something inside of her.

She didn't know what it was, but she couldn't ignore her instincts.

Now to convince Oliver Sullivan he needed to hire her.

Oliver Sullivan knew regret too well.

He wasn't about to let a Help Wanted sign earn a place. Hiring help before the season opened made sense. Get someone trained before business picked up. And Jonah had agreed.

Less than ten minutes after hanging his sign, a dark-haired dynamo blew into his shop like a strong wind and expected to be hired on the spot.

And she'd been the only person in the shop since he opened three hours ago.

"I'm here to save you hours of tedious interviews by giving you the opportunity to hire me right now." Eliza Quinn raised a perfectly arched eyebrow as she leveled him with her brown eyes. "I'm a hard worker. Easygoing. I love books. I can work a flexible schedule. Well, except Sunday mornings—church, you know."

"We're closed on Sundays."

"Even better." She pulled off her white knitted hat with a fluffy pom-pom that released a faint crackle as her hair clung to the fibers, untied the bulky matching scarf, and dropped both on the counter, messing up one of his displays. Then she unzipped her white coat, revealing a yellow hoodie with *Just a girl who loves books* written in some sort of script font. Her dark jeans emphasized her long legs and slight curves.

"And I'm never late. In fact, you should give me a key because I'll probably beat you to work."

He scoffed. Couldn't help it. "Not likely."

She didn't need to know he practically lived at the store . . . or at least above it. His eyes shot to the ceiling, then redirected back to her.

He'd known Eliza and her family since they took over the 3Q Ranch and stables nearly thirty years ago after her grandparents chose to retire. And she used to hang out with his baby sister, Dani, when they were growing up.

Eliza trailed a finger over a round oak table by the checkout counter that highlighted Victor Holt's latest fantasy release, *The Defender*, and then moved and stood in front of the electric fireplace on the right wall and rubbed her hands together. Two armless brown couches held pillows featuring Shakespeare's and Edgar Allen Poe's faces.

She returned to the counter, her footsteps tapping against the polished hardwood floor. "This is a cute place."

He raised an eyebrow. "Cute wasn't the vibe Jonah and I were going for."

"Were you going for dark and tomb-like?" She waved a hand toward the closed curtains. "How can customers see what you have to offer if you close them out?"

"Buttering up the manager won't get you hired any faster."

She looked at him a moment and crossed her arms, hands on her elbows. "I heard about your wife. I'm sorry. Losing someone you love is the hardest thing to endure."

The softness in her eyes arrowed him in the gut. Not pity like so many others. But understanding, maybe?

"Thanks. I heard about Jared. I'm sorry. I always liked your brother."

Nodding, she bit her bottom lip and lowered her head. "Everyone did. He was a great guy." Then she lifted her chin, a wide smile on her face as if the past ten seconds hadn't happened. "So, when do I start?"

"I haven't hired you yet." Oliver moved from behind the counter and leaned against the front of it, ankles crossed.

"Minor detail. When do I start?" She stood in front of him, hands clasped.

He ran a hand down his face. "You're persistent."

"One of my best qualities."

"That's debatable."

"Like your hiring process?" She shot him a grin. "What are you looking for?"

"Someone part-time—"

"I can do part-time." Her words came out in a rush. "In fact, I can start right now, if you want."

He stared at her a moment, then lifted his hands and dropped them back to his sides. "Fine, you're hired. But I can't do paperwork right now. I close an hour early on Saturdays for a children's story time, and they'll be here shortly. You're welcome to stay, and then I can walk you through how things are done."

She jerked a thumb toward the door. "I have to pick up an order from Kelley's and run it back to the ranch. Then I can come back."

He waved a dismissive hand. "No need. Come in on Monday. We open at noon during the offseason."

She grinned as she zipped up her jacket. "Thanks, Ollie. You won't regret it."

He held up a hand. "One rule."

"What's that?"

"Don't call me Ollie."

"But everyone does." She headed for the door and waved. "Bye Ol—Oliver."

Bells clanged against the glass as she closed the door behind her.

He dragged a hand through his hair.

What just happened?

That was the most unconventional interview he'd done. If he could even call it an interview.

Was his quiet bookshop ready for someone like Eliza?

Blowing out a breath, he pushed away from the counter and opened the curtains in front of the windows. Gray light drifted over the empty display platform.

The scent of paper and coffee-scented candles from a display drifted over him as he straightened a carousel of last-minute purchases to catch customers' attention—bookmarks, magnets, and postcards of the island—and the stack of upcoming events that had been messed up when she tossed her hat and scarf on the counter.

He wandered through the rows of books, his Converses tapping lightly against the walnut flooring as he inspected the shelves. He righted a mug on one of the rotating cases that held mugs with quotes from famous authors, bookmarks, highlighters, and sticky notes.

He moved past the fiction section, walked into the side room, and flipped on the light. The woodland theme came to life as air blowing through the heating vents stirred the mobiles of birds hanging from the ceiling. The Kids' Cave, as he liked to call it. His twin sister Kate had used her artistic eye and helped him design it.

A lifelike tree trunk sat in the corner with stuffed squirrels and birds sitting on the limbs while a fox sat at the base next to a colorful mushroom wearing glasses and holding a book. Done in a woodland theme, the room held shelves made of tree bark that lined the walls while several small tables and child-sized chairs sat in the middle on a large, grassy, green area rug.

Oliver crossed to the M-section and pulled out the book he

planned to read, then he set another copy on one of the easels on top of the waist-high shelves.

"Cute book."

His head jerked up, and he found Eliza walking toward him, no hat, and jacket unzipped. "Didn't you have an order to pick up?"

He didn't even hear the door open.

"Mom and Dad took a load to their new cottage and decided to pick it up. Apparently they texted me, but I didn't see it while talking to you. So…" She lifted her arms and dropped them again. "I'm back."

He glanced at her, taking in the brightness of her cheeks, the scatter of freckles across her nose, and the light in her brown eyes.

"I heard they sold the ranch and bought a place on Rose." He tapped the hardback book with the watercolor dust jacket of a battered bear sitting in the grass. "The Teddy P. Bear series is classic. I pre-ordered multiple copies of this one, hoping parents will want copies to take home. I reached out to the author for autographed bookplates, and she sent stickers and an activity sheet to go along with the story. The kids will do those after story time."

"Great marketing strategy. Sounds like she knows what she's doing." Eliza picked up the book he'd set on the easel. "Chrissy Monroe. She's one of Candace Bishop's authors. I met her at the agency retreat last year in Port Joseph that I attended while still working for my aunt."

Oliver lifted a shoulder. "Don't know her. Just emailed when I planned out the books for the month."

His phone vibrated in his pocket. He pulled it out and silenced the alarm that signaled he had five minutes before kids were due to arrive. "Kids will be coming shortly."

He left the Kids' Cave and headed for the front of the store.

The door flew open. He caught it before it could crash into the wall.

Three-year-old Maggie Franklin raced past him, her boots leaving squashed bits of snow in her wake.

He was going to need a mop. Or perhaps that would be a good job for his new employee.

He caught Maggie in his arms, then tapped her on the nose. "Good afternoon, Miss Maggie."

She gave him a heart-melting smile as she pushed her blonde curls away from her face. "Hi, Oliber."

Her five-year-old brother Finn raced past them, then stopped, turned around, and waved. "Hi, Ollie."

Oliver ruffled Finn's dark hair, the little boy looking more and more like his deceased dad every day.

Mia Franklin, their mom and his cousin, followed behind. A blue bandanna wrapped like a headband held back her dark hair. She took Maggie from him and smiled. "Hey, Oliver. How's it going?"

"Can't complain. How's that fiancé of yours doing?"

"Cody's good. Busy getting his fishing business ready for opening season."

Oliver's Aunt Mary came in with her grandson Sam, and Mia gestured that she was heading for the Kids' Cave.

Aunt Mary flicked her usual blonde ponytail over her shoulder, then wrapped an arm around Oliver and gave him a squeeze. "Afternoon, sweetheart."

"Hi, Aunt Mary." He kissed her cheek, then crouched and held out his fist to the little boy with Down syndrome. "Hey, Sam. How's it going?"

Shrugging, Sam adjusted his glasses, then gave him a rather wimpy fist bump.

Oliver ruffled the little boy's red hair, then Sam shuffled toward the kids' section as if he carried the weight of the world on his tiny shoulders.

Aunt Mary tracked her grandson's movements. "Don't mind

Sam. He's been having a rough go of it since he and Ethan returned on island. But he did want to come to story time."

"Maybe he'll feel better after he hears the story."

The door opened again, and Ivy Dawson, owner of Hair Haven Salon, walked in holding hands with her seven-year-old daughter, Zoey. Their matching strawberry blonde hair had been arranged in the same sort of messy bun. Zoey's bangs covered her forehead, while Ivy had loose hairs framing her face.

"Well, if it isn't the Dawson ladies." Oliver smiled at Ivy, then crouched in front of Zoey. "I have a new book, and I think you're going to like it."

Ivy rested a manicured hand on his shoulder. "You sure it's not a problem? I have a quick blowout, then I'll be back to get her."

Oliver pushed to his feet and smiled at the struggling single mother. "Ivy, you ask me the same question each week. It's fine. We'll take good care of Zoey."

Ivy pressed a kiss to Zoey's cheek, then opened the door. She breezed through, then held it for Iris and Violet, six-year-old twins, who drifted over to him as they raced through the door ahead of Doug Manning, their grandfather and owner of the market next to the bookstore.

"Hi, girls." Oliver smiled at them as they shot past him, then nodded to the older man. "Hey, Doug."

"Hey, Ollie." He finger-combed his brown hair that had been teased by the wind. Then he wiped his thick glasses with the hem of his green Doug's Market T-shirt and put them back on his face. "The wind's pretty strong today. More snow is coming."

Shaking his head, Oliver took Zoey's hand and followed them into the other room.

He was ready for snow to be gone for good, but living on island for a large chunk of his life had taught him the weather was as unpredictable as the islanders themselves.

He glanced at Eliza, who chatted with Mia.

"Okay, guys. Grab a rug and have a seat."

The twins chose matching flower rugs, which didn't surprise him. He and Kate, his twin sister, older by eight minutes, made a lot of the same choices. Maggie chose a squirrel while Finn chose a fish. Again, not surprising considering Cody's influence over the boy. Zoey chose a mouse and kept her distance. Fitting for the quiet child.

Sam, on the other hand, didn't want to sit with the other kids in a lopsided semicircle in front of Oliver's green reading chair. Instead, he leaned against Aunt Mary and kept his head on her shoulder.

Oliver settled in his chair and pulled out a tattered and matted teddy bear from the basket next to him. "This is Teddy P. Bear. He's very special and well loved. But there was a time when Teddy did not feel loved, and that's what our story is going to be about today. Can you tell me about a time when you didn't feel loved? Or when you felt forgotten?"

He waited patiently while the kids shared their moments. Zoey didn't like it that her mommy had to work so much. Finn grew serious, mentioning not having his dad around for his birthday.

Then his face lit up. "But now I have Cody. And he's awesome. Right, Mom?"

Mia smiled and nodded, but Oliver still caught a shadow that flashed across her eyes.

A shadow he knew all too well.

Unfortunately, grief remained a constant reminder, no matter how much a person tried to move past it.

"Today's book is called *The Day Teddy P. Bear Got Left Outside*. And it's written by Chrissy Monroe. Who can tell me what we call a person who writes books?"

Violet's hand shot into the air. "An author."

"Very good, Violet."

For the next ten minutes, he read the story and paused to answer questions or listen to their comments.

He caught Zoey's eye and raised the book. "Did you like the story, Zoey?"

The little girl shook her head. "I didn't like it."

His heart squeezed at the sad look in her eyes. "Well, I'm going to find a story you do like. Wait and see."

The same conversation they'd had every week for the past month since he started the reading program.

Directing the kids to the small tree trunk tabletops, Oliver pulled little metal pails of crayons and colored pencils out of his supply closet. He shared the stickers and activity pages.

Eliza moved away from the doorway where she'd been standing while he read. "Well, that was the most fun I've had on a Saturday afternoon since returning on island."

Her praise warmed something inside of him. "Glad you enjoyed it. I do it every Saturday. A lot of parents read to their kids, which is great because it's one of the fundamental building blocks to their education, but I like to offer additional opportunities where they can socialize with other kids and be exposed to learning opportunities the bookstore has to offer."

"Oliver Sullivan, who would've thought?"

He scowled. "What's that supposed to mean?"

Eliza lifted a shoulder. "Nothing. Just surprises me that you're aware of that."

"Meaning what?"

Her cheeks darkened to a light pink. "Well, not many single guys know much about early learning foundations."

He wasn't single by choice.

Eliza didn't know the half of it.

Not many guys spent six months of their late wife's pregnancy reading daily to their unborn child so he could be the father his kid deserved.

Not that it mattered now.

Grief had a way of rewriting this chapter, no matter how carefully he planned the story.

Two

THE BEST PART OF HIS WEEK ALWAYS ENDED too quickly.

Once the last child left, Oliver returned the crayons and colored pencils to the supply closet. Eliza gathered the leftover stickers and coloring pages.

"Thanks." He set them on a shelf in the closet, closed the door, and flicked off the lights in the Kids' Cave. He turned to Eliza, who moved to the doorway. "I'll have paperwork ready for you on Monday."

He brushed past her, and she followed him to the front of the store. She retrieved her jacket from behind the counter, put it on, shouldered her tote bag, and waved. "Thanks again. See you on Monday."

As soon as she exited, Oliver closed the curtains in the display window and turned the Open sign to Closed.

As he was about to flip the deadbolt, Dani, his younger sister, appeared at the door and pressed her way in.

"We're closed. Didn't you see the sign?"

"It's as dark as a cave in here." She flicked on the overhead lights and glanced at the clock on the wall behind the register. "It's not even four. How can you close so early? That's no way to run a business, Ollie."

He gritted his teeth against the use of that ridiculous childhood nickname. "I've had two customers all day. Besides, I'm the manager. I can close when I want."

"Fine. Gives us more time to talk."

"About what?"

She leveled him with a look as she unzipped her winter coat, revealing a light-blue hoodie with the Tourism Bureau logo. "You know what. I texted this morning and said I'd be by this afternoon to discuss the booklovers' festival. I planned to be here sooner, but then Zach called about the catering for my wedding. By the time I got off the phone with him, someone walked into the Tourism Bureau needing directions."

"How's our brother, by the way?"

"Still grumbling about his job and fighting with Chef Louie. Zach is destined for bigger and better things than a restaurant in Chicago. I'm trying to talk him into entering the island cook-off competition this summer. Listen, Ollie, about the book festival—" Dani put on her serious "tourism director" face.

"I'm not doing the festival."

"Why not? I signed you up already."

"Without asking me first. I've never even organized a card game. How will I coordinate an entire book festival?" Oliver waved a hand over the now quiet store. "And I have a business to run."

"A business that's failing if you don't do something soon." Dani raised an eyebrow and rested her hand on her hip. "You've been open a month, and you've barely sold any books. Mom and Aunt Elise are your best customers."

"You don't know that."

"Seriously, Ollie? You're not denying it."

"A lot of businesses struggle at first."

"And coordinating and hosting the festival will help you to go from barely surviving to thriving. Besides, it's only a few days—Thursday night to Saturday morning." She tugged on the sleeve of her light-blue winter jacket, then tossed her long blonde braid over her shoulder. "And I wouldn't ask if it weren't so important. Liam's getting on me to stop spreading myself so thin. And with the wedding coming up . . ." Her words trailed off as her shoulders sagged.

"Dani, are you sure the island is ready for more festivals? Are they even necessary? Sure, there were a lot growing up, but the island's changed since . . . well, it's changed. And it feels too early. The ice just started melting and the ferries aren't even running on a regular schedule yet. And why have it so close to your wedding date? The closing brunch is that same morning. That's just crazy."

"We had great success with the few we did last year. We need to remind the tourists that we're here and open for business. I put a lot of planning into reviving the island and bringing everyone back together." She gestured toward the nearly empty street. "I planned this year's festivals last year before Liam proposed. We decided to get married before the season opened because of how busy I am already at the Tourism Bureau. As it is, I have to dive into the Apple Blossom Festival right after our brief honeymoon to Napa. So if you aren't willing to do it, then I'll find someone else." Dani crossed her arms over her chest and jutted out her chin.

He gripped the back of his neck.

She looked up with those big green eyes that tugged at him . . . just like they did when she was a kid. Imploring her big brother to do something for her.

And like his past interactions with her, he couldn't say no.

Maybe, just maybe there was hope for the store . . . if they could hold on for another month. But man, coordinating a festival was not in his wheelhouse.

"Listen, Ollie, if you funnel the festival through the bookstore, then it'll generate more income with book sales and increase exposure."

Oliver scrubbed a hand over his chin. "That's all well and good, but I'll need to determine the logistics—coordinating authors, setting up signings, getting the local businesses involved, and figuring out what type of engagement we want."

"See, you're thinking like a coordinator already." Dani grinned, then bit her lip as she gave his arm a little tug. "Does this mean you'll do it?"

He put his hands on her shoulders and gave them a little squeeze. "You, of all people, deserve time to focus on your wedding. Because of you, more people are visiting again. I need to run this by Jonah and get his input, but it's late in Germany. I'll give you an answer on Monday."

The light dimmed in Dani's eyes, but she flashed him a smile anyway. "Meet me at the Tourism Bureau at nine a.m. on Monday, and we'll work out the details." Then she gave him a hug and headed out the door.

He stood there a moment and viewed the late-afternoon busyness on Main Street. Hooves clopping, voices talking, and children's laughter penetrated the glass.

Oliver locked the door, turned out the lights, then headed through the shop and down the short hall. He opened the last door on the left and stepped into his office.

Reaching above his wooden executive desk, he turned off the mellow jazz music that streamed through the shop.

Identical black square frames containing typed first lines of some of his favorite novels written by Mark Twain, Madeleine L'Engle, Ursula K. Le Guin, F. Scott Fitzgerald, and Victor Holt lined the walls painted the color of old parchment.

His vintage Remington typewriter sat on top of an old oak bookshelf that had once belonged to his grandfather, the former journalist who inspired him to become an editor.

His former colleagues could have their black industrial decor, but Oliver preferred wood and traditional furnishings.

You're an old soul, Ollie, and I love you for it.

Melody's voice filtered unhindered through his thoughts before he had time to capture it and keep it locked in his memory bank, where it needed to stay. Safer that way.

His eyes flickered to the photo in a wooden frame sitting next to his monitor. He picked it up and ran his forefinger over his late wife's face. In the photo, his hands cupped her swollen belly as she smiled up at him. Her cherry red lipstick should've clashed with her strawberry blonde hair, but somehow it made her even more beautiful and accentuated the short-sleeved cherry-printed dress she wore.

Gone too soon.

Her and their unborn baby.

Blinking back a sheen of wetness, Oliver returned the photo, but then his hand hit the monitor, and the frame fell down the gap between his desk and the wall.

He wrestled the memory back where it belonged, turned off the light, and closed the door.

He headed up the back steps to the second floor. The left door opened into the apartment of Bronte Parker, Jonah's girlfriend, while Oliver's smaller unit was on the right.

Oliver unlocked the door and stepped inside, his nose twitching at the scents of fresh paint and wood. The door closed, echoing in the nearly empty space.

He turned on the light.

Even though Dani had invited him to crash on her couch, he'd wanted his own space so he could work on it after closing the store for the day.

Drop cloths covered a large section of the old floor still needing to be redone. Paint cans, trays, and washed brushes sat on the counter separating the living room from the kitchen. He walked around the boxes of laminate flooring stacked in the middle of the room.

The white oak flooring would go well with the textured off-white walls he'd painted a couple of days ago . . . despite Dani's and Kate's opinions that the space needed more color.

He was a dude who liked basic things. He didn't need the pops of color they recommended, like a soft yellow. What did that even mean?

It wasn't like anyone other than family would see the place anyway. Even then, that time would be limited now that Dani, the queen of hospitality, would have her own place with Liam once they got married.

Even with Dani's upcoming wedding, Dad and Oliver's brother James would stay at the Grand. Oliver's other brother Zach would probably bunk on their younger brother Tyler's boat. Oliver's older sister Ashley and his nephew Benny would probably stay with Mom while Kate, his twin, crashed at Dani's.

He dropped on the chair he'd taken from downstairs, and his foot brushed against his air mattress—the only two pieces of furniture in the place. A few books sat on top of an overturned cardboard box—a handyman's manual, a Graham Lee novel he'd just finished, and an illustrated copy of *Pride and Prejudice* that he'd given to Melody for her last birthday and she'd challenged him to read.

He hadn't cracked it open in three years, not since receiving the news she'd been killed.

Three months ago, he packed up his shell of an apartment where he lived after selling the house he and Melody bought two years before her death, put his furniture in storage, then crashed on

Dani's couch until he opened the bookstore. Then he moved upstairs and started working on his apartment.

He fished out his phone and texted a message to Jonah.

Oliver
____

Hey. Something's come up. Let me know when's a good time to talk tomorrow.

A moment later, his phone chimed, signaling a video call.

He accepted the call, and Jonah, his bookstore partner and longtime friend, appeared on the screen. A blue scrub cap covered his military-short dark hair, and a mask hung around his neck. "Hey, man. How's it going?"

"Dude, this can wait until tomorrow."

Jonah pulled the scrub cap and mask off and tossed them in the trash. He jerked a thumb over his shoulder. "Just got out of surgery. Figured I'd call and talk while heading back to the barracks. I have about five minutes before I need to grab some chow then hit the rack. Just finished removing shrapnel from a nineteen-year-old soldier's leg. I'm beat."

"Night, Major." A soldier dressed in fatigues saluted as he passed by Jonah in a brightly lit hall.

Jonah returned the salute. His eyes bore dark circles of not enough sleep. He dragged a hand over his face. "So, what's up?"

"Sorry, man. That's tough. If you want to talk tomorrow, I get it."

"No, we can do it now."

"Okay, I'll make this quick." Oliver shared about the festival.

Jonah's phone bounced as he walked out of the Army hospital. Darkness shrouded his surroundings. "Sounds doable. So what's your beef with it?"

Oliver stared at the guy who used to spend Saturday mornings with him at the bookstore when they were kids as they pored over Mr. Johnson's impressive comic book collection.

He considered his words a moment, then said, "It's a lot to take on, especially with getting the store up and running. And in thirty days, no less."

"Listen, life's about taking risks. We bought the store, knowing it was a risk. It just opened. Who knows what great things the Lord has in store for it? And for us. Do the festival. Let's do a grand opening at the same time. You've got this, man. The bookstore's going to be a success, but you've got to go all in and take advantage of this opportunity to show people what we're about."

Partnering with Jonah had been a lifeline after his small press business crashed and burned, but Oliver didn't want his past failures to affect what could be a solid venture.

Maybe that's where he needed to focus his time and energy—redefining what success meant to him.

"Listen, I'm being paged and need to head back to the hospital. Looks like chow and rack time will have to wait. I left the bookstore in your capable hands. Don't screw it up."

Jonah gave him a laid-back two-finger salute and ended the call, leaving Oliver to stare at his own reflection in the black screen.

He had a bookstore to run, and a festival *was* the best way to drum up new business.

Time to get to work and make it happen.

His phone chimed again. This time, a text from his twin sister, who lived in Benton Harbor, Michigan, flashed on the screen.

Kate
____

Just talked to Dani. Heard you're
taking over the festival. You good?

He texted back.

Oliver
____
Fine. Just fine.

He pushed out of the chair and flopped belly-first on the air mattress.

Yeah, he was fine, all right. Absolutely fine.

Eliza needed to figure out her future.

Getting hired at the bookstore had been unexpected but still felt right. At least for now, the part-time job would be enough until she decided what to do next.

Her comment to her aunt about becoming an agent tried to take root, but Eliza wasn't sure if that was what she truly wanted to do.

Deciding her future needed to wait a few hours because she'd promised to have the cottage's living room walls painted tonight. That way, they'd be dry by morning, and her parents could move furniture in tomorrow after church.

She needed to dig in and finish what she'd started.

She dipped her small brush into the plastic paint cup she held in her left hand and cut a line of Natural Linen paint along the edge of the stained wooden window frame, careful not to get paint on the trim.

The neutral color added light and warmth to the room and contrasted well with the dark hickory original flooring with its unique knots, grain patterns, and color variations, and covered the faded rose from the previous owners.

Pop music streamed softly through Eliza's phone propped on the windowsill. The scent of fresh paint filled the air, combating the staleness from the cottage being closed up.

"Okay, this wall is done." Sadie Quinn, her cousin's wife of only a few months, pushed to her feet, the drop cloth covering the hardwood floor swishing behind her. She pressed the backs of her wrists against her hips while she surveyed her work.

Standing a couple of inches shorter than Eliza's five feet seven, Sadie's dark hair had been twisted and clipped in place to keep it out of the paint. A few tendrils escaped and framed her face. Then she turned and looked at Eliza with bright blue eyes and smiled, dimple creasing her cheek. Streaks of paint smeared her faded jeans with holes in the thighs and the hem of her long-sleeved red T-shirt with #SEO across the chest.

She pointed to the other wall. "Want me to paint that one now that you cut in around the trim?"

"Sure, that would be great. Thanks again for helping. I can't believe they're hoping to be settled in here by the end of the month. I'm sure you and Asher are looking forward to having the ranch all to yourselves."

Sadie held up a finger. "First, I love painting, so thanks for asking me." She held up another finger. "Second, just because your parents are moving into the cottage, that doesn't mean you have to leave the ranch. Asher and I would love to have you stay."

Sadie grabbed a corner of the drop cloth and dragged it across the floor. She refilled her paint tray and then wiped her hands on a wet rag they'd been sharing for spills.

"You guys are still newlyweds and need your privacy. I'll figure out where I belong soon enough."

Or at least she hoped so.

Eliza finished the left side of the window and bent backward to release the tightness in her lower spine and glanced at the time on her phone. "I thought Dani would've been here by now."

Sadie thunked the heel of her hand against her forehead. "Oh, I forgot—she texted me while Asher was driving me over in the golf cart and said she was running late. She had to swing by the bookstore and talk to Ollie about something."

"Oh!" Eliza's head jerked up. "Speaking of the bookstore . . . I got a job there today. It's only part-time but something until I figure out what's next."

"You did?" Sadie eyed her. "Does that mean you're staying on island?"

Eliza added more paint to her brush. "I don't know. Honestly,

I've felt a little lost since leaving my job as Aunt Sally's assistant and returning to help Mom. I'll stay until they get settled here, then figure out what to do. Aunt Sally mentioned her agent is retiring, so I may talk to Candace Bishop and see what it takes to become one." She shrugged. "I really dislike feeling so unsettled, but at least working at the bookstore will help pad my bank account until I can decide what to do."

"Listen, I get it. I came back late last summer to help Gran after her hip surgery. I was working remotely, but coming back to the island brought me to Asher. So who knows—you might meet someone special on island."

Eliza laughed and glanced out the window toward the empty street. "I doubt that, but I'm glad your situation from last summer turned around. Now you and Asher are married." She swallowed a sigh as she cut her brush around the corner of the frame.

"There's a man out there for you. I just know it. I've been to the bookstore a couple of times since it opened. A little darker than I remember from my summers spent with Gran, but Ollie's been great helping me find books I needed."

"Don't you mean *Oliver*?" She enunciated his name, then shook her head and rolled her eyes.

"Why do you say that?"

Fisting a hand on her hip, Eliza took a breath and recited her earlier conversation with her new boss. "What's up with him anyway? He's been Ollie for decades, and now, all of a sudden, he makes up this rule that I have to call him Oliver."

Sadie paused painting and looked at Eliza with serious eyes. "You know about his wife, right?"

"He was engaged the summer the Grand burned, and that's really the last time I'd seen him on island. I kind of fell out of touch with island news and didn't really know when he got married, but Mom mentioned something about him losing his wife."

Sadie rolled a swath of paint on the wall. "Dani said Oliver and his wife went to college together, interned at the same publishing company, and ended up scoring editor positions for different lines. When his wife was pregnant with their first child, she and their unborn daughter were killed in some freak accident."

Eliza sucked in a breath. "When was that?"

"About three years ago, I think."

Eliza turned back to the wall and puffed out her cheeks as unexpected tears rushed to her eyes, her mood subdued. Her brush blurred as she trailed it along the edge of the window. "A tragedy like that would change anyone. I'd assumed he'd gotten married off island and took the literary world by storm like he'd always wanted." She swallowed the thickening in her throat, then faced her cousin-in-law. "Instead, the fun-loving, lighthearted Ollie I knew disappeared, and this broody, grumpy Oliver emerged in a Rochester sort of way."

Sadie sat cross-legged on the drop cloth and set her roller back in the tray. She rubbed dried paint off her finger. "Explains so much, doesn't it?"

Eliza took in the sadness on her friend's face and set her paint cup on the windowsill. She moved to the drop cloth, sat next to her, and wrapped an arm around her shoulder.

Neither she nor Sadie were strangers to grief, both having lost siblings in the same accident.

The doorbell rang, and Eliza jumped to her feet, nearly sliding on the drop cloth, eager to drop the funk that descended on the room.

She opened the door and found Dani Sullivan bouncing on the balls of her feet on the white covered porch. She cupped her gray mittened fingers around her mouth.

"Hey, Dani. Glad you could make it. Get in here so you can warm up."

"Thanks. I wouldn't be surprised if we got more snow tonight."

"Welcome to spring on island." Eliza held the door as Dani

passed by. She untangled her scarf and shrugged out of her winter jacket.

She flipped her long blonde braid over her shoulder and stepped out of her wet boots, revealing white socks covered with Eiffel Towers all over them.

Eliza waved toward the living room. "Sadie's here, and we're nearly done, but we'd love the company."

"Sorry I'm so late. I had to swing by the bookstore and talk to Oliver, then head back to the Tourism Bureau and finish up a few things. Time got away from me." She waved to Sadie. "Hey, friend."

Sadie smiled, then jerked her head toward Eliza. "Since you were at the bookstore, did your big brother tell you about his new employee?"

"Employee?" Dani frowned. "No, it didn't come up. Who'd he hire?"

Sadie pointed her roller over Dani's head. "Eliza."

Dani whirled around, her green eyes wide. "Are you serious? When did this happen?"

Eliza lifted a shoulder. "This afternoon. Saw his Help Wanted sign and kind of sort of demanded that he hire me."

Dani threw her head back and laughed, the sound bouncing in the empty room. "That's awesome." Then she clasped her hands together and held them close to her chest. "Sooo, that means you can help with the festival."

Eliza shrugged. "What festival?"

Shaking her head, Dani sighed. "That brother of mine. Of course he didn't mention it. The booklovers' festival next month. A couple of days before my wedding, actually. When Ollie opened the bookstore, I signed him up to coordinate the festival, but he's been dragging his feet. Now we're getting down to the wire."

Eliza moved past her friend and picked up her paint cup. She dipped the brush into the paint and cut another line of Natural

Linen along the other side of the window. "I can't imagine Oliver coordinating a festival."

"That's what he says too, but he was in publishing, and now he runs a bookstore. Makes perfect sense. Now that you're working for him, maybe you'd be willing to help?"

At her friend's questioning tone, Eliza glanced over her shoulder and found Dani looking at her with those wide eyes she used to get what she wanted. "D, I haven't officially started working for him yet. He may even change his mind about hiring me by Monday."

"Why would he do that?" Sadie handed Dani a clean paintbrush and a blue paint cup. "Here, paint around Eliza's cut lines so I can roll paint on the wall without messing up the trim."

Dani took the brush and cup and moved to the opposite side of the window from Eliza. "El, I think you'll be a great asset to the bookstore . . . and the festival. Especially after hearing about the events you planned for your aunt in the past."

"I think you will be too." Sadie shot her a pointed look. "And you just said you needed something to do."

"You two are a bunch of parrots." Eliza laughed. "Okay, okay. I'll talk to Oliver about the festival."

"Great! I have a meeting with him at nine a.m. on Monday at the Tourism Bureau. Join us."

It wasn't a request but more of a command. Still, Eliza found herself nodding. "Sounds good."

She set up the ladder next to the window, then climbed up to cut around the top of the frame. "So, you think Oliver can handle this festival?"

"With you in his corner, he can. Besides, I'm only a text or call away." Dani set her brush on top of her paint cup and shifted until she stood in front of the windows that overlooked the intersection of Rose Road and Jonathon Boulevard.

She waved a hand toward the snow-covered cobblestone street. "The island needs this festival to happen. All of the festivals I have planned for the year—the Apple Blossom Festival, the Flavor Fest and cooking competition, the Theater Festival, the Sip and Sail Festival, the Harvest Festival, just to name a few, and I've even put in a call to my cousin Ariel and Miss Dahlia to see if they'd be willing to do a benefit concert."

"Having two mega country superstars will be a guaranteed draw. The island was packed last year when Miss Dahlia came for the Summer Sunset Music Fest." Sadie wiped the back of her wrist across her forehead, pushing hair out of her eyes. "Asher loved closing out the concert with her last year when they sang 'Amazing Grace.'"

"See, the festivals bring the island to life, and we need that if our small businesses like the bookstore are going to thrive." Dani's eyes grew serious. "To be honest, without this festival, I don't know if Ollie's store will make it. And without that, I don't know what he'd do."

"Other than correct people about his name, you mean?" Eliza spoke the words under her breath.

Okay, maybe she wasn't being fair. Especially after their conversation about his loss.

But then Eliza remembered the way his face lit up during story time. The way he engaged the kids. The way she used to browse the aisles for hours while growing up on island.

So yeah, she'd do whatever she could to ensure the festival was a success.

"I used to love going to the bookstore when the Johnsons had it. Lucinda always found a book I hadn't read yet and saved it for me. My dad used to joke he'd need a second job to support my reading habit." As the sweet memories filled her head, Eliza sighed and dipped her brush into the paint. She swiped another stroke of color onto the wall, the brush bristles scratching lightly against the surface. "Oliver has that same passion for story. He read a story to a handful of kids this afternoon, and he really got into it. It was fun to see that side of him."

"Oh, really?" Sadie raised a brow, amusement flickering in her eyes.

Shaking her head, Eliza pointed the brush at her. "Don't get any ideas. He's my new boss."

"Believe me, romance is the last thing on my brother's mind." Dani paused her painting and looked at Eliza. "I just had a thought. Well, it was something that Sadie said a moment ago that triggered it—how big names draw people in. What about your aunt? I'm sure readers would flock to the island to meet the legendary Sally Jo Wilson."

Eliza smiled. "I could call and ask if she'd be willing to participate." She nodded toward the small half bath off the kitchen. "I'll wash my hands and give her a call now."

After washing her hands, Eliza called her aunt. While waiting for her to answer, she folded the ladder and tucked it out of the way.

"Hey, El. What's up?"

"Hey, Aunt Sally, I have a quick question for you." She explained about the bookstore job and the booklovers' festival. "Would you be interested in participating in the festival?"

"When is it?"

"In three weeks." Eliza bit the corner of her lip as she exchanged looks with the two girls.

"Wow, why so soon?"

She shared the conversation with Dani with her.

"So you're doing it on your own?"

"No, I'll be working with Oliver Sullivan."

"Ollie! How is he? I always did like him. Such a nice young man with a level head on his shoulders. Although I don't like what his business partner did to my friend Constance."

"Constance King?"

"Yes, that slimy Dennis Wahl took advantage of her. Stole her rights to a movie deal and money that was owed to her. But then Oliver stepped in and got everything back for her. This industry … I'm telling you—it can chew up good people."

Whoa.

Eliza didn't know what to do with that information, but she'd certainly try and process it later. "Oliver's fine. He and Jonah White bought the Island Bookstore from the Johnsons and re-opened last month."

"I remember Martha Kelley mentioning that. We chat about once a month, and she catches me up on the island gossip."

"Well, gossiping is one of Martha's superpowers. I'm sure she hears plenty at her restaurant. If you're on board, then we'll have a huge draw right away."

"You know how much I love meeting my readers. Count me in."

Anything to be the center of attention. One of the many ways Eliza and her aunt were polar opposites. Yet, somehow, they'd made it work for five years.

"You're a natural. I'll send details to you and Kimberly once we finalize them." Eliza ended the call and thrust a fist in the air. "We have Sally Jo Wilson!"

Dani and Sadie cheered and high-fived her. "Way to go."

Sadie grabbed her hand. "I think you're right where you're meant to be."

Folding her arms in front of her, Eliza gazed out the window and watched snowflakes drift in the lamplight.

Maybe remaining on island wouldn't be so bad after all.

Helping with the festival felt like a step in the right direction, and hopefully her new boss felt the same way.

But they had only three weeks to pull everything together.

Three

EVEN THOUGH SO MANY THINGS WERE CHANGing right now, Eliza was than   was the one place on island where she'd always felt she could just be.

Today was no different.

Eliza slid her arms into the sleeves of her white winter coat, grabbed her Bible and purse off the wooden pew, and followed her parents down the middle aisle toward the back of the sanctuary. Arched stained-glass windows behind the wooden pulpit and along the side walls scattered jewel tones of light across the scarlet carpet.

She waved at Dani Sullivan and Liam Stone, who talked with Dani's Uncle Seb, who was also the island mayor, his wife Elise, and Dani's mom Becky MacBride, who was also Seb's younger sister.

She shook hands with Pastor Arnie Chamberlain, who had taken over the pulpit when Augo Kennedy retired a number of years ago. "Thanks for the sermon, Pastor Arnie."

"You're welcome, Eliza. Remember—the Lord always meets our

needs." Dressed in a dark-gray suit, the trim fiftysomething man with red hair, who modeled what he preached, smiled.

Eliza turned to his wife, Tara, whose silver-blonde hair had been pulled back into an elegant French twist. She wore a long-sleeved white sweater, gray slacks, boots, and a silver heart pendant. "Good to see you again, Tara."

Tara placed a hand on Eliza's arm. "You too, Eliza. Let us know how we can help with the move."

Not "do you need help" but the expectation to be called to serve.

Yes, that described the Chamberlains.

Eliza stepped outside, and the cold sweeping across the lake nearly stole her breath. She pulled up the collar of her coat to ward off the wind spilling down her back.

Her cousin Asher and Sadie stood on the sidewalk talking to Henrietta Hudson, Sadie's grandma. Sadie left the group and met up with her. "Hey, mind if Ash and I catch a ride back to the ranch?"

Eliza eyed Gus and Ginger, hitched to the polished black touring carriage with the hard top, metal wheels, two benches, and coachman's box, and nodded. "Of course. Dad brought just Mom and me today."

"Great." Sadie looped an arm around her shoulders and squeezed. "Thanks. Gran, Mom, and Dad are going to check on Jacob Kennedy, who hasn't been in church for the second week in a row. Augo mentioned his older brother wasn't feeling great, so since Jacob and Grandpa Hank used to be pals, Gran's been keeping an eye on him."

Eliza glanced at the Island House Inn next to the church. "I remember. I hope Mr. Kennedy is okay."

Asher held his wife's hand while she stepped into the carriage. With his short dark hair, brown eyes, and square jaw, when he turned just right, he reminded her of her older brother Jared. Too much. The cousins had been mistaken for brothers more than once. Except now Asher wore a beard that covered the faded scars on the left side of his jaw and neck.

He helped Eliza's mother into the carriage, then held his hand out to Eliza.

"Thanks, Ash. You're such a gentleman."

"Well, your dad's right there, so I have to put on a good show." He winked at her.

She laughed as she settled on the bench next to her mom and shared the soft fleece blanket that covered their legs.

Mom sighed and leaned her head against the side of the carriage cover.

"You okay, Mom?"

Her dark-brown wavy hair threaded with silver had been pulled back into a ponytail and emphasized her lovely cheekbones and green eyes. She smiled. "Just a little tired. Nothing a nap after lunch won't cure."

Dad climbed into the coach box, checked to ensure his passengers were comfortable, then flicked the reins and guided Gus and Ginger up Blueberry Boulevard toward Sugar Maple Lane.

As the carriage bumped over the cobblestones, Mom leaned closer to Eliza and gave her arm a gentle squeeze. "Becky MacBride mentioned you were helping with the upcoming festival."

"Dani came by to paint last night and invited me to help Oliver since I'll be working at the bookstore."

Mom squeezed her arm. "I'm glad you're staying, honey. At least for now." She waved a hand toward the rows of houses. "It'll be good to see the island come back to life again. We got a taste of it late last year, and it gives us hope for what's to come. Do you think you can handle coordinating a festival?"

"Of course. I've organized book signings, writers' retreats, and conference get-togethers for Aunt Sally, despite her worry that I couldn't pull them off. The festival is simply a series of events handled one at a time. Plus, Dani said she'd be only a call away."

"It is a large undertaking, but I know you'll do well. Your dad and I stopped in the bookstore a couple of times. Oliver was always so welcoming and quick to help us find what we needed."

"Last night, I couldn't sleep, so I started thinking about a new online marketing campaign. Can you believe the bookstore doesn't even have a website? In today's technological age, that's almost unheard of."

"Honey, remember where we are. That's not unheard of for business on island. They like to keep things simple, move at a slower pace, remember?"

The residential streets gave way to more snow-flocked trees and less activity.

"I get that, but last year Sadie was even able to talk Martha Kelley into a new website for the sake of growing her business at the restaurant. Websites attract viewers from all around the world." She shrugged. "Maybe they don't have one up because they just opened. Still, I'm going to talk to him about it."

"Bob and Lucinda didn't have one either. The store thrived when they owned it."

"Yeah, but things were different before the Grand Sullivan burned and the pandemic hit. The Johnsons had close to fifty years tied into the bookstore, so word of mouth was their best advertiser. After they closed down, people kind of forgot about it. So now it's time to let customers know that Oliver and Jonah have reopened the Island Bookstore."

Mom laughed, then stifled a yawn. "You always saved your allowance and wanted to spend it on books."

"They've always been my escape. One thing Oliver and I have in common."

"Oh, really?" Mom nudged her shoulder. "What else do you have in common?"

Eliza scowled. "Mother. Really? He's going to be my boss."

"Workplace romances have been known to happen." Mom nodded toward the back of Dad's head. "That's how your dad and I met. Thirty-six years of marriage and two kids later—"

"Not with me." Eliza cut her off. "I have no desire to get hooked on a guy I work with again, only to be tossed aside."

"Honey, just because Tim broke your heart doesn't mean you have to close it off to romance. Not all men are like him."

Casting a discreet glance over her shoulder, Eliza found Asher and Sadie so caught up in each other they weren't paying any attention to her conversation.

"He didn't just break my heart, Mom. He cheated with my so-called best friend and called off our engagement. He chose her over me. I'm tired of being somebody's second choice."

Mom tucked a lock of Eliza's hair behind her ear. "I know it hurts. I won't pretend to understand that kind of pain, but you are always my first choice."

Eliza leaned into her mother's tender touch. "You have to say that. You're my mom."

Dad guided Gus and Ginger through the gate and stopped in front of the ranch house. He jumped down and helped Eliza and Mom down while Asher practically lifted Sadie from the carriage.

While Asher and Sadie headed for the stable with Dad, Eliza and Mom started toward the house.

"So tell me the truth. Why do you really want to do this festival?" Mom hooked a hand around Eliza's elbow.

Eliza opened the front door and stepped back as Mom passed by her. "I've been thinking about what I really enjoy, and that's connecting readers with authors whose work is underappreciated. I think I can help them step out of the shadows and gain more exposure for their work. With the festival, I can see if I have what it takes to connect readers with authors and prove this could be the right career path for me. And prove I can organize an event of this magnitude."

"Then you need to do it. You know your dad and I will help

you in any way that we can." Mom shrugged out of her jacket and hung it in the coat closet to the right of the front door. "Your dad wasn't happy when Sally wouldn't let you work remotely, but after talking to her, he saw her point."

"Wait—he called Aunt Sally?" That was news to her.

"Not about that, directly. He called her about something with the carriage business, and it came up in conversation. He just doesn't want to see you get hurt."

"But he can't protect me forever."

"I know, honey, but you have to look at it from his perspective. After losing Jared, the last thing we want is to lose you too." Mom's eyes shimmered.

Eliza nodded. "I can understand that."

The mention of her brother created the same ache in her chest as it always did. She missed his laugh, listening to him sing, and the way he teased her. She'd give nearly anything to have him back again.

"Your dad's going to be busy in a couple of weeks when the horses start returning on island for the season, but he and Asher are now able to run the carriage tour business full-time."

Eliza kicked off her boots and set them in the closet. "Well, when Asher and Sadie aren't writing music and heading off to Nashville, you mean?"

Mom sighed. "How do you feel about that?"

"Me?" She scrunched up her face. "Well, I'm happy for them."

Mom tilted her head, studying her. "And?"

"And nothing. They both deserve it. How do you feel about all the changes, Mom?"

A shadow flickered in Mom's eyes as she swept a hand over the room. "I'll miss the ranch, but it's too big for two people. I love the cottage and look forward to getting settled." Then her eyes dimmed as they reconnected with Eliza's. "I'm also happy for Asher and Sadie. I'm so thankful they're healing over their losses.

They deserve the fresh start God has given them." She sighed. "Even though Asher's band Phoenix is no more and I'll always miss hearing Asher and Jared performing together, I'm excited for this new road for Asher and Sadie to walk down."

Tears pricked the back of Eliza's eyes as her throat tightened. She nodded, not quite sure if she could actually speak.

Mom lifted her face to the ceiling. "It's been five and a half years, but there are days when the grief hits in such a wave that I feel like my heart is breaking all over again. I miss my son." She blinked rapidly and then turned back to Eliza, a soft smile parting her lips. "But I just hold on to the knowledge that Jared's love for the Lord continued even as he toured and we'll have an eternity with him in heaven."

"That's the best kind of hope." Eliza wrapped her arms around Mom, who stood a couple inches shorter than Eliza, but at that moment, Mom appeared to have shrunk a little as grief caught hold once again.

For a few minutes, they stayed in each other's embrace as the past wound around them. Then Eliza gave her mother a final squeeze and stepped back. "I'm heading upstairs to change."

"I'm going to make some lunch, then do more packing. Or maybe take that nap." Mom picked up a knitted afghan off the leather couch. "I know you don't want to, but we need to start packing up Jared's room, honey. It's time for a fresh start . . . for all of us. Even you, El." Mom folded the blanket and set it on the end of the couch. "Even though we're moving, we'll always have room for you in our new home."

Problem was, that wasn't Eliza's home. It was a place her parents chose together. While Eliza appreciated her mother's offer, she needed to find her own place in the world . . . wherever that might be.

Even after a halfway decent night's sleep and spending the morning painting the bedroom in his apartment, Oliver still needed to clear his head.

Best way to do that was to throw on his gloves and go a few rounds with the heavy bag.

The men's locker room in the Jonathon Island Fitness Center smelled of sweat, shampoo, and a slight tang of disinfectant. Long wooden benches sat in front of rows of blue lockers—small square ones on top and longer ones below them—that lined the cement walls painted a light gray.

Oliver sat on the bench, tied his sneakers, adjusted his black T-shirt over his black athletic pants, then grabbed his gym bag and slung it over his shoulder. He headed out of the locker room and down the hall, his feet nearly silent against the gleaming tile.

Bulletin boards advertising local events, motivational posters, and framed photos of award-winning athletes hung on cinder block walls painted a light blue. He turned the corner and passed the gym where the thumping of basketballs and squeaking of sneakers against the polished gym floor echoed through the open doors. At the end of the hall, he stopped at a locked metal door and punched in a code to access the weight room.

The sounds of grunts, clanking of metal against metal, and '80s rock pulsing through the sound system filled the room. Exposed pipes ran along the ceiling, and mirrors cracked in the corners ran along the cinder block walls painted the same color as the locker room. Industrial fans cooled the sweat running down the faces of the bodybuilders lifting free weights.

Oliver crossed the thick mat covering the floor and passed the racks of dumbbells, free weights, and weight machines. He dropped his bag on one of the long wooden benches, sat, and unzipped it.

Asher Quinn, former rock star and now future owner of the 3Q

Ranch, pulled himself up on the chin-up bar, his biceps bulging and sweat running down his red face.

Spying Oliver, he lifted his chin, pulled himself up a couple more times, then dropped to the mat. He grabbed a towel and ran it over his face. Then he snatched one of the disinfectant wipes from the tub in the corner and wiped down the bar . . . one of the rules for using the equipment—wipe it down after each use.

Chest heaving, he strode across the mat and sat next to Oliver on the bench. He held out a fist, and Oliver bumped it. "Hey, man. What's going on?"

Asher grabbed a water bottle and chugged half of it. He wiped his mouth with the back of his hand, then ran the towel over his head. "Getting in a workout while Sadie's helping her parents design new menus for the bakery."

"Glad to hear they're reopening it. Hudson Bakery's been a mainstay on island for decades." Oliver dug his black hand wraps out of his bag and wrapped his wrist. He flexed his fingers to ensure he had good circulation without the wrap being too tight.

The door to the weight room buzzed. Oliver looked up from wrapping his other hand as Hunter and Waylen Barrett stepped inside.

"What up, party people?" Waylen, one of the island cops, wore bright-orange jersey shorts and a white T-shirt with a large smiley emoji on the front. His hair was a wild mess of curls he didn't bother to tame. He fist-bumped everyone he passed, then dropped his bag next to Oliver. "Ollie, my man. What's up?"

Hunter, his younger and much calmer brother, nodded to Oliver. A backward blue Barrett Construction ball cap covered his dark hair, and a touch of scruff darkened his chin. He eyed Oliver's hands and lifted a brow. "Bad day? You only hit the bag when you're mad."

Other hand wrapped, Oliver slid his hand into his glove and Velcroed it in place. He repeated with the other glove, using his teeth to fasten the hook and loop closure. "Not mad. Just need to work out some things."

"Have at it, man." Hunter held out a fist, and Oliver hit it with his glove.

He strode to the black heavy bag hanging from the steel beam in the corner of the room. Clenching his jaw, he rolled his tight shoulders, then drew in a deep breath. He released it slowly, then ground his footing against the mat.

"Let's do this."

Standing in front of the heavy bag, Oliver extended his arm until his glove touched the bag. He rocked back on his feet for a couple of steps to find his rhythm, then he snapped the bag with his right hand and drew it back.

"Whip that punch, Sullivan! Your sister can hit harder than that," Waylen heckled from the bench.

"I'll just pretend it's your face, Barrett."

"Hey now, remember, assaulting an officer will land you in cuffs."

"It's worth the risk." Oliver grinned at him, then refocused on moving with the bag. He shifted and jabbed the bag, harder this time. With each steady thump-thump of his glove hitting the bag, the stress drained, and Oliver's muscles relaxed.

His arms quivered as sweat ran down his temples. The bag swung away, and as it came back, he caught it in the center with his left glove to stop the swinging.

He tuned out the noise and focused on his movements for the next twenty minutes. Chest heaving and shirt soaked, he brought the bag to a stop, then leaned at the waist and balanced his gloves on his knees while he caught his breath.

"Hey, Rocky." Hunter grabbed the bag. "You working something out or trying to take down the bag? That was an intense workout. What's going on?"

Oliver glanced around the room that was filling up, which was odd for a Sunday afternoon, and shook his head. "Not here. I'm beat."

"Go shower off your stink, and I'll grab some burgers from Kelley's. We can meet up at my place."

He rolled his neck. "Sounds good."

An hour later, Oliver carved out a corner on Hunter's worn dark-brown couch in his open-concept apartment above Hudson Bakery. He propped his socked feet on the scarred coffee table and faced the seventy-five-inch flatscreen. Probably the most expensive item in the room.

Oliver folded back a corner of the foil around his bacon cheese-burger and took a large bite. As the smokiness of the meat filled his mouth, he rested his head against the back of the couch, closed his eyes, and let out a groan. "That's some good beef."

Hunter dropped on the other end of the couch and reached for the remote. He found a football game and muted the sound. "Yeah, Patrick Kelley knows his way around a flat top."

As they ate, the only sounds were the crinkles of foil and slurps of pop.

Hunter wiped his mouth and balled up his wrapper. He pitched it into the empty take-out bag standing on the table. "So what's going on with you?"

"Dani needs me to take over a book festival."

"Yeah, dude, organizing festivals sounds right up your alley."

"That's what I tried to tell her, then she played the wedding card. I talked to Jonah last night, and he's on board. Says it will generate business for the store."

"So what's the problem?"

"I need to come up with a plan, man. Oh, and the festival's in three weeks."

"When you put your mind to it, things happen. Look how fast you got the store open. Get out of your own way and just do it. You may be surprised by what happens."

"Jonah text you and pay you to say that?"

Hunter leaned his head back and laughed. "Haven't talked to the major since we finished Bronte's apartment. Oh, and speaking of apartments, now that your flooring is in, want some help installing it? I'm sure I can get my meathead brother to lend a hand."

"Yeah, that would be great. Thanks. I'm ready for my place to be finished so I can get my stuff out of storage in Port Joseph. Sleeping on the air mattress is getting old."

"I hear you." He waved a hand around the room. "This pad's been fine, but I'm looking forward to moving into the Barrett House with Daisy as soon as we're married."

"You two deserve it. All kinds of engagements and weddings happening lately." Oliver finished his burger, balled up the wrapper, and pitched it into the bag.

"Thanks. And yeah—some of us have gotten snatched up. And I'm not complaining."

"Enjoy every minute, and don't take her for granted."

"I won't."

Despite his body wanting to do otherwise, Oliver pushed to his feet. "Thanks for the chow. Burgers are on me next time. I gotta head out. I have a meeting with Dani tomorrow to discuss the festival."

Between tonight and tomorrow morning, he needed to find enthusiasm he didn't feel for the festival, because too many people were counting on him, and anything other than success wasn't an option.

Four

S AYING YES TO COORDINATING THE FESTIVAL was a no-brainer, yet Oliver still couldn't ease the pit in his stomach. Even though he cared about the bookstore and wanted it to succeed, he was so out of his comfort zone.

But he wouldn't let his sister pull double duty before her wedding. He'd man up and be the brother she needed right now, especially since she rarely asked for help. He didn't want to be the reason she stopped.

He opened the door to the one-story, hundred-year-old building that housed the Tourism Bureau, where his younger sister worked as director. Passing the large wooden desk in the reception area and the oak case containing updated brochures of businesses and activities that were now available to tourists, he strode down the short hallway past the closed conference room.

Laughter spilled out into the hall from the next open door.

So either Dani was on the phone, or she had a visitor.

He pulled in a breath, then let it out slowly and stepped inside the room that smelled of old books, Dani's favorite hazelnut-vanilla candles he bought her last year for Christmas, and something else he couldn't figure out.

Dani and Eliza leaned against the desk and laughed at something on Dani's phone.

Eliza wore a white V-neck sweater with a pair of black jeans and black ankle boots. Her dark hair had been pulled up into some sort of tangle on top of her head, giving him a clear view of the curve of her neck.

Dani wore gray pants and a navy sweatshirt with Stone Developers embroidered in white block letters.

Clearly swiped from Liam. Hopefully, the dude was fine with his wardrobe being fair game after they got married.

He cleared his throat. "Hey. I'm here."

Dani pushed off her desk and strode toward him, her smile wide as she stretched out her arms and wrapped them around him.

Over her shoulder, he noticed she'd finally removed the vintage anchor wallpaper and painted the walls off-white that went well with the stained wainscoting and worn secretary desk she wasn't ready to replace.

Potted plants lined the windowsills that looked over Main Street. Another plant sat on top of the wooden file cabinet, its leaves hanging down the side. A picture of Liam and Dani on the beach at sunset sat on top of her desk strewn with papers, books, a Good Day Coffee mug, and colored pens.

He didn't know how his sister found anything.

Organized chaos, she called it, especially when she was in the midst of a project.

He released his sister and found Eliza watching them, an expression on her face that he couldn't quite decipher. Longing, maybe?

But she shuttered it quickly and replaced it with a smile. "Hey, Oliver."

He nodded at her. "What are you doing here?"

"I'm helping with the festival."

"Once I learned you hired Eliza to work at the bookstore, I figured she could help you with the festival." Dani reached up and cupped his chin. "Since you're the best brother ever."

He held out his hands and lifted the corner of his mouth. "Well, I am. And not because you're trying to butter me up."

"I'm so glad you're doing this." She pulled in her lips, clasped her hands, and shot him a look he'd seen so many times growing up.

He blew out a breath and raked his fingers through his hair. "You're sure we need this festival?"

She clutched his arm. "Definitely, Ollie. Wait and see what it does to bookstore sales."

He glanced out the window, released another breath, then looked at her. "Yeah, Jonah's on board, so let's get rolling."

Dani's face lit up. "Now that's the attitude I was hoping for."

He shoved his hands in his pockets and shook his head. "I have no idea what I'm doing."

Dani stepped back, crossing her arms. "And when has that ever stopped you from trying something new?"

Since his last big risk nearly cost him everything . . .

"Most of the time? It's my number one reason for staying out of trouble."

Dani leaned in, lowering her voice. "Not always. Remember when you and Jamie—"

He walked into that one. His hand flew up to stop the jaunt down memory lane. That was a story for a different day. A time when Eliza wasn't around to witness his humiliation when his oldest brother got him into trouble.

Dani moved over to Eliza, who remained next to the desk, looped an arm through hers, and pulled her toward Oliver. "And that's why you have Eliza. Not only will she be an asset to the bookstore, but she's also going to share her expertise and be your all-star for coordinating this festival. Between the two of you, you're going to knock it out of the park."

He schooled his tone and flashed her a real smile. "We'll give it our best shot."

Dani grinned at him. "You *are* the best brother ever."

"Can you put that on a T-shirt so I can wear it to our next family reunion?"

She snorted. "If only we had a family reunion."

His smile slipped. "Yeah, our family is a little too fractured for that to happen."

Dani's expression softened. "I'm still holding on to hope that we can bring everyone back together."

"We?" Lifting an eyebrow, Oliver shifted his weight and shoved his hands under his arms. "That's your plan, not mine."

"Don't you want our family back together?"

He shot a look at Eliza, who seemed to be watching them with interest. "It's not about what I want. The last time our family was together, the hotel burned down. Remember?"

Dani closed her eyes a moment, then reopened them, but the flash of pain remained. "Don't remind me."

She picked up a photo of the Sullivans taken about fifteen years ago on the beach after their brother Tyler's graduation. Kate had set up her tripod and captured the moment.

A happier time. Back when his parents loved one another. Before his mom cheated on his dad. Before she married Ryan Mac-Bride. Before his dad burned down the hotel.

"All of that is changing. Thanks to Liam, the hotel is being rebuilt." She waved toward Main Street. "We're bringing tourists back. We'll restore the island. And we will restore our family."

The last sentence had been spoken with so much hope that Oliver didn't want to be the one to squash her dreams. She'd proven herself over the last year that she was going to accomplish what she promised.

Their family though? Well, that would take a miracle.

Dani brushed past him and pulled one of her infamous binders off the built-in behind her desk. Returning and standing between Oliver and Eliza, she flipped through the page protectors filled with typed notes. As soon as she started talking about hotel room layouts, food vendors, and registration ideas, the words blurred on the page, and her voice sounded like she was talking underwater.

"Oliver, are you even listening to me?" Dani elbowed his side.

He pushed her arm away. "Hey, keep those bony elbows to yourself."

"My elbows aren't bony." She closed the binder and glared at him. "You're zoning out. This is important. I need you to pay attention."

"I am paying attention."

"Prove it. What did I just say?"

"'This is important. I need you to pay attention.'" He grinned.

She made a face and stuck out her tongue.

He laughed. "What are you, eight?"

Dani rolled her eyes. "Whatever. At least Eliza is paying attention."

Oliver looked at Eliza, who smirked at him. "Scoring points already, huh?"

She shrugged. "This is my jam."

Yeah, she was definitely on board, though he didn't quite share her excitement. His brain was trying to work out the details, and it made his head pound.

"I'd rather have a root canal."

Eliza laughed—a musical sound that hit him in the chest.

Well, that was unexpected.

He turned his attention back to the binder of doom and tried to focus on his sister, regretting stepping foot inside the building.

"I have an idea." Eliza shoved her hands in the back pockets of her jeans.

Dani tucked her binder into the curve of her arm. "Oh yeah? What's that?" She shot a look at Oliver. "At least someone is bringing something to the table."

He made a face.

Eliza ignored him. "Well, Dad said the horses will be returning to the island in a couple of weeks. What if we do some sort of horse-themed scavenger hunt for the kids? I'm sure my dad and cousin would be willing to help, and we could make it a fun family event."

Oliver thought about her suggestion a moment, then an idea sparked. "We could create a horse-themed window display at the store and read a couple of horse-related books during Saturday afternoon story times leading up to the festival."

Dani fisted her hands and pressed them against her mouth. "See, I knew you could do this."

"I can do a window display, Dan. Far cry from a festival."

Eliza grabbed one of her colored markers and a sticky note pad. She jotted something on the pad, tore it off, and tucked it in her pocket. "That's a great idea! We could create activity sheets and picture clues for those who can't read. Everyone who brings in their activity sheet can receive a fun little prize."

Oliver rubbed a hand over his chin. "What did you have in mind for prizes?"

"We could invite local businesses to offer gift certificates."

Dani crossed to her whiteboard, picked up a blue dry-erase marker, and wrote *Prizes*. "I'm sure Lily would do gift certificates for ice cream or fudge from Fudge Shop on the Corner."

"Oh, that would be great! And we could advertise her shop. Maybe she'd offer a discount coupon if we make the fudge shop one of the stops during our scavenger hunt."

For the next few minutes, Dani wrote as Eliza tossed out more ideas.

He had to admit—she seemed to know what she was talking about.

When the two women paused to take a breath, he looked at Eliza. "How about if *you* read to the kids on Saturday?"

Frowning, she took a step back. "Me? To be honest, I don't have a lot of experience with kids."

"You don't need to. Besides, I'll be there. Read the story and ask questions to engage them in conversation. Tell them about your experiences with the horses returning to the island and growing up on the ranch."

"I don't know . . ."

Her hesitation took him back a little. Did the Queen of Confidence actually have a flaw?

Dani capped her marker, tapped it against her chin a moment, then pointed it at Eliza. "Sadie helped me with marketing strategies for last year's music festival. You could ask her for some ideas. I'm sure she wouldn't mind dusting off her copywriting skills."

"Good idea. I'll run my thoughts by her and see what other suggestions she has." Eliza turned back to Oliver. "We need to get you online."

"Online? For what?"

"Well, I went to find the Island Bookstore's website." She shook her head. "And there wasn't one."

"Right . . ."

"I think a website and social media platforms would generate more exposure for the bookstore."

Oliver frowned. "People can buy books anywhere. How will a website help? It's not like they're going to hop on the ferry just to buy the latest copy of the Pike Sisters series when they can have it delivered to their home."

"No, but we offer them the full experience. Brick-and-mortar stores are dying out, and what you have is a true gem. Let's create an atmosphere they won't want to miss. And your kids' section is adorable."

Oliver rolled his eyes. "Yeah, *adorable* was what I was going for."

Eliza folded her arms over her chest and glared at him. "Are you always this sarcastic?"

"Only on days that end in *y*." He made a face.

"Ollie, knock it off." Dani hip-bumped him and held her binder out to Eliza. "I think this festival is going to be in great hands." She eyed him. "Are you going to get on board, Ollie?"

Eliza touched his arm. "You're not alone in this, Ollie. Trust me."

"I'll trust you when you stop calling me *Ollie*." Then he flashed another smile to soften his words.

Maybe they could make this work.

And maybe, just maybe, Eliza *wouldn't* be the worst person to be stuck with after all.

Besides, what did he have to lose?

Well . . . besides his bookstore and his future.

Minor details.

Eliza couldn't sleep last night.

Maybe it was from completing her first day at the bookstore or from the ideas tumbling over in her head.

And when sleep eluded her, she planned.

Planning meant she was in control. And if she wasn't in control, then, well . . . she didn't even want to think about it.

After leaving the bookstore at the end of her shift yesterday, she spent last evening poring over the notes in Dani's binder and made her own notes to share with Oliver.

Hopefully, he'd be on board with her ideas.

She opened the back door of the Island Bookstore and headed

to Oliver's office. She shrugged out of her coat and hung it on the hook behind the door. She dragged Dani's binder and her notes out of her tote bag and set them on the small kitchenette counter.

Another door opened and closed. Then whistling sounded down the hall, breaking into the quiet. The same low, almost absent-minded tune she'd heard yesterday while she filled out paperwork and Oliver stocked shelves.

He came into his office wearing a black shirt tucked into black pants and black Converses.

"Good morning." She moved out from behind the door.

The whistling ceased, and he jerked. "Where'd you come from?"

"Just got here." She reached for Dani's binder. "So, I made some notes last night."

His back to her, she didn't miss the way his shoulders tightened. Or his hand stilled from scooping coffee grounds into the filter. "Notes for what?"

"The festival." She kept her tone light and fought the "duh" that clawed at her throat.

"Right." He brushed past her, and she caught a whiff of something woodsy and clean. Body wash? Shampoo? The overhead light glinted off his damp, wavy hair.

He flipped a switch above his wooden executive desk against the wall, and soft music filtered through the air from the store's old sound system. Then he tapped his mouse and brought his computer to life.

The screen cast a light over his face. When he glanced up, his eyes widened, almost as if he realized she was still there, and he straightened. Something flickered through his eyes, but then he schooled his features into a neutral mask. "What are your thoughts about the festival?"

She gripped the edge of the binder a little tighter than necessary. Clearing her throat, she leafed through the book and found her notes from last night. "I created a mock-up of a website for the store. I figured we could take some pictures today and upload them. And we'll need to create accounts on a few social media platforms. Then, I was thinking we could kick off the festival with the horses' return to the island, followed by the kids' scavenger hunt, then close out the evening with a book signing—something big that would build excitement and bring readers to the island right away. My Aunt Sally will do it. She loves hanging out with her readers. Maybe we could highlight Michigan authors like her and even Bronte Parker."

"Bronte's from Oklahoma." He returned to the counter and pulled a couple of mugs from the cabinet above the coffee maker.

Eliza set the binder on the edge of his desk and gripped the back of his chair. "Okay, so she's a transplant Michigander. We can mention she loved the island so much that she moved here."

"What else?"

"On Friday, we could offer a variety of different events and stops around the island, almost like a literary tour. We could talk to Annabelle Kennedy about doing a historical tour, highlighting historical novels featuring the area. Maybe Jacob and Augo Kennedy would allow us to do a reading in the parlor at the Island House Inn."

"Parlor's been closed since Jacob's son and daughter-in-law drowned a handful of years ago."

Eliza's mouth formed an O. "I didn't realize that. Okay, scratch that idea. We could do some rom-com readings at the fudge shop—something sweet to go with a sweet romance."

Oliver's eyes narrowed as if she'd suggested lighting the bookstore on fire.

"We could conclude on Saturday with a brunch at the Grand. Show how we're rebuilding our island and invite our readers to come back again." Her words came out in a rush, but she couldn't stop the speed. She glanced at him, but his face gave nothing away.

Her heartbeat thundered in her ears as she turned the page and reviewed the rest of her notes. "How about a workshop for aspiring writers? Or even advance writers, since many will be on island. I could talk to Aunt Sally and her agent, Candace Bishop—she lives on island—about teaching. I also suggest an author panel where readers can ask questions, and maybe even roundtable discussions at the Grand. Imagine speed dating, but instead of finding a date, readers get to spend time with different authors."

She glanced up from her notes and found he hadn't moved. Or changed expressions.

Did he like *anything* she'd suggested?

Surely he understood the importance of a variety of engaging activities, didn't he? Her ideas could work. She needed them to.

Oliver poured coffee into the mugs, set one on his desk, then handed the other one to her. He jerked his head toward the kitchenette. "There's cream and sugar next to the pot."

She wrapped her hands around the ceramic and nodded.

"You didn't sleep at all last night, did you?" His tone remained light as he raised an eyebrow and sipped his coffee.

While he probably meant it in jest, if he only knew . . .

"Why do you ask that?" She stared at her reflection in the brew.

He tapped the binder. "That's a lot of information. You might even put Dani to shame."

Heat crept up her neck. She hated how his words made her feel ridiculous, even if that wasn't his intent. She shrugged. "I had some time. Like I said, I enjoy this kind of thing."

"I think it would take me a couple months to come up with all that." He lifted his mug to his lips, but not before she caught a shadow of a smile.

The knot in her stomach eased. She walked over to the counter and added creamer and sugar to her coffee. "We all have our gifts."

Like seeing possibilities for this festival. Or knowing how to make something work. And fighting obstinate bookstore owners for things that mattered. Hopefully, he'd listen.

"Well, that's all I have for now."

She lifted her eyes and breathed a prayer of forgiveness for the lie.

He didn't know about the other notes, the maps she'd drawn, or any of the brochures she designed.

He seemed to be overwhelmed already.

Oliver set his mug on his desk and folded his arms over his chest. "You do have a gift. One that I definitely don't share. I'm still trying to wrap my head around pulling this thing off in such a short amount of time."

Eliza eased her way over to him. Almost as if she made a sudden movement, then he'd bolt like a skittish dog. "Like I've repeatedly said, you're not in this alone. Besides, once we do it this year, next year's festival will be much easier."

"Next year?" His head snapped up, his eyes wide.

She swallowed the grin at the look of disbelief on his face. "If it's a hit, why not repeat it?"

"I was hoping for something on a smaller scale. Maybe the book signing. And that's about it."

Eliza dug her nails into her palms.

He couldn't see what she envisioned. How the festival could transform his quiet bookshop. How it could bring back a joy of reading to the island. How it could feel to partner with someone.

She thought through her words before opening her mouth. Then she looked at the man who was her current employer. As she searched his face, she saw a spark of something in his blue eyes before he caught her gaze and looked away.

Oliver was afraid.

But of what?

"You want your bookstore to thrive, don't you?" She spoke without judgment as she touched his arm. "Let's partner up and show your readers that you're here and ready for business. Bringing in big-name authors and having a social media campaign will raise awareness for the festival, boost tourism, and get other business owners involved. A stronger community means stronger businesses."

Oliver blew out a breath. "Well, when you put it that way . . ."

She eyed Dani's binder. If she bopped her boss over the head with it, would that be grounds for dismissal? She wouldn't be able to help with the festival if she lost her job and got charged with assault.

His stubbornness frustrated her, but she'd figure out a way to deal with it.

This seemed like a perfectly good opportunity to bring necessary exposure to the bookstore. Problem was, he hadn't asked for her help. His sister did.

Simply put, Oliver didn't trust her.

Yet.

So she had to be smart and remember it wasn't just about keeping her job or pulling off the festival but showing she was more than capable of doing what she said.

Not just to Oliver, but also to herself.

She needed his trust and partnership to do that.

Five

IN THE TWO DAYS SINCE SHE STARTED WORK-
ing at the bookstore, Eliza put a lot of time and energy—not to
mention her heart—into this festival only to have Oliver challenge
her at every turn.

The clock was ticking, and if she couldn't convince him to ex-
pand their offerings, then their festival was going to be a dud.

Afternoon sunlight streamed through the large bay display window to the right of the front door and warmed Eliza's face as she
added vinyl letters to the glass to spell *Saddle Up for a Scavenger
Adventure.*

When she'd come into the store shortly before noon, the place
resembled a cave with too many shadows and not enough lighting.

She didn't just slide back the gray curtains in the display windows—she removed them.

And judging by Oliver's thinned lips when he saw the curtain
rods sitting on the counter, he didn't approve. But he didn't tell
her to put them back either.

Besides, having them gone made it easier to create her display.

After adhering the final letter, she stepped back and checked the alignment, nearly bumping into the large barn cutout she and Sadie had created last night out of foam core and cardboard. A stack of hay bales held books about horses written by children's authors that she and Oliver selected yesterday for the reading adventure. She moved a stuffed gray horse and set it in front of the barn.

With a sigh, she turned and stepped away from the window and faced her stubborn boss. He stood at the checkout counter, arranging a revolving display of stationery and writing supplies.

"I still think sponsors are the way to go. I'm trying to see your point." Eliza brushed hay from her hands. "But why don't you think they're needed? The Tourism Bureau doesn't have a coffee can full of cash stashed under Dani's desk to fund the different events. And if we don't offer a variety, then readers will be bored and leave." She tried to keep her tone neutral, but working with Oliver had a way of poking her last nerve. "That would impact the store and create unnecessary stress for Dani."

Clenching his jaw, Oliver grabbed a stack of journals off the counter he'd just priced and jammed them into the carousel rack. "All right. Fine. What sponsors are you thinking of? I don't want to beg business owners to give us money for a festival that may or may not work out."

Even though his words had an edge, Eliza caught a sense of uncertainty in his tone.

It wasn't about the money. Was it more about him? But why?

Her shoulders loosened as she moved over to the counter and grabbed a handful of packaged notebooks out of the box at Oliver's feet. "Let's talk to the businesses on Main Street and see if they'd be interested in putting together coordinating gift baskets—items tied to a particular theme or genre. We'll offer ad space in the festival booklet and ask if they'd sponsor specific events. Sadie said that's what they did for last year's music festival she and Asher worked on."

"So you talked to Sadie?"

Eliza jerked her thumb toward the display window. "Yes, last night while I put the barn together. She had some wonderful suggestions."

"Such as?"

"We could give the participants tote bags advertising the bookstore. Authors could sign them, and people could use them to carry purchases. Plus, I have contacts with some publishers through my aunt. They might be willing to donate giveaway copies. I called Candace Bishop before work this morning, and she agreed to reach out to some of the houses she works with for her authors to see if they'd donate books."

"Doesn't that defeat the purpose of funneling sales through the store?"

"Not necessarily." Eliza priced the notebooks and slid them into the display rack. "We'll order books for the signings. Those sales stay local. But some of Candace's authors aren't big names yet. I want to help them get more exposure. The festival offers that opportunity."

"You have a heart for authors, don't you?" His words came out softer, almost . . . admirable.

"I want to see them succeed."

"What does their success look like to you?"

"Getting their work in front of readers, letting their voices be heard." She glanced at him. "Writing is a solitary venture. No one else can get the words out of their head and onto the page. It's all on them. And that's brave."

"You sound like you're talking from experience." Oliver reached in front of her and pulled a stack of plastic-wrapped bookmarks out of the box. He set them on the counter and picked up the price gun.

Eliza laughed as she removed the plastic from the bookmarks and handed them to him. "I'm not a writer. I don't have that gifting. But I've seen my aunt's journey up close. The highs and the gut-wrenching lows."

"Bronte's shared some of her struggles."

"See?" Eliza leaned a hip against the counter. "That's why we need to make this work. Writers deserve to be seen. Readers deserve to discover them. Let's do what we can to help make that happen."

Oliver priced the bookmarks and slid them into their place on the rack. "Fine. You win."

"It's not about winning, Ollie—"

"Don't call me Ollie." His tone cut sharper than expected.

Eliza blinked and took a step back, hands in front of her. "Sorry. Habit. You were always Dani's big brother Ollie—the one who was going to take the literary world by storm."

He scoffed, his jaw tightening. "Yeah. By storm, all right."

She frowned but remained quiet.

He walked to the front door and flipped the sign from Closed to Open. "I'm sure you have a list of businesses to contact in that binder of doom Dani handed off. Let's divide and conquer and get this over with."

"You make it sound like I'm sending you off to be executed."

"Feels like it."

"It's not that bad." She flashed him a smile. "I promise."

He lifted an eyebrow but didn't reply.

Eliza moved behind the counter, pulled the binder from her tote bag, and flipped it open. She handed him Dani's list of business contacts.

Oliver stared at it. "Leave it to my little sister to color-code the apocalypse."

"Dani likes to be organized."

"Have you seen her office?" Oliver looked up, a smirk on his face. "Poor Liam. The guy doesn't stand a chance."

"He seems pretty on board with everything she does."

"He's a good guy." Oliver scanned the list, then plucked a pen and started marking names. "After closing, let's hit these first and go from there."

Eliza took the marked-up list and tried not to grin like a fool. It wasn't a total victory, but it was something.

Maybe, just maybe, working with Oliver wouldn't be as difficult as she thought, and they'd both come out unscathed.

Oliver had hired Eliza as a part-timer at the bookstore, but he didn't expect her to start transforming his whole world.

Light had flooded the bookstore the moment she removed the curtains soon after clocking in. Then she created the window displays without asking for permission.

And why did she bring cookies? He eyed the container on the counter. They were there to work, not socialize.

And did she really have to talk so much?

He missed the quiet.

He had to admit, though, the displays looked pretty good. And the chocolate chip cookies weren't bad either.

So he needed to get on board . . . or move out of the way so Eliza didn't trample him. As much as he hated to admit it, her ideas were good.

Dani . . . and the success of the bookstore . . . counted on him to give the festival his best efforts, which was why he was spending his evening soliciting donors for the festival.

Someone had come in close to closing, so they stayed open a little later than usual.

After the last customer left, they closed and decided to visit

Good Day Coffee, Kelley's Bar & Grill, and Martha's on Main before the day ended.

Might as well get the Kelley clan—and probably the most stubborn ones except for Jill—out of the way.

He opened the door to Good Day Coffee and held it while Eliza stepped inside. He followed her into the bright shop that smelled of coffee beans, vanilla, and sugar.

His glucose levels spiked with every sniff, but it was worth it.

Jill Kelley, the pleasant owner of Good Day Coffee, had a smile in place as they stepped up to the counter. "Hey, guys. What can I get you?"

"I'll have a black coffee. And whatever Eliza wants." Oliver pulled out his wallet and laid a twenty on the counter.

Jill looked at Eliza. "Anything for you, hon?"

"How about a chai latte?"

"Coming right up." Jill rang up the total, slid Oliver's twenty in her drawer, then handed him the change along with the receipt.

Eliza glanced at Oliver, then turned back to Jill. "We're co-ordinating the upcoming booklovers' festival, and we'd like to feature your shop in the booklet we're sharing with all registered participants." She removed Dani's binder from her tote bag and pulled out a sheet of paper they'd put together with advertising opportunities and prices. "We're offering ad spots for sale, but if that's not your deal, we're also looking for gift card and basket donations in exchange for advertising."

Jill took the paper and glanced over it while Eliza shared more of the festival ideas she'd pitched to Oliver a couple days ago. "I love this idea. Can I have a day or two to decide what I want?"

"Absolutely. And if you have more questions, please don't hesitate to ask."

Jill made their drinks, then set two paper to-go cups on the counter. "We work with a roaster in Port Joseph who distributes our coffees and teas. If you'd like, I can offer a couple of specialty blends with literary themes for that weekend only. We can have bags of coffee to sell and single purchase items on a select menu board."

"Scarcity marketing." Eliza smiled wide. "I love it. What do you think, Oliver?"

Oliver lifted his cup off the counter. "Sounds good to me."

"Great. Let's do it." Eliza reached for her cup.

After thanking Jill for her time, they headed back out into the cold and paused on the sidewalk as a carriage being pulled by Gus and Ginger passed by them. Eliza's dad, Terry Quinn, waved from the coach box.

They waved back and crossed behind the carriage.

"I'm surprised Dani didn't have sponsors lined up already," Oliver said.

"When I talked to her this morning, I asked that same question, and she admitted to being embarrassed about that detail falling through the cracks. To be fair, though, she has a lot on her plate."

"Dani thrives with a full plate."

"Or maybe she wants you guys to think that to bring everyone together."

They reached Kelley's Bar & Grill, and Oliver opened the door. He held it while Eliza moved past him, leaving a light floral scent in her wake.

They stepped inside. The door to the left opened into the bar, and the door to the right opened into the dining room. Oliver reached over Eliza's head and pushed the door to the dining room open.

Patrick Kelley, the owner, stood next to the hostess stand talking to Mindy, one of the twentysomething servers. He lifted a chin. "Oliver. Eliza. Good to see you."

"Hey, Patrick. How's it going?" Oliver extended a hand.

The older man shook it. "Another day, another dollar."

"I hear you." Oliver lifted his nose and breathed in the tangy scent of sauce. Then he glanced at the chalkboard easel advertising seventy-five-cent chicken wings. "It's wing night?"

"Sure is." Patrick nodded to Eliza. "Want me to drop a couple of baskets for you two while Mindy shows you to a table?"

Oliver turned to Eliza. "Want to stay for some wings?"

She shrugged. "A girl's gotta eat. Sure."

Eliza ordered honey mustard, and Oliver ordered mild.

Mindy tapped a pile of menus on the hostess stand. "You probably won't need these, will you?"

"Probably not." Placing his hand on the small of Eliza's back, they followed Mindy to a booth along the side wall.

A few other customers sat in booths or round tables filling the middle of the room.

They slid into their seats and gave their drink orders. Oliver glanced at the table tent showing a selection of burgers, handhelds, tacos, and varieties of chicken wings. Then he moved it to the edge of the table and leaned back in his booth.

He scanned the exposed beam ceiling, earth-tone brick walls, hardwood floor, and pendant lighting. A retro jukebox in the corner played an old Patsy Cline song.

Then he returned his focus to Eliza. "My buddy Jonah and I used to come here when we were in high school and see who could eat the most chicken wings. We had this stupid little rubber chicken we bought from Doug's Market that the winner kept."

"Who has it now?"

Oliver lifted a shoulder. "Who knows? We kind of grew out of that silly contest. We haven't had wings together in a few years."

"Kind of hard when he's in Germany."

Oliver frowned. "How'd you know that?"

Eliza raised her eyebrows. "Um, duh. I'm an island girl, remember? I spent most of my life here. I know Jonah and his four sisters. Dr. White was my physician growing up. Plus, I've met Bronte."

"Right." Oliver ran a hand over his face. "I keep forgetting just how small this island truly is."

"You haven't been back in quite a while, have you?"

Mindy arrived with their iced teas, set them on the table, then shot them a wide smile before walking away.

Oliver removed his straw from the wrapper and plunked it in his drink, then curled the paper around his fingers. "I wanted to make a name for myself in publishing and couldn't really do it while on island." Then he scoffed. "I just didn't expect things to happen the way they did."

"What do you mean?"

Man, why did he open his big mouth?

Before he could say anything, Patrick headed toward them carrying two red plastic baskets of wings lined with red-checked wax paper in one hand and two plates in the other.

The smell reached them before the food, and Oliver's stomach growled.

Patrick set everything on the table. "Need anything else? Let Mindy know."

"Thanks, Patrick." Oliver handed a plate to Eliza.

She took it and set it next to her honey mustard wings, then looked up at the owner. "There is one thing."

"What's that?" He straightened and crossed his arms over his chest.

Oliver cleared his throat. "Eliza and I are coordinating the booklovers' festival set for early April, and we're looking for advertisers for the booklet each reader will receive in their bag. You interested?"

Eliza opened her binder and pulled out a sheet of paper like the one they'd just given Jill with their rates and more information. "You can read this and feel free to ask us any questions."

Taking it, Patrick raised an eyebrow and ran a hand over his chin as he skimmed the page. Then he looked between the two of them. "You're coordinating a festival for booklovers? Doesn't seem to be your thing, Ollie."

Heat climbed up his neck. Man, he hated that childhood nickname. "Why not? I spent nearly a decade in publishing, and now I'm running a bookstore. Dani was in charge of it, but with her upcoming wedding, she asked me to take it over."

"Makes sense. But what doesn't make sense to me is why you took a step back in your career and bought the store from ole Bob in the first place."

"Jonah and I bought it. I'm running it until he's back stateside." As soon as the words were out of his mouth, Oliver wanted to snatch them back and shove them down his throat. Why had he given the man more ammo?

"So you're his employee?" Patrick shook his head. "That's another thing I don't get—the man's an officer in the Army, and a surgeon at that. He should've taken over his father's practice just like George had done when his father retired. Now Nova Lake—a stranger to the island—is running it."

"Nova used to vacation here every summer with her family. Just because she didn't grow up on island doesn't make her a stranger. George White was more than happy to let Jonah make his own decisions and live life the way he wanted. As for the bookstore, no, I'm *not* an employee—we're partners, like I said."

He didn't need to defend himself. Patrick Kelley could think what he wanted. The grouchy bar and grill owner had been doing it for years.

Patrick snorted and slapped him on the back. "Okay, kid. Whatever you say. Before the hotel burned, you were gung ho on heading to New York. What happened? But then, you Sullivans have a knack of destroying a good thing, don't ya? From what I hear, you and your ex-partner had a falling out. If that happened to me, I'd be a bit leery jumping into a partnership with someone else.

Now you're selling the books you helped make it to the shelves. Interesting twist of events, if you ask me."

Oliver ran his hands over the legs of his khakis, doing everything in his power not to ball his fingers into fists and take a swing at the guy.

But he wasn't a brawler. Never was. But the next time he did his heavy bag workout, it wouldn't be too hard to imagine Patrick's face in the center of the canvas. Anything to wipe that smirk off Patrick's face. Especially after the crack about his family.

Working his jaw, he nodded to the paper Patrick still held. "Feel free to drop that off at the bookstore or give me a call and I'll swing by and pick it up." With that, he turned his attention to his wings, hoping the older man would get the hint and leave so Oliver would have one less person being witness to his humiliation.

Patrick made a noise in his throat and dropped the paper—now sporting a saucy thumbprint in the corner—on the table and walked away.

Eliza made a face at Patrick's retreating back. "Well, I guess we can count him out as a sponsor."

"Good riddance, if you ask me." Oliver picked up a wing, then dropped it in the basket and pushed them away.

"Something wrong?"

"Lost my appetite."

Eliza pushed the basket back toward him, her eyes fierce. "Don't allow him to get under your skin. Patrick Kelley's been rattling people's cages for as long as I can remember. The man owns a restaurant, yet he loves to tell my dad how to care for horses."

Oliver smirked. "He's been a know-it-all for as long as I've known him. Being on the town council, he had plenty to say after Dad burned down the hotel, as you can tell. That's one of the reasons I didn't come back. To escape the island gossip."

"My parents always said island gossip spreads faster than the flu." She wiped her saucy fingers and took a drink of her tea. "But it is hard to take the book world by storm when you're on island, I'm sure."

"There is that." Oliver picked up a wing and took a bite, more out of hunger. He'd been anticipating the tangy richness of Patrick's signature sauce, but now the flavor tasted bitter.

"Losing your business sounds like a terrible thing. I'm sorry that happened to you."

He dropped the half-eaten wing on top of the others and pushed the basket away again. He wiped his fingers with a napkin and drained the rest of his tea. He wanted to get out of here and head back to his apartment, stream something on his laptop, and crash. Or head to the gym and do a few rounds with the bag. Anything to forget about his conversation with Patrick.

"After losing my—" No, he wasn't going there. "I worked as an editor at a reputable publishing house but needed some personal time off. But before I returned to Palmer & Jones, Dennis Wahl, a former colleague, approached me with an offer to start our own small press. His business plan looked sound, and the idea of owning a small press appealed to me, so I got on board and sunk a chunk of savings into our venture. About six months ago, I learned he was engaging in some unethical business practices, including signing away rights for one of the debut authors I contracted when we first started."

"Constance King?"

His head jerked up. "How'd you know?"

Eliza looked at him, but there wasn't judgment or even pity in her eyes. Just . . . understanding. "She's friends with my aunt, and Aunt Sally mentioned Dennis had taken money and rights from Constance."

"I called him on it, and the jerk laughed in my face. Told me to grow up—that was how business was done." Oliver reached for his glass, then realized it was empty and set it back on the table. Catching Mindy's eye, he raised his glass, signaling the need for a refill. "I was the one who offered Constance her first contract, and her debut novel was a huge success. When Constance learned what had happened, she was crushed, and I was humiliated. I'd had enough and wanted out. He tried to sue me for breach of contract, but I got Ryan MacBride, my former stepfather, who is a practicing attorney, involved. We dissolved the partnership. And I forced Dennis to give Constance what was due her. Needing a job, I reached out to my previous employer, but rumors about what had happened spread through the industry. My reputation was tainted since it was tied to his. When Bob Johnson finally wanted to sell the bookstore, Jonah made an offer. We used to hole up in the back corner on Saturdays and read through Bob's stash of comics. After Christmas, Jonah called and said he made an offer to Bob, who accepted it."

"And that's how the Island Bookstore reopened."

"Pretty much. Jonah's leave was up, so he had to return to Germany. I came back and crashed at Dani's for a couple of weeks."

Mindy returned with two full glasses of tea and set one in front of each of them.

Eliza smiled at the younger girl, then switched her straw from the empty glass to the fresh one. "Didn't there used to be a couple of apartments above the bookstore?"

"Yes, Bronte lives in one. She was on deadline at the time, but she planned to move from Tulsa. While she was back in Oklahoma packing up her apartment, I worked with Hunter Barrett and Cody Hart to get the bookstore revamped and her place ready."

"What about the other apartment?"

Oliver reached for his glass and drained a third. He set it back on the coaster, then wiped the back of his hand across his mouth. "That's my pad. It had some water damage from a leak in the roof and needed more extensive repairs, but that's been fixed now, so I'm crashing there while working on the place at night after closing the store. Hunter's been lending a hand in his free time, but he's also been helping Henrietta Hudson's son and daughter-in-law—"

"Sadie's parents."

"Yes, right. Her parents are reopening the Hudson Bakery, which Henrietta closed after the death of her husband Hank. Now they want to have it ready by the time the season opens. Hunter's been helping Colonel Hudson with the bakery and lending a hand with my place in his spare time."

"You do remember Sadie's married to my cousin, right? Why not stay with Dani until it's done? Or even your mom? I heard she bought a cottage recently."

Oliver leaned back in the booth and listened to the country song blaring from the jukebox as he formed his next words. "Mom found a place on Poppy Place and invited me to stay in her guest room."

"And you told her no?"

"With Dani's apartment above Island Pizzeria being on Main and kitty-corner from the bookstore, staying with her while getting the bookstore up and running made more sense. Easier to get to and from work. Plus, things with my parents are a bit dicey, to put it mildly. I get along with both of them, but I don't want to be caught in the middle."

"Is your dad coming up from Florida for Dani's wedding?"

"Yes. My oldest brother, James, too. He's been working with my dad in Florida, but he'll take over as the Grand Sullivan manager in May. Having both parents at the same event will be a treat. But we'll all be there, so we'll keep them apart . . . and Dad in line. He has a habit of running his mouth at the worst times." Oliver noticed Eliza's basket of wings was empty and nodded toward the pile of bones on her plate. "Want some more?"

She wiped her mouth and shook her head. "No, thanks. I'm full. I should be heading back to the ranch anyway. I promised Mom I'd get busy with packing up my room."

"Does it feel weird leaving the ranch?"

Eliza paused a moment, her eyes on her drink, then nodded. "It's the only home I remember. I wasn't born on island, but we moved when I was a toddler. After Asher's Phoenix tour bus crashed, killing my brother, I couldn't wait to leave. From the time we were kids, Jared and I were going to take over the ranch and run it together. After his death, though . . . well, that wasn't going to happen. My aunt's assistant left to get married, so I moved to Pittsburgh and lived with Aunt Sally and became her assistant. She lost my uncle during the pandemic and hated living in their townhouse by herself, so it worked out for both of us. Her daughter—and only child—just graduated college in December and took over my job when I moved back to help Mom after her thyroid surgery."

"Your family's had several losses over the last handful of years."

Eliza lowered her head and nodded, then she lifted her face and flashed him an overly bright smile. "We managed to get through them."

"Grief changes you."

"Not always in a good way." Eliza dumped her plate of bones in her basket, then did the same with his, stacked the plates, and then moved everything to the edge of the table. "I hold on to the hope that our family will be reunited in heaven someday."

Mindy returned, gathered their dishes, and left the check.

Oliver reached for it as Eliza did, and her hand touched the top of his. She jerked it back as if she'd gotten stung. He swiped the check and pulled out his wallet. "The bookstore will cover dinner—it's a business expense for the festival."

He pulled out the company credit card, then handed the ticket and card to Mindy as she walked past. He reached for his jacket.

Mindy returned a moment later. He signed the receipt, pocketed his card, and then slid out of the booth.

Eliza zipped her jacket, then pulled her trapped hair out from beneath her collar. "Ready to hit up Martha?"

Oliver swallowed a groan just as his phone vibrated in his front pocket. After pulling it out, he found a text from Dani.

Dani
> Hey, what's the name of the publishing house you worked for? The one that publishes Victor Holt's books?

Oliver
> Palmer & Jones. Why?

Dani
> That's what I thought. They responded to a call I made a few weeks ago and offered sponsorship for the festival. Thoughts?

Oliver's pulse spiked. Yes!

Oliver
> Take it, but you'll need to be the one to contact them. Keeps me from having to solicit more sponsors. Leaving Kelley's now. I'll call in a bit.

Dani sent him a thumbs-up emoji, and Oliver pocketed his phone. He relayed the information to Eliza.

Her eyebrows shot up. "That's good news, right?"

He gave her a curt nod, then headed for the exit door. He needed some air.

Standing on the sidewalk, he breathed in the chilly night air and allowed Dani's text to tumble through his head once again.

Eliza touched his elbow. "Dani's text sounded like a good thing, but the look on your face says otherwise."

"What look on my face?"

She eyed him. "Right now, it's a cross between annoyance and deep in thought."

Oliver stuffed his hands in his jacket pockets and looked up the empty sidewalk. Flakes of snow drifted from the dark sky. Then he lifted a shoulder. "With a corporate sponsor, we don't have to put as much work into trying to get local businesses, but it adds more pressure to ensure this festival goes off without a hitch."

"We want that, no matter who sponsors. I know it still feels overwhelming. Let's just focus on the next thing that needs to be done." Eliza pointed over his shoulder. "I'm heading back to the ranch. Let's talk tomorrow and determine our next goal. Thanks for dinner."

She cut across the empty street and walked up the sidewalk to the bookstore, then turned left and headed up Blueberry Boulevard toward the 3Q Ranch.

Their conversation over dinner was the most Oliver had opened up to anyone in a long time. Eliza made it easy. And he was still standing.

As she grew smaller as the distance widened between them, he had a thought that kind of shook him.

Maybe Eliza could be a real friend. She was proving to be an excellent festival partner. Maybe they could get through the next few weeks without a problem.

Once she disappeared from sight, Oliver headed to Dani's.

However, with each step, the pressure to succeed mounted.

Now that his former employer was involved, even indirectly, he had an even stronger reason not to fail.

Six

AFTER TALKING WITH DANI LAST NIGHT ABOUT P&J's sponsorship, Oliver wanted to prove to Eliza that he could be a team player and pull in a big-name author too. He didn't want to be left in the dust.

Not that it was a competition or anything, especially since she was related to one of the biggest names in the writing biz.

He pulled his laptop off Dani's coffee table and slumped in the corner of her couch, where he'd crashed last night, too tired to return to his empty apartment.

Oliver typed in the URL for Victor Holt's website, then scrolled to the fantasy author's Connect page and drafted a quick note to Logan Kingsley, the real person behind the pen name, letting him know about the festival and inviting him to participate. Oliver left his cell phone and the store numbers, then signed off.

Closing the laptop, he returned it to the coffee table and scrubbed both hands over his face. With less than six hours of sleep under his belt, he stripped Dani's couch, folding sheets and blankets, and made quick work of transforming it back into her living space so it would be free once she woke up.

Once everything was stacked in the closet, he made a cup of coffee and then headed down the back steps, breathing in the scents of Italian seasoning, yeast, and marinara brewing from inside Island Pizzeria below Dani's apartment.

With his ears shoved into the collar of his navy winter jacket, Oliver trudged across Main toward the bookstore as the wind nipped at his face. His breath puffed out in front of him.

Last night's snow drifted against the old-fashioned light posts and the Victorian storefronts. According to his weather app, today was gearing up to be in the high 30s or even low 40s, so hopefully the couple inches of snow would melt by lunchtime.

A dog barked, and Oliver glanced in the direction of the livery on Blueberry Boulevard next to the Island House Inn. Jack, the scruffy island dog, raced across the street and pawed Oliver's leg, leaving a muddy paw print on his khakis.

Swallowing a sigh, Oliver crouched in front of the Jack Russell terrier and ran his fingers through the dog's brown and white coat. "Good morning, boy. Did you sleep well? Scrounge up anything for breakfast yet?"

Jack's ears perked as he cocked his head. Then he let out a small yip.

Oliver scooped him up, headed up the back stairs to his apartment, unlocked it, and entered.

He set Jack on the floor, and the dog took off, exploring every corner, his toenails clicking against the old vinyl tile still needing to be removed.

"Be a good boy. I'll be out in a minute." Oliver patted Jack on the head.

Oliver headed for the bathroom, took a quick shower, and changed into clean clothes.

Whistling for Jack, he scooped him up again, headed downstairs, and unlocked the back door.

"How about some breakfast, Jack?"

He drew in a deep breath as the warm shop chased away the chill. Light shone through the glass rear exit door and cast shadows across the light gray slip-resistant floor runner.

Oliver opened his office door, pulled out his black ergonomic mesh chair, and set Jack on the seat. Reaching above his desk, he flipped the switch that piped mellow jazz music through hidden speakers into the shop.

He eyed his wooden executive desk against the wall. Without taking the time to analyze his decision, he turned the heavy desk, careful not to yank his monitor onto the floor and left enough space for his chair.

He left the office, and Jack jumped off the chair and followed him to the storage room on the other side of the fireplace. He found a standing desk that one of Jonah's sisters had donated. He moved it back to his office and turned it perpendicular between his desk and his wooden bookcase. The leg bumped against something.

He reached down and found the framed photo that had fallen off his desk the other day.

He picked up the photo of Melody in his arms, brushed off the dust, and ran a finger over her face. Releasing a sigh, he set it next to his monitor.

He returned to the storage room and grabbed a dusty secretary chair. Hopefully, it would do.

Back in his office, he wet a rag in the small sink and wiped them down. He opened the cabinet above the kitchenette and found a mug with covers of banned books. Grabbing it, he moved to his desk, rummaged through the drawers, and added a few pencils, pens, and an extra pair of scissors.

Stepping back, he assessed the changes. He still had room to move around, and he didn't spend that much time in here anyway.

Should be fine.

He started a pot of coffee, then pulled a dozen eggs from the dorm fridge nestled under the counter. Until his appliances were hooked back up in his apartment, he'd been using the kitchenette in his office for meals.

He reached for a small glass bowl off the drying mat next to the small sink and cracked an egg on the rim. After beating it with a fork, he placed it in the microwave for a minute. Then he retrieved English muffins from the cabinet above the microwave and popped one in the toaster. The microwave dinged. Oliver removed the egg and scooped it onto a paper plate.

Once it had a moment to cool, he set it on the floor and whistled. "Want some breakfast, Jack?"

The dog raced to the food, gobbling it down as if it was his last meal.

Oliver made another egg, added a slice of cheese and deli ham, then blanketed them within the hot English muffin. He reached for his favorite snarky mug—a gift from his twin sister Kate—that read *I'm sorry I offended you using facts & logic*. Carrying everything to his desk, he sat down and booted up his computer.

His phone vibrated in his pocket.

He pulled it out and found a text from an unknown number.

Unknown number

Hey, man! It's Logan Kingsley.
Good to hear from you. I'd love to
know more about the festival. On
my way to the airport now. Will call
once I get through security, and
we can talk.

Oliver

> Sounds good. Thanks, man.

Jack's ears perked up, then he let out a bark and raced to the front of the store.

Oliver pocketed his phone and followed the dog to the door, where Eliza was coming in.

Spying Jack, she dropped her oversized tote bag on the floor and knelt in front of him. Jack licked her face in greeting, and she laughed as she picked him up. "Good morning to you too, Jackie boy. How are you today?"

The laugh arrowed Oliver in the chest.

Eliza looked up at him with bright eyes, her cheeks pink from the morning chill. "What's he doing in here?"

Oliver jerked a thumb over his shoulder. "I was heading over from Dani's, and he greeted me along the way. So I brought him in and made an egg for him. I figured he could keep me company while I did some bookkeeping. What are you doing here so early?"

Eliza set Jack on the floor, then pushed to her feet. She brushed dog hair off her jeans and glanced at Oliver as she unzipped her white puffer jacket. "I wanted to restock shelves and get some other things done before we got busy today."

Oliver scoffed, a sound that sounded more like a choke, and raised an eyebrow. "Busy? You're an optimistic one, aren't you?"

She shot him a grin as she removed her coat and fluffed her long, straight hair that fell down her back.

He had a sudden and uncharacteristic desire to run his fingers through the strands and see if they were truly as silky as they looked.

What was his problem today?

Not enough sleep, apparently.

Pushing past her and trying not to focus on Eliza's citrusy scent or the way her yellow sweater and jeans curved in all the right places, Oliver opened the front door, letting in a blast of cold air, and whistled. "Okay, Jack, time to head out. Thanks for being a good breakfast buddy."

The dog barked, then raced past him as something on the sidewalk caught his attention.

After closing the door, Oliver secured the deadbolt once again and glanced at the clock above the checkout desk that Dani had fashioned into a clock with twelve book covers in a circle, each one representing a number.

He had less than forty minutes before it was time to open.

Just enough time to finish his breakfast and check his accounts.

She followed him back to his office, then stopped in the doorway, pointing to the standing desk. "What's this?"

He brushed Jack's dusty prints off his chair and sat. "What's it look like?" He nodded toward the counter. "There's fresh coffee in the pot if you want some."

"You thought about me."

He looked up from his computer and found her watching him with a wide grin and blinking rapidly.

Was she tearing up? Over a dumb desk?

"More like I didn't want you messing with my stuff." He shrugged.

"Whatever." She rested a hand on the back of the chair. "Thank you. I appreciate it."

"It's just a table and a chair." He lifted a shoulder. "Nothing special."

"If you say so."

For some reason, though, he got the impression it was more than that.

Women. Go figure.

After filling a cup with coffee, Eliza left the office, humming something light and catchy.

Oliver tried to focus on the numbers on the screen, but his attention drifted down the hall.

Releasing a sigh, he pushed back from his desk, palmed his mug, and headed to the front of the store.

Eliza came out of the storage room carrying a large box.

Leaving his mug on the counter, he hurried over to her and reached for it. "Let me get that."

She twisted, moving it out of his grasp. "Oliver, I can handle this." Shooting a smile, she headed to the kids' section.

His phone rang. An unfamiliar number appeared on the screen. He thumbed over the accept button. "Oliver Sullivan."

"Hey, Oliver. It's Logan Kingsley."

"Logan, good to hear from you. Thanks for calling. Wasn't sure you'd remember me or not."

"Remember you? Are you kidding? Dude, I owe my career to you. You're the one who discovered me when you requested an R&R on my first book. I just wish you'd been the same editor when I sent back the revise and resubmit proposal."

"Yeah, sorry about that." Oliver gripped the back of his neck. "I had some personal stuff come up."

"I heard about your wife. I'm sorry, man."

"Thanks. Listen . . ." Oliver explained the festival and the different events he and Eliza—mostly Eliza—had planned, including the initial book signing to draw readers to the island the first evening. "So what do you say? Interested?"

"For sure. Count me in. I'll talk to Devin, my girlfriend, and get back to you with the details. I'm sure she'll want to come with me."

"It'll be great to see you again."

They ended the call, and Oliver couldn't stop the grin spreading across his face.

Eliza came out of the children's room and stopped. She cocked her head and gave him a quizzical look. "You look pleased about something."

Oliver waved his phone. "I just got off the phone with Logan Kingsley. He agreed to be a part of our festival."

She frowned. "Logan Kingsley? Not sure who that is."

Oliver laughed and jerked a thumb toward the table displaying his fantasy series. "You may be more familiar with his pen name—Victor Holt."

Eliza's jaw dropped, and she stared at him a moment. "Shut up. Victor Holt is not coming to the island."

Oliver slid his hands under his arms and leaned against the counter, still grinning like a fool. "Logan Kingsley, a.k.a. Victor Holt, just agreed to be a part of our festival."

He wanted to punch the air and let out a whoop, but he tried to appear calm and collected, even if his insides felt like they were doing jumping jacks.

Eliza sucked in a breath as her hands flew to her mouth. Then she rushed over to him and grabbed his arms, those serious eyes bright and animated. "You know what a big deal this is, don't you?"

Without waiting for him to answer, she swept her arm over the room. "We'll need a much bigger venue because this space won't be large enough for Victor Holt fans. After six years of no public appearances, he did his first one when his new book released in January. People camped out overnight to be a part of it. They traveled from all over the country to be there." She paused and pulled out her phone. "We could do an author meet and greet with his readers. I'm texting Dani to see if there's any open space at the Grand. She's allowing us to use a few rooms that are away from the renovations for our festival events." Then she looked up at Oliver, and her mouth downturned. "We don't have a lot of time to get word out."

Time.

His gut clenched as he realized they were a week closer to the festival. He glanced over at the front window that overlooked

Main Street. A few people walked in front of the store, but no one stopped.

Well, technically, they were still closed. And sure, the season hadn't opened yet. When it did, more people would be coming.

"Oh no. Bummer." Eliza's shoulders slumped as she looked up from her phone. "Dani said the larger spaces are booked already."

"Not surprising since most of the Grand is still undergoing renovations. So maybe getting Victor Holt to be a part of our festival wasn't such a great idea." He held out his hands.

"Are you kidding me?" Eliza grabbed one of his hands and high-fived him. Her fingers curled through his and gave a light squeeze. "It was a fantastic idea. Really good. And keep 'em coming. That's how we're going to get things done, partner. Trust me."

He looked down at the long fingers with neat, unpolished nails, then back up to the hopeful look in her brown eyes.

She released his hand and headed back to the children's department.

Partner. Trust me.

Simple words. Powerful impact.

Eliza hadn't let him down yet, so maybe he needed to shove his doubt away and believe this thing just might work.

Eliza had another plan to grow the festival. She just needed to get Oliver's feedback. Now that he'd seemed excited after the Victor Holt score earlier this morning, she hoped he'd be more on board with the new ideas she proposed.

Hopefully, he'd see she had the bookstore's—and the island's—best interests in mind.

After putting out new books in the kids' section, she returned to the register and managed to knock over Oliver's mug and spilled half a cup of coffee down her pants.

He sent her home to change. While she was there, she grabbed her iPad, where she'd transferred Dani's notes she'd transcribed last night into a digital work plan so she didn't have to haul that huge behemoth binder around.

What was it with this island and dragging their feet into the digital age?

Not wanting to waste any more time than she had already, since she was running late, Eliza borrowed her parents' golf cart and drove it down Blueberry Boulevard, the sun warming her face against the chill sweeping across the lake. She waved to Tommy McIntyre, the fire chief, as he exited the station.

Seagulls plucking at something tossed on the street scattered as she made it to the bookstore. She parked behind the shop, then rounded the side of the building.

As she reached the door, Doug Manning came out of the market next door.

He steadied a chalkboard easel that highlighted the weekly specials outside his old-fashioned grocery store with empty flower boxes waiting for the annuals he added every year in memory of his late wife.

"Hey, Doug. How's it going?"

The fiftysomething man peered at her through his thick glasses and smiled. "Hey, Eliza. How's it going?"

"Good. Good. Busy with the festival prep."

He chuckled. "This island loves their festivals."

"It's a people draw, and that's what we need right now to revitalize. We'd love to talk with you about participating as one of our sponsors. You could advertise the market in the booklet we're handing out to readers."

"Could I include a coupon they could use at my place?"

"Absolutely. If you know the discount you'd like to offer, I could create a few graphics and run them by you."

He scratched his clean-shaven chin. "Let me think about it. It would be good to have more foot traffic. Stop by after work, and I'll let you know what I need."

"Sounds good, and thank you."

Eliza pivoted and reached for the door to the bookstore as an older woman pushed it open on her way out. Eliza held it for her, then bounced inside. And stopped.

Oliver had opened the curtains.

Even though she'd taken down the curtains to create the window displays the other day, he ended up putting them back up.

For the last week, she opened them every morning after clocking in. And he closed them after their days ended.

Since she'd hurried off to change clothes, she hadn't opened them.

But he did.

Would a dance in the middle of the room be too much? Probably. She didn't want to scare him off.

Between the curtains and Oliver making room for her in his office, she wasn't quite sure what to think. He'd claimed it wasn't anything special.

Maybe not to him. But she couldn't read too much into it.

She was not getting caught up in a "workplace romance" as her mom called it.

Oliver looked up from behind the counter, his phone in his hand and a scowl on his face. "You're back."

"Hello to you too, Grouchy Pants."

"I'm not grouchy." His words came out as a growl.

"Could've fooled me."

He sighed and gave her that look she interpreted as she was getting on his nerves.

She moved to the front of the checkout counter, set her tote bag next to the register, and pulled out a container of cookies. Popping the lid, she held the container out to him. "Here, try one of these. It'll sweeten you up. Mom was making them when I went back to change."

"You think I need sweetening up?" He took one of the chocolate no-bakes and bit into it.

"After her thyroid surgery and learning she has Hashimoto's, Mom went gluten-free and dairy-free to manage her illness. She made these with gluten-free oats and almond milk."

Oliver stopped chewing and raised an eyebrow.

Eliza laughed. "They're good, I promise." She broke one in half and popped it in her mouth. Then she wiped her fingers on the seam of her jeans and dug out her iPad. "I grabbed my iPad while back at the ranch so I could show you what I did last night."

"Creating more big plans for the festival keeping you awake again?"

She dropped her gaze to her tablet, then peered at him out of the corner of her eye. "I . . . slept."

He folded his arms over his chest. "Actually, I was kidding. You've been coming in here with new ideas almost every day. Made me wonder if you actually sleep at night." He looked at her, his eyes serious. "So just how long *did* you sleep last night?"

"Five hours." Her words sounded like a squeak.

"Eliza, that's not healthy." He dropped his arms and took a step toward her. "You're going to wear yourself out planning this festival."

"I'll be fine." She waved away his words. "I came up with a name for the festival. What do you think about Novel Connections? And I created a new social media campaign along with some graphics and reels to upload to the store accounts. Oh, and I just saw Doug Manning." She nodded toward the market. "I think he's going to advertise in our booklet and offer a coupon for the readers to use in his market. Pretty smart, huh? Maybe we should do something like that for here."

"I thought the purpose was to bring in sales, not give things away."

Eliza fisted a hand on her hip. "You're not giving away anything—well, not unless you want to—but you could include a percentage-off coupon in the readers' bags that would bring them back into the store. Or you could do a store-wide coupon and have it for limited merchandise. And it's just for that weekend. Scarcity—"

"Marketing. Yeah, you've mentioned that before. I'll think about it."

What was it with these males and needing to think about marketing decisions? She saw it as a win in the long run. But whatever.

She tapped on one of the bookstore's social media accounts to show the graphics she created and scheduled, but then she let out a little gasp when she noticed the number of notifications.

"What's wrong?"

Eyes still on the screen, Eliza shook her head as she scrolled through the notifications. "Nothing. I don't think . . ."

"You don't think?"

Her head shot up and she grinned. "I think all the time, actually. Too much, at times."

He gave her that "you're being annoying" look again, and she swallowed a giggle.

But her amusement was short-lived as she read a scathing post from a popular book reviewer complaining about the festival. Her stomach tightening, Eliza scrolled to the woman's page and her heart flipped over.

The woman posted a rant about trying to purchase tickets on the store's new site but then she got locked out. When she tried to communicate with the bookstore through email and a phone call, she hadn't gotten a response. She ended her tirade with #scam and other hashtags that reflected poorly on the shop. People jumped on her bandwagon and posted negative comments.

"You got quiet. What's going on? You're never quiet."

Feeling the blood leave her face, Eliza handed him the tablet.

"What's this?"

"Just read it." Her fingers curled into fists.

As he read, his jaw tightened as his nostrils flared, and his lips thinned.

Forcing a neutral tone, she looked at him. "Did anyone call or email you about the festival?"

Oliver lifted a shoulder and handed the iPad back to her. He dragged a hand through his hair, rumpling the waves. "I don't know. I've been getting calls, and I couldn't always get to them, so I let them go to voicemail. Then I don't always remember to check."

"I'll handle them from now on. I'll check the answering machine when I come in each day and go through the store's emails. Just give me the password." Eliza gestured to the iPad. "And I'll take care of this too. The last thing we want is for anyone to pull out of the festival. I'll reach out to the reviewer and offer her something special."

"So we're giving in to cyberbullies now?"

"She's not a bully, Oliver. Sure, her words are a bit harsh, but this is on us. We need to offer clear communication. Besides, it's a win-win for all of us. She has a large circle of influence, so we could use her on our side."

"If you say so."

Eliza swallowed her frustration and shoved her iPad back into her bag. Leaving the cookies on the counter, she nodded toward the office. "Well, I'll leave you to your busyness and go take care of this."

Without waiting for him to respond, she headed down the hall and moved to her desk. Her phone rang, and she dug it out of her back pocket. Her aunt's agent's name and number appeared on the screen.

"Hey, Candace."

"Hi, Eliza. Hope I'm not bothering you at work. I expected to leave a message."

"It's fine. What's up?"

"Well, I just had a surprising call with Sally Jo. She mentioned she's planning to come on island for the festival, which is great. She also said you're thinking about becoming an agent. Is that true?"

"I tossed the idea around, but I haven't settled on it." She rested an elbow on the standing desk.

"Would you be willing to meet for breakfast on Saturday at Good Day Coffee and we could discuss a few things?"

"Sure, I'd love that. I'd also like to talk to you about a writing workshop, if you don't mind."

"Not at all. Let's add it to tomorrow's breakfast agenda."

Spoken like a true publishing professional.

They ended the call, and Eliza stared at her silent phone, contemplating Candace's offer. She loved working at the bookstore, and the festival was temporary busyness. Would she be able to manage working for Oliver and Candace?

Well, she'd know more soon . . . and maybe have a better idea for what was next.

Seven

ELIZA HAD LESS THAN AN HOUR TO MEET WITH Candace Bishop to discuss her future.

Problem was, she wasn't sure if that was the career path she wanted to take, but maybe breakfast with Candace before work could sway her one way or another. Plus, Eliza needed to discuss her participation in the writing workshop for the festival.

Despite her good intentions of heading to bed at a decent hour, that hadn't happened.

Again.

She'd stayed up late fixing the glitch with the website, festival registration, and writing a very apologetic note to the frustrated book reviewer.

She'd finally fallen asleep around two a.m.... and slept through her alarm.

After showering and dressing in jeans and her blue Island Bookstore polo shirt that Oliver ordered for her, Eliza dried her hair, twisted it, and secured it in place with a clip. As she applied her makeup, her mother's laughter drifted up the stairs.

She tidied her space, half-heartedly made her bed, throwing the white eyelet comforter left over from her teen years over the rumpled blue-and-white striped sheets, then grabbed her tote bag. She closed the door behind her . . . and the guilt of not being packed up yet.

Soon, the only bedroom she remembered having was about to become a memory. Being back on island for the past few months, she'd spent more time in the room than in the last ten years or so. Part of her was ready to say goodbye to the white walls, framed photos of family and friends, ribbons and trophies from horse shows, and cases of her beloved books from childhood until she graduated college.

But another part wanted to hold on to what was. But that wouldn't be the same again.

She stared at the closed door across the hall from her room. Jared's room.

Mom was right—they needed to pack it up, but Eliza couldn't bring herself to touch the doorknob, let alone step inside and dismantle the room that had remained untouched since her brother was killed.

While she understood her parents' desire to slow down, that didn't lessen the sting of saying goodbye to her safety net.

Things might have been different if Jared were around, but he wasn't.

God had other plans. And Eliza needed to trust Him.

She released a sigh, then stiffened her spine and headed for the polished wooden stairs. Scents of fresh coffee and cinnamon rose up the steps.

Following the sounds of voices, she moved through the living room devoid of the family photos and horse pictures that used to hang on the walls. They'd been wrapped and packed for the new cottage. The furniture remained, but not for long.

Eliza walked into the kitchen and found Mom with a full coffeepot in her hand, refilling the cups of her visiting friends, Henrietta and Joanne Hudson.

Sunlight shone through a trio of windows along the east wall, stretching light across the reclaimed wood flooring. The creamy white cabinets contrasted with the exposed beam ceiling and natural wood trim. The kitchen was twice the size as the one in her parents' new cottage. How would they fit everything in the new place?

The glass doors to the built-ins were open, with half of Grandma Quinn's milk glass collection remaining on the shelves. Judging by the boxes and pile of newspapers in front of the cabinet, Eliza suspected Mom was packing the vintage collection.

"Good morning, ladies. You're up early." Eliza kissed her mother's cheek, trying not to let the shadows under Mom's eyes give her pause, then hugged Henrietta, her mother's longtime prayer partner and Sadie's Gran, and Joanne, Henrietta's daughter-in-law and Sadie's mother.

"Morning, honey. We're doing our weekly Bible study. Care to join us?" Mom lifted the pot as if to ask if Eliza wanted some. Her dark hair had been twisted and clipped like Eliza's. Bangs and soft fringe framed Mom's face. The scar at the base of her neck was fading from bright pink to soft rose. The dove necklace Dad had given her the day of Jared's funeral lay in the hollow of her throat.

Shaking her head, Eliza held up a hand. "Thanks, but I have a meeting before work." She turned back to the table. "Henrietta, how's Georgie doing? I haven't seen your little dog lately."

Henrietta brushed her white hair off her forehead and flashed one of her warm smiles. "Oh, the little rascal is as mischievous as ever. Since Gregory and Joanne moved back home, though, he's been following Gregory around and even managed to finagle a trip to the bakery this morning."

Eliza laughed as she tore a corner off one of the cinnamon rolls smothered in a sugary glaze and popped it in her mouth. "Joanne, how are things going at the bakery? Still on track to open by the beginning of the season?"

Joanne added cream to her coffee and nodded, her dark bob bouncing against her chin. "Yes, Greg and Asher are there now, installing a new oven. After the pipe burst in the kitchen last September, we decided to replace the equipment. Now that the ice has thawed, our orders are shipping again."

"I'm looking forward to a fresh-from-the-fryer Hudson Bakery raspberry-filled doughnut again." Shouldering her tote bag, Eliza kissed her mother's cheek again, waved to the ladies, and reached for her coat and scarf on the hook by the back door. "Have a good day."

Winding her scarf around her neck, she headed for the garage and retrieved her aqua single-speed cruiser. Steering it toward Sugar Maple Lane, she pedaled in a light flurry of snow. The cold air pebbled the skin on her hands and face. She'd forgotten to grab her gloves.

Ten minutes later, she parked her bike behind the bookstore, crossed Main Street, and headed for Good Day Coffee.

Her phone vibrated in her bag. She pulled it out and found a message from Candace saying she'd arrived and found a table for them.

Opening the door, she stepped inside and breathed deeply as the scents of coffee, sugar, and vanilla swirled around her as her face thawed.

Behind the counter, owner Jill Kelley rang up a customer and laughed at something the woman said. A lighthearted sound that bounced off the walls and competed with the sounds of coffee grinders and espresso machines.

Much nicer than most of her relatives, Jill had a way of making people feel at home. And that was one of the reasons Good Day Coffee was always packed.

Waving to Jill, Eliza scanned the airy, cozy shop with its pastel teal walls until she spotted Candace by the large front window that overlooked Main.

Of course. She should've known.

Candace loved people watching. Called it keeping her pulse on what was happening on island.

Forcing herself to bypass the pastry case, Eliza walked over, set her tote bag on the wooden table, pulled out a black iron chair, and shrugged out of her coat. "Morning, Candace."

Candace turned from the window, her green eyes bright beneath her crown of pixie-cut white hair. "Hello, dear. Your cheeks are red, but you'll warm up in no time. It's toasty in here."

"A chai will definitely help." Eliza peeked briefly at the pastry case that held muffins, scones, cookies, and probably slices of cheesecake before averting her eyes to the chalkboard menu. She glanced at Candace's teal mug stamped with the Good Day Coffee logo in white. "Are you eating or just having coffee?"

Candace lifted her cup, gold bracelets tumbling from her wrist to forearm. "Just coffee for now. I was up at five, worked out, had some eggs, and then sent off a few proposals."

Goodness, she made Eliza feel like a slug.

"What will you do when you retire?" Shaking her head, Eliza grabbed her wallet and headed to the counter. She ordered a hot chai tea and a breakfast sandwich.

Jill flicked her bright red ponytail over her shoulder, then handed Eliza a steaming paper cup with a corrugated collar. "I filled out the sheet for the ad in the reader booklet. Want it now, or should I drop it off at the bookstore?"

"You can give it to me now. I'm headed there after this."

"Great. I'll bring it out with your food."

"Thanks." Smiling at the fiftysomething woman, Eliza took her chai and returned to her seat.

Candace folded her hands on the table. "So, as I mentioned on the phone on Thursday, Sally said you expressed interest in becoming an agent."

Eliza removed the plastic lid from her cup. "Honestly? I'm not sure. When Aunt Sally said you were retiring, I considered the idea of becoming an agent. I'm staying on island and looking for an apartment, so I'll need to figure out something soon. In addition to working at the bookstore, that is."

"Yes, I heard your parents sold the ranch. That's quite a change."

Nodding, Eliza blew on the tea. "To my cousin and his wife. Mom and Dad found a cottage on Rose Road. We've been repainting while Dad and Asher handled the updates. They want to move in next month."

"That'll be here before you know it."

Eliza didn't need to look at the calendar to know her days on the ranch were coming to an end. She squashed down the rush of sadness and took a sip of her tea. "I love helping authors and getting their stories in front of readers, especially those underrated books with little exposure. I have some contacts because of my aunt, but those are limited."

"I'm hosting my final author retreat in a week or so. You should come. Get to know the authors I manage." Candace reached inside her designer handbag and pulled out a tablet. She tapped on the screen and turned it toward Eliza. "This is my schedule for today. Each color represents a specific author."

Eliza's eyes widened at the rainbow plastered across the screen. "How do you keep it straight?"

"Organization. Focus. Doing one thing at a time. But I'll admit—I get tired easier these days. My husband wants more time together, so I'm retiring after my seventieth birthday. If you're serious about this, I'd be willing to take you on as an assistant.

Teach you the ropes. Share a few clients. Then you can grow from there. Your aunt is highly respected, and you learned a lot while you worked for her. But you don't need to ride her coattails. You have your own strengths."

Knowing what a sharpshooter Candace was, Eliza's heart swelled. "Thank you. I just . . . I don't know if I have what it takes."

Candace leaned in, her eyes sharp and direct. "You are more than capable. And remember—the good Lord gives us the courage and the confidence to do what He's called us to do."

"You're right. Anything worth having takes hard work."

"Exactly. And you have what it takes. But is it what you want to do?"

The question tumbled around inside Eliza's head as Jill arrived with Eliza's food and an envelope. "Here's my check for the ad in the reader's booklet."

"Thanks, Jill." Eliza smiled at her, then tucked the envelope in her tote and looked at Candace again. "Once I'm done with the festival and helping my parents move, could I take you up on your offer?"

"Of course." Candace took a sip of coffee, her ringed fingers cupping the mug. "You mentioned a writing workshop. Tell me more about it."

Eliza pulled her own tablet out of her tote and found her festival notes. "I've found a group of readers on social media who are interested in becoming writers. I talked to Aunt Sally, and she's willing to give a presentation on basic story-crafting skills. I'd like to invite you to share what writers need to know before querying and submitting to agents and editors."

"Sounds easy enough. Sure, I'll take part in that." Candace drained her cup and pushed to her feet. She picked up her handbag and hooked it over the crook of her elbow. "I'm sorry to cut this short, but I must catch the ferry with my husband. We're heading to Port Joseph to see our grandchildren."

Dressed in black pants, polished boots, and a white turtleneck sweater paired with a floral silk scarf, Candace looked tall and elegant. Eliza felt a little dumpy compared to her. But what set Candace apart was her kindness and professionalism in an industry where both needed to be held in high regard.

"I need to head to work anyway. Thanks for meeting with me." Ignoring her untouched sandwich, Eliza stood and reached for her coat. She wrapped her sandwich in a couple of napkins and dropped it into her bag. Grabbing her tea, she followed Candace outside.

They parted ways as Candace headed for the ferry while Eliza walked to the bookstore. Snow dusted the cobblestone streets and settled on awnings and windowsills of the shops lining Main Street.

A dray wagon passed, and Eliza waved at Finley Campbell, an old friend of the family whom her dad rehired now that business was picking up. She admired the strength and skills of the two black Percherons pulling the load.

At the bookstore, she battled the wind and hurried inside. With her back against the door, she found Oliver lifting a box over his head. His forearm muscles flexed as back muscles rippled beneath his polo shirt.

For a moment, all of the words fell out of her brain.

Where had he been hiding *those*?

"Good morning."

She blinked, then found her tongue. "Good morning."

As her cheeks heated—hopefully from the warmth inside the bookstore—she headed to his office and hooked her coat and bag next to his on the back of the door. She paused a moment and pressed her cold hands to her warm cheeks.

Get a grip. You've seen guys with muscles before.

She returned to the front of the store, lukewarm breakfast

sandwich in hand. "I just left Good Day Coffee. Want half of my sandwich?"

Shaking his head, he lifted another box of books, set it on an empty table near the display window, and used a box cutter to slice it open. "Thanks, but I already ate. You go ahead."

Eliza clocked in at the register, then broke apart her sandwich and ate it quickly. She washed it down with several gulps of still-hot tea. She wiped her mouth and tossed the napkins in the trash.

She glanced around the quiet shop. "What more can we do to attract customers?"

"Just hold on and hope the festival brings in more business, I guess." Oliver brushed his hands together, then leaned folded arms on the counter. "Let's open a little later today and head to the Grand."

"For what?"

"Based on the lack of customers lately, I'm surmising it's going to be another slow day. Don't worry—we'll be back for story time." He looked out the window and sighed.

Oh, right. She was supposed to read today.

He pushed away from the counter. "On our way to the hotel, we can review the events that will be held there—Victor Holt's meet and greet and Sally Jo Wilson's writing workshops. Between the bookstore, the Grand, and the informal gatherings on Blueberry Hill Park, we'll need to create a map for the booklet."

"So . . . surmising, huh? Steal that from your Word-of-the-Day calendar?" Eliza shot him a grin.

Oliver lifted a shoulder. "Nah, just a leftover spelling bee word when I was ten that never left my head." Clearing his throat, he straightened, legs together and hands down at his sides. He lifted his chin. "Surmising. Verb. Definition—suspecting something could be true without evidence to confirm it. S-U-R-M-I-S-I-N-G. Surmising."

Laughing, Eliza clapped as she tried to imagine ten-year-old

Oliver at a spelling bee. "Well done." Then she opened the drawer beneath the register and found stickers they handed out to the kids. She peeled off a gold star, rounded the corner of the counter, then stuck it to his chest, smoothing the points in place.

Her palm tingled, and she jerked her hand back, curling fingers into fists.

What was her problem today?

She needed to pay more attention to Oliver's words than his physique, especially since he was actually taking an interest in the festival.

She returned the stickers to the drawer and bumped it closed with her hip. "So when do you want to go?"

"How about now?"

"Sounds good."

"Great, let's grab our coats and head on over. I borrowed a golf cart from Dani since she's going to be working in her office for several hours. Let's head out the back and then take the hill up to the hotel."

Nodding, Eliza returned to Oliver's office and grabbed her jacket off the hook. As she headed back out the door, he started to enter. She shuffled to the side to get out of his way just as he moved in the same direction.

"Trying to dance with me?" Then he laughed, a rich sound that melted over her like cream swirling into coffee.

He brushed past her, his arm touching hers, and she forced herself not to act like some giggly fifteen-year-old.

Good grief. Get a grip.

But part of her couldn't stop her imagination from wondering what it would be like to dance with him.

She headed outside and took a seat in the very cold cart. Oliver followed, pausing to lock the door. Then he slid into the driver's side and started the golf cart. He maneuvered them out of the parking spot and headed up the boulevard toward the Grand Sullivan.

She held on to her seat to keep from knocking into him. With every bump, her arm brushed his, but he didn't seem to be fazed. He stared ahead as he maneuvered the golf cart up the hill toward the hotel.

Leafless trees, pines, and old-fashioned lamp posts flanked the slope leading to the hotel. The expansive stately Grand Sullivan crowned the hill and stretched across the lawn speckled with snow. White columns grew taller as they approached. An American flag rippled in the breeze, and empty white rocking chairs moving without patrons lined the community porch.

The fragrant spring air smelled clean and crisp. To the left, the steel-blue lake met the pale sky.

"I've lived here most of my life, and the scenery of the island still takes my breath away." Eliza lifted her face to the sun trying to peek through the clouds.

Oliver glanced at her. "Feeling poetic this morning?"

"More like appreciative."

Oliver drove to the back of the hotel and parked in the employee lot. They rounded the front and stepped inside, the indoor heat chasing away the chill.

Eliza breathed in the fresh flower arrangements from Holly's Flowers perfuming the lobby. The chandeliers sent glitters of light across the bold-patterned carpet in tones of red and gold.

While much of the hotel was still under construction, the main lobby had been completed and was open for business.

Josh Colvin, the interim manager, came around the reception desk and moved toward them, his hand out. Dressed in a well-fitted dark suit with a silver-and-blue striped tie and his blond hair slicked away from his face, Josh's warm smile was welcoming.

Oliver shook the man's hand. "Morning, Josh." Then he turned to Eliza. "You know Eliza, right?"

"Of course. We went to school together." He extended his hand to her. "How's it going?"

Smiling, she shook his hand. "Good to see you, Josh. Thanks for all you're doing to help with the festival."

"Hey, anything to bring tourists back on island is a win for all of us. What can I do for you today?"

Oliver glanced at Eliza, then cleared his throat. "We were hoping to talk with Chelsea, the events coordinator Dani was working with before she passed the festival over to us."

"Of course." He pointed to a hall on his right. "Head to the Rose Room, and you should find her preparing for a luncheon being held there this afternoon."

As they headed down the hall, Eliza trailed her fingers along the yellow wallpaper trimmed with white molding.

Growing up, the hotel always seemed like a fairy tale to her. And rich in history, especially this part that survived the fire.

They reached the Rose Room. Heavy wooden doors were closed, and Oliver pushed one open, then stepped back, allowing her to pass.

Eliza stepped into the room, but Chelsea wasn't there. Maybe she'd be back shortly.

Eliza turned slowly to take in the stage cloaked in heavy burgundy curtains, rose-patterned walls, and tall windows framed with dusty-rose drapes that had been pulled to allow the morning light to sweep across the deep rose carpeting. Round tables had been covered in white linens and held blush-pink rose centerpieces that fragranced the room.

She sighed and pressed a hand to her chest. "I don't know what's happening in here today, but I'd love to be a part of it."

Oliver stood behind Eliza—so close she could inhale his woodsy scent. "This was my mom's favorite room. And Dani's."

"I can see why." Eliza touched the embossed roses in the wallpaper. "I wonder just how many celebrations have taken place here over the years."

Oliver moved in front of her, hands in his pockets as he turned slowly. "We held my mom's fortieth birthday here. Dad planned this elaborate surprise party, and she cried when he brought her in. I remember my parents dancing, and she rested her cheek against his chest. In that moment, everything seemed . . ." He shrugged. "Right, I guess. I wanted to dance with my wife in this room. Maybe raise our children on island. But the fire changed that."

He spoke those last words so low they were almost like a whisper. Almost as if he hadn't meant to say them out loud.

Sighing, he turned and looked at her with a somewhat sad smile tugging at his lips. "Doesn't matter. Not going to happen now."

As Eliza did a slow walk around the perimeter of the vast room, one thing became very clear.

She'd misjudged Oliver Sullivan.

He wasn't grumpy. He was a heartbroken man who was trying to climb his way back to the light.

She returned to him and touched his sleeve. "Let's talk to Josh and see if we can host the closing luncheon in this room."

Oliver looked at her fingers a moment, then smiled sweetly. "Doesn't hurt to ask."

As they moved to the door, she glanced over her shoulder one more time and took a mental picture to add to her notes once she was back at the shop.

More than anything, she wanted the festival to be perfect, and this room would be a wonderful way to conclude the whirlwind two-day event.

She turned back to the door and found Oliver watching her, something unreadable in his eyes. As she moved past him and back into the hall, her shoulder brushed his as he turned and closed the door.

Their footsteps padded by the carpet, they headed back to the main lobby to find Chelsea. Ideas tumbled over in Eliza's mind, but they had nothing to do with the festival and everything to do with the man next to her.

While she appreciated Candace's offer, training to become an agent would have to wait.

She couldn't bring back Oliver's wife, but she'd do whatever it took to make the festival work so the bookstore would succeed and he could rebuild his life on island.

Just inviting her to the Grand had shown he'd taken another interest in the festival, and she was determined to make sure the event highlighted Oliver and his store in the most positive light.

Oliver *really* needed his apartment to be finished. He wanted more than an air mattress, an old chair, and a couple of books in his living space.

After getting Hunter's text that he and Waylen were available to put down the flooring, Oliver finished what he was doing, then headed out the back door of the bookstore. He glanced at the golf cart still parked from when he and Eliza had visited the Grand that morning.

Watching her take in the Rose Room had tugged at something in his chest—something he hadn't felt in a long time. He needed some time and headspace to explore what that meant, but not right now. He was on a mission.

He jogged up the back steps behind the store, headed to his apartment, and opened the door. Tapping and a low rumble of conversation echoed through the empty space.

Hunter and Waylen crouched on their knees, tapping planks of flooring in place.

"Hey, man, what's up?" Waylen lifted his chin and adjusted the navy bandanna holding his hair in place.

"Your brother has you working on your day off?" Oliver leaned against a support beam that separated the living area from the small kitchen.

Hunter lifted a shoulder, then adjusted the backward ball cap over his dark hair. "Bro needed some cash, and I needed a second pair of hands. Sounds like a win-win to me."

"Hey, if it gets me my digs done faster, I'll pay for a third set of hands. Or even offer mine after the shop closes."

"Sounds to me like you have your hands full as it is." Waylen waggled his eyebrows and flashed a cocky grin.

"What do you mean by that?"

"I heard you hired Eliza Quinn. She's ho—"

"Don't finish that sentence, man." Oliver's fingers curled into fists, then he shoved them under his arms.

Why was he getting so defensive about Eliza all of a sudden?

Waylen lifted his hands. "Dude, no offense meant."

Hunter grabbed a rag and flicked his brother with it. "Knock it off, bonehead."

"Hey, I could arrest you for assault."

Hunter dropped the rag and did a backward wave gesture. "Bring it on, tough guy."

While the brothers bickered, Oliver pushed away from the beam and reached for the open box of white oak laminate. He laid out the rest of the pieces so the guys just had to tap them into place.

Hunter sat back on his haunches and ran his forearm over his brow. "The floor will be done tonight, and the place is starting to come together. Once you bring up your furniture, it'll be a solid living space. What do you think?"

Oliver thought back to the earlier moment with Eliza in the Rose Room. It'd taken everything in his power not to take her into his arms and dance to the music playing in his head as he watched her explore the room with wonder—and maybe a bit of longing—in her eyes.

But he'd remained rooted by the door. No need to look like a fool. And she was his employee.

He was having a harder time remembering that.

Yes, he could see a future on island, beginning with having a real living space.

"I finished the painting, so I guess all that's left is to get my stuff on island and grab some help to cart it up the stairs."

Waylen pushed to his feet and swiped the half-empty water bottle off the floor. He chugged the rest then crumpled the plastic. "Buy a round at Kelley's, and I'm in."

"Sounds good." Oliver held out a fist, and Hunter bumped it. "Thanks, man."

"Sure thing."

A knock sounded on the open door.

Oliver turned and found Bronte standing in the doorway. He waved her in. "Hey, neighbor. How's it going?"

Standing around 5'8" or 5'9", the top of her head came to his nose. Her dark, curly hair was held in place by a fabric headband that matched her gray eyes and fair skin. She wore an oversized olive-green Army hoodie, probably stolen from Jonah, and a pair of patterned leggings.

She shot him a wide smile. "Pretty good. Just emailed my manuscript to Jonah. He'll read through it before I send it to my agent Lexi."

"Another Pike Sisters story?"

Bronte shook her head. "I wrapped up that series . . . and did something completely different. A rom-com, if you can believe it. I started it last Christmas when I got snowed in at Holland's cottage."

"Yeah, Jonah mentioned that."

"I hear you and Eliza are making good strides with the festival."

"It's coming along. I know you're not a fan of in-person events, but we're planning to kick off the festival with a book signing featuring Sally Jo Wilson. Plus, Victor Holt will be joining us for other events."

"Whoa, seriously?" Bronte's eyes widened. "How'd you score

Victor Holt? The man is just now stepping out of the shadows. Bringing in the big guns, for sure."

Oliver brushed imaginary dirt off his shoulder. "We don't do things halfway at the Island Bookstore."

Bronte laughed. "You mean Eliza doesn't do things halfway."

Oliver rolled his eyes. "Whatever. Let me know if you're interested."

"I'll think about it. If Jonah were here, I could handle it. I'll let you know after I talk to him tonight."

"Thanks, B." Oliver's phone vibrated in his pocket. He pulled it out and found Logan Kingsley's name on the screen. He glanced at Bronte. "Excuse me, I have to take this call."

She jerked a thumb toward the door. "I have to go anyway. I'm meeting up with Holland, Amy, and Mika Beth. See you later, neighbor."

He lifted a chin as he answered the call and followed her out into the hall. "Hey, Logan. How's it going, man?"

"Hey, Oliver. I'm sure you're busy, man, so I won't take up much of your time. I met a promising new writer at my book signing in January, and she emailed me the other day. She's looking for an editor for her first book and asked for suggestions. She's considering going indie since receiving several rejections due to her low social media numbers. I wondered if you'd be interested in taking a look."

Oliver dragged a hand over his face. "Thanks for thinking of me, but I'm out of the editing business, remember?"

"I get that. It's just that she shows so much promise and deserves to have someone steer her in the right direction. I wasn't sure if you've considered doing any freelance work, but I do know I owe my career to you. She and her husband aren't really hurting for money, and she's willing to pay well for your time." Logan named a price that caused Oliver's breath to catch.

Man, the offer was tempting. But Oliver had sworn off editing, sworn off being a part of the world that he'd allowed to define who he was.

But the money the writer was offering…well, that was hard to turn down. Especially if it could help get his apartment finished sooner than expected.

What would it hurt to read a few pages?

He blew out a breath. "Yeah, okay, have her send it, but I make no promises. I have a lot going on the next couple of weeks with the festival, and my little sister is getting married."

"Thanks, man. I appreciate it. I'll have Jolene get in touch with you."

After they talked through a few more details, they ended the call, and Oliver headed back to the bookstore.

As he strode past his office and into the shop, he heard singing. He moved through the chest-high shelves and found Eliza singing along to the music streaming into the room as she arranged a stack of books in the other display window.

He slipped his fingers in his front pockets. "Your brother and cousin weren't the only ones with musical abilities in your family."

Eliza yelped, whirled around, and fumbled the stack of books in her arms. Her cheeks darkened to a deep red.

A sight he found endearing.

And that bugged him more than surprising her.

"Oliver." Sounding a little breathless, she brushed her hair away from her face. "I didn't hear you come back."

"Apparently." He folded his arms and leaned against the counter. "Pretend I'm not here. I don't mind a free concert."

She scrunched her face. "I just sing for pleasure. And when I'm *alone*."

"Don't underestimate yourself, Eliza. You have a lovely voice."

Her eyes widened as she fluttered her hands in front of her face. "Is the great Oliver Sullivan actually paying me a compliment?"

"Knock it off. I meant it."

"Thanks. I appreciate your kind words." She set the books on the floor of the display window and crossed to the counter. She rounded it and pulled something out of the cabinet under the register and handed it to him.

He took the paper. "What's this?"

"The solution to our disgruntled book reviewer. I offered her a free ticket to Victor Holt's event, and she agreed."

Oliver scanned a printed email conversation between Eliza and the annoyed book reviewer. "Did you ask her to take down her post?"

"We don't want it to look like we're offering a bribe. I sent her a lovely email apologizing for the issue and asked her to direct future correspondence to the new store email I set up and can check."

"Thanks for handling that." He set the paper on the counter.

"Oh, and I arranged a lunch with you and Graham Lee, who has agreed to be a part of the suspense-writers' panel."

"Graham Lee." He reached for a hardbound copy of *Midnight Silence*, featuring one of Oliver's favorite crime-fighting protagonists, and thumped the cover. "This Graham Lee? How'd you manage that?"

She lifted a shoulder as if it was no big deal. "He's one of Candace Bishop's clients, so I called and asked her to help set it up. He's an excellent writer, but his books are woefully underappreciated. I decided to do a window display of her clients and put his books in the center." She waved to the window display she'd been creating.

Oliver returned the book to the stack and opened the front door. Leaving it ajar, he walked outside and viewed the display from the sidewalk.

She'd draped boxes in black and gray fabric and set out Graham Lee's new detective collection along with a tattered red umbrella that matched the one on the cover of *Midnight Silence*. She'd recreated Detective Joe Sterling's evidence board and hung it on the side wall with the words *Guilty of Keeping You Reading Past Your*

Bedtime and pinned pictures of Candace Bishop's clients looking like mug shots.

Something rose inside his chest, something that told him hiring Eliza had been the right decision. In the past couple weeks, she'd breathed life into the store, shining fresh light . . . and another set of eyes. The subtle changes didn't go unnoticed.

He returned inside and looked at Eliza. "The display looks impressive. You have a good eye for design. Thanks."

She waved off his words. "I just want good books to get the attention they deserve . . . and more exposure to underappreciated authors like Graham."

"I get that. When I was an editor, there was always this excitement of finding great manuscripts in the slush pile. Especially with those debut authors who had the courage to submit the stories they spent so much time writing."

"Hand me one of those books, please." She pointed to the stack of *Midnight Silence* hardbacks.

While Eliza finished the display, she shared details with Oliver about his upcoming lunch with Graham Lee at Martha's on Main and a few more details about the festival.

Just watching her face light up, the way she talked with her hands, and the way her voice rose when she was excited stirred something deep within him. Something he hadn't felt when Dani asked him to take over coordinating the festival.

Excitement.

Instead of the dread that seemed to pool daily in his gut, he now looked forward to what was coming.

But the one thing he wasn't too sure about was how quickly Eliza was getting under his skin.

He was trying not to care for her more than as an employee, fellow coordinator . . . or even a friend. But he was failing, and to be honest, it scared him.

He couldn't risk liking her. Not now, when he was just getting his feet back under him after his life had unraveled so badly in the last few years.

She was his employee, and he knew better than to cross that line.

Eight

GROWING UP WITH SIX OTHER SIBLINGS, OLiver had no choice but to learn to share. Even if it wasn't his favorite thing to do.

Even though he was the one who suggested Eliza do this afternoon's story time with the kids, he still wasn't crazy about giving up that hour.

He looked forward to it all week—the wonder in their faces and their laughter as he read the featured story using different voices. It was the one time of the week when he could tap into that side he didn't get to share too often—that side that longed for story time with the daughter who would've been around Maggie Franklin's age by now.

But he had to admit Eliza was killing it reading a story about the horse who was afraid to jump.

She'd admitted earlier to being nervous, which he found a little endearing considering her confidence on so many other levels. He'd promised to remain by her side.

But she didn't need him.

Her eyes bright and her right hand gesturing as she held the book in her left, she read the final page about the horse having the courage to jump and doing it despite being scared. Then she closed the book and looked at the small circle in front of her—Finn and Maggie Franklin, Iris and Violet Manning, Zoey Dawson, and even his cousin's son Sam appeared engrossed with Eliza this week.

"Zoey, did you like the story?" Eliza held up the book with the toon-like horse on the cover.

Zoey looked at the cover a moment, then shook her head quickly, her two braids hitting her cheeks.

Eliza exchanged looks with Oliver. "We'll find one you do like." Then she turned to Maggie and tapped her on the nose. "Miss Maggie, what are you afraid of?"

Maggie ducked her head, then she turned and pointed to Cody Hart, who stood next to Oliver. "It's dark in my room. My Cody gabed me a new nightlight. Now I not scared."

Oliver elbowed the younger guy. "Way to go, Super Dad."

"Not their dad yet, but soon." Cody shot him a grin that showed his love for Mia's two kids. He nodded to Eliza. "She's really great with them."

"Yes, she is." His eyes connected with hers, and she flashed him a smile that arrowed his chest.

One more trait to add to the *Eliza is awesome* column. Not that he was counting or anything . . .

Man, he was going to be in trouble if he didn't get his head on straight.

As Eliza directed the children to the small tables where she'd set up markers and a horse craft, Oliver reached for the flyers Eliza had designed and passed them out to the parents and grandparents. "The horses will be returning on island in a few days. Everyone is welcome to welcome the horses back on island. It will be the kickoff for the Novel Connections festival. We'll be having a horse-themed scavenger hunt for families to enjoy."

"Cute name." Aunt Mary gave his hand a little squeeze as she took the paper from him. "This looks like fun. I'll be sure to tell Ethan. Thanks, Ollie. I'm sure Sam will love it. You know your Uncle Bryan and I will be there."

"Don't thank me—Eliza's the one who put it together."

The bell above the front door jangled against the glass, and Oliver headed to the front of the store.

Dani stood by the counter and removed the hood of her jacket, a pinched expression on her face.

"Hey, Dani. What's up?"

"I tried to text you, but my phone says the message wasn't delivered. I'm really hoping the town council can do something about improving the internet on island." Sighing deeply, she shoved the phone in her pocket, then flicked her long blonde braid over her shoulder and looked at him. "We have a problem."

"What sort of problem?"

"You and Eliza will have to move your closing brunch from the Rose Room to a different place. Did you forget that my wedding reception's going to be held in there? I planned to decorate that morning. I paid for the whole day." With each word, her voice rose a little higher. "Chelsea called me this morning when she saw the booking on her calendar. Apparently, Josh made it without consulting her."

Oliver stepped back until his hip hit the counter. "Sorry about that. We'll find another place for the closing brunch."

"Why didn't you run it by Chelsea?"

"Well, we tried. When we visited, she was supposed to be there, but she'd left to run an errand and hadn't made it back yet. So we set it up with Josh and planned to connect with her at the beginning of next week. Why'd she call you instead of us?"

Dani lifted her arms, then dropped them. "She tried contacting you but didn't get an answer."

Oliver looked toward the children's section. "I'll see if Eliza can reach out to her after she's done with story time."

Dani crossed her arms over her chest and gave him a look he knew too well. "Ollie, I thought you were handling the details and she was helping you."

"More like the other way around. She's so much better at this thing than I am. I told you that when you asked me to take it over."

"You're right. I'm sorry for sounding snarky. I'm just tired. There's still so much to do." She rubbed a hand over her forehead. "Jamie wouldn't let anything like this happen."

"Well, James isn't the manager yet, and our big brother isn't perfect, Dan. People make mistakes, so cut Josh a break."

Her shoulders slumped and she pressed her forehead against his chest. "Getting married is exhausting."

"Been there. Remember?" Oliver wrapped his arms around his little sister's shoulders and perched his chin on top of her head. "But it doesn't have to be, sis."

She scoffed. "Try telling that to Becky MacBride. Mom is intent on the entire island plus some being in attendance. Well, she did say Dad didn't have to come, but I put a stop to that nonsense."

Oliver chuckled and shook his head. "Your wedding is going to be interesting, that's for sure."

She grabbed on to his shirt. "Promise me you won't let our parents ruin my wedding."

Oliver removed her fingers and gave them a squeeze. "I promise. Your day will be perfect."

She stood on tiptoe and planted a kiss on his cheek. "Thanks, Ollie. I must go. I have a thousand things to do today. By the way, I haven't received your RSVP to the wedding."

He raised an eyebrow. "Uh, I'm one of the groomsmen. I kind of figured it was a given I'd be there."

"Yes, but are you bringing a plus-one?"

Oliver waved a hand toward Main Street. "I've been back on island for less than two months. When I'm not fixing up my place or raiding your fridge, I've been here. Who would I even ask?"

"What about Eliza?" Dani raised an eyebrow and flashed a sly smile. "You can even bring her to the family dinner at the Island Pizzeria diner Wednesday night, if you want."

"What *about* Eliza? She's my *employee*." He drew out the last word, but was that more to remind Dani or himself? "And family dinners are for family."

"Uh-huh. And?" Dani lifted a shoulder. "You two look cute together. I don't mind if family shows up with a plus-one."

"Cute is for kittens and puppies. Besides, I'm not ready to date."

"You're just scared." She touched his arm.

"Thanks, Dr. Phil, for that amazing revelation. I'm fine."

"I didn't say you weren't fine. I'd just hate to see you miss out on what could be a wonderful relationship."

Oliver ran a hand over his face. "Listen, sis. I get that you're excited to walk down the aisle and now you want to pair up the rest of the world, but I did that once already, remember?"

"I know, and I'm sorry for your losses. But you don't have to spend the rest of your life alone, though."

"I'm not alone. I'm surrounded by people." He gestured toward the Kids' Cave, where parents and grandparents helped their children with the horse activities.

"You know what I mean."

"Yes, and I appreciate the concern. I love you, but butt out of my love life. I'm not inviting Eliza, and I'm not dating. Remind me again why everyone's coming in a week before your wedding? How will they get the time off? Especially Zach—Chef Louie drives him crazy as it is."

A smile spread across Dani's face. "Blame it on Liam. He knows how much it means to have my family at my wedding, so he's paying to fly Ashley and Benny in from LA. Since Zach took vacation to cater the wedding, he's coming in early to ensure everything is ready. He and Tyler are bunking on Tyler's boat. Ty wants to spend some time with Ray and Peggy Martinez while he's here—I think they want him to rebuild their patio or something like that." She took a breath and let it out slowly. "The last time I talked to Kate, she sounded like she needed a break. She's coming in early to help with the last-minute details."

"Right. Thanks for catching me up." He glanced at the clock above the checkout counter. "Don't you have some place to be?"

"Right. I do have to go. Have Eliza check with Chelsea and see if there's another spot at the Grand where you can host the closing brunch. Otherwise, you'll need to find a different place because the Rose Room is finally all mine." She flung out her arms and spun around. "At least for the day." Dani's phone chimed, signaling a text. She read it, her eyebrows pulling together. "Huh. So Dad's coming up with James, after all. The last I talked to him, he wasn't sure if he'd make it in time for the family dinner or arrive next Friday right before the wedding. Apparently, he and Jamie are going to work with Josh so Jamie can take over the hotel in May rather than waiting until the end of the year."

"Makes sense with tourism picking up this year." Oliver's lips thinned as he shoved his hands in his pockets. "Having Dad and Mom back on island together should be an adventure."

"I'll handle Dad. You check in with Mom. Just remember your promise."

Nodding, he moved to the door and opened it, then stepped back for Dani to pass by. He closed the door behind her and kept his hand pressed against the wooden frame.

He loved his family, but nothing good came out of having his parents in the same room together. He'd make sure Dani's day would be everything she'd imagined it to be.

"Everything okay?"

Oliver turned away from the door as Eliza set the rest of the flyers on the edge of the counter.

He jerked his head toward the sidewalk, then shared his conversation with his sister. "We'll need to find another place for the closing luncheon."

Eliza's shoulders slumped. "Man, I really liked that room. I'll start looking for a different venue. It would've been the perfect ending to an amazing festival."

Amazing because of her.

Oliver's gut tightened. He hated hearing the disappointment in Eliza's voice. What could he do to fix it?

Before he could think on it a second longer, the door opened again, and several people filed into the store.

Oliver exchanged surprised looks with Eliza, then fixed a warm smile in place. "Welcome to the Island Bookstore. Let us know if we can assist you with anything."

One of the women glanced at her friends. "We read about this place online and decided to take the ferry over and check it out." She picked up a handmade candle from the ladder shelf near the door. "What a cute place."

Eliza held up a fist, and Oliver bumped it.

Yeah, bringing her on was really paying off.

As the customers dispersed between the shelves, the door opened again.

For the next several hours, they spent more time ringing out purchases and helping locate books than they had in the whole last week combined. He wasn't complaining.

While trying to find a graphic novel for a couple of teen girls, Oliver's phone vibrated. His fingers landed on the right book. He handed it to the girls, who squealed and thanked him before rushing to the counter.

He pulled out his phone and quickly scanned a message from Jonah.

Oliver stifled a groan. He took a moment and blew out a breath.

He really needed Jonah here for the grand reopening. After all, the dude was his business partner. But Oliver understood the Army took a higher priority over his civilian duties.

Finally, Eliza turned the deadbolt, flipped the Open sign to Closed, and leaned against the glass door. "Phew, I haven't seen it that busy since I started working here."

Oliver started cashing out the register. "I think the thanks go to you and your new social media campaign. Several people mentioned the reels you posted and decided to check us out."

"See—social media isn't all that bad."

"I didn't say it was bad. I just don't have much time for it." He looked up at her. "Thank you, by the way. I should've led with that. You were a great help today, and I appreciate you staying over. And you're doing a great job with the festival."

"Even with the double-booking?"

"That wasn't your fault." Oliver lifted a shoulder as he oriented the bills in the same direction. "We'll find a place."

"Wow, that's . . ."

"That's what?"

Eliza looked down at her feet, then lifted her eyes and looked at him with a touch of vulnerability or something. "It sounds almost like you trust me."

Oliver stared at her for a moment, slid the money back into the drawer, then closed it. He rounded the counter and stood in front of her. Gripping the back of his neck, he glanced at the toes of his Converses, then back at her. "I do trust you, Eliza. You've shown me time and time again that you're a person of your word. I'm sorry if I've been a knucklehead about the festival."

"Knucklehead is a good word for it." She shot him a smile that arrowed his gut.

Oliver sifted through the words filtering through his head. "Dennis soured my trust in partnering with others. When Jonah asked me to partner with him to open the bookstore, I really hesitated, then finally agreed to a one-year partnership. Once he's stateside for good, we'll determine what's best for us and the store."

"After what you've shared, I can see why trusting could be challenging for you." Her voice, soft and smooth, lacked any judgment.

"The people who are supposed to be in your corner aren't always there for you."

"Does that include God too?" Eliza sucked in her lips. "I'm sorry. Your faith is none of my business. It's just that I haven't seen you in church. And I've often wondered if you hesitate for fear of making a mistake."

"Yeah. I guess I don't think God really has my back. If I make a mistake, it's on me to bail myself out."

"Oh, Ollie—I mean, Oliver. That's simply not true."

"True or not, that's my reality." Oliver gripped the back of his neck, then paced next to the counter, a long-ago memory resurfacing.

"When I was twelve, my dad and I were hitting balls at the golf course by the Grand. I liked a girl who was there with her grandpa. When my dad found out that I liked her, I begged him not to say anything, and he promised he wouldn't. That night, my mom asked me to drop something off to Dad at his office. Instead of being there, though, I found him in one of the restaurants, sitting at the bar, laughing about my crush with his buddies from the golf course, including the girl's grandfather. At that moment, I realized even the people closest to you can't always be trusted to keep their word."

He hadn't thought about that moment in years.

"That really stinks." She touched his arm.

He looked at her, his gaze roving over the compassion in her eyes, the frown between her perfect brows, and the downturn of her lips.

"So it's not really you." Oliver straightened and adjusted the papers on the counter. "I can trust my siblings . . . most of the time. And Jonah. But it takes a while to warm up to others."

She pressed a hand to her chest. "I know what it's like to be hurt by others, and I promise I will never do anything to betray your trust."

"I'm sorry you were hurt. What happened?"

She lowered her gaze to the floor, then lifted her face and stared over his shoulder. "Candace Bishop's granddaughter Bethany was my best friend from kindergarten until we were ten. We did everything together until her family moved to Port Joseph. I was so sad because I wouldn't get to hang out with her as much. She invited me to her eleventh birthday party, and I couldn't wait to go to her new house. She also invited a bunch of girls from her new school. I didn't know any of them. I struggled to fit in, but they just kept rolling their eyes at me and saying I was being annoying. I went to the bathroom, and when I came back out, they were gone."

"Gone? What happened?"

"They ditched me and went to the park. So instead of spending the night, I called my mom, crying. She took the ferry to Port Joseph and came to get me. Bethany never apologized, and we stopped talking. The thing is—her grandma is one of the sweetest people I know. She apologized for her granddaughter's actions, but Bethany cut me off. People can reject you for no reason. Even if I'm helpful enough or do a great job, people can still walk away. Part of me wonders if God will reject me too."

"You? Never. Mean people just plain stink."

"They sure do. Sounds like we both have issues."

"Yeah, but you're better about seeing the best in people." Oliver tapped her nose. Then he fisted his hands.

He shouldn't have touched her.

But he had.

And now the nerves in his fingers thrummed.

His eyes settled on her slightly parted lips. What would it be like to kiss her?

He longed to reach for her again, to run his fingers through her hair, to trace the curve of her ear, or cup her shoulder, and draw her close to him.

And that shocked him more than anything.

But that would be reckless and all kinds of stupid.

And he didn't need to make another mistake that risked his new business or created friction between them.

He returned to cashing out the register.

Keeping a distance between him and Eliza was the safest choice.

Problem was, his heart wrangled with his head, not wanting anything to do with safe.

He didn't know what to do with that.

If Eliza was any kind of gambler, she'd bet a box of Jill Kelley's caramel-frosted cinnamon rolls that Oliver Sullivan—her boss and festival co-coordinator—had wanted to kiss her yesterday after they closed the shop.

And she'd wanted him to.

Just the way he looked at her with compassion in his eyes, stepped toward her, and then touched her nose of all things.

In that moment, everything—the festival, the bookstore, leaving the ranch—all of it faded away. All she could think of was bridging the distance between them.

But she'd remained where she was. She couldn't risk falling for him. Not when they'd come this far. With the festival. With their partnership. And his trust in her.

With that in mind, she'd had an epiphany about another event while she tossed and turned last night, reliving that almost kiss.

As she sat on one of the benches in Blueberry Hill Park after church and waited for him to show, she watched kids race around the playground and charge up the ladder to the twisty slide. Their laughter drifted through the air and reminded her of yesterday's story time.

She'd enjoyed that more than she expected. Kids weren't scary. They just wanted attention. Why had she been so nervous?

Her gaze shifted to the sunshine streaming a silver glow over the lake fringed with snow and ice.

With the warmer temps coming this week, maybe, just maybe, they could get horses on island without complications.

A long shadow stretched across the bench. Eliza turned and looked up, her heart thudding.

Oliver stood behind her dressed in faded jeans that fit in all the right places, a cream-colored sweater that emphasized his broad chest, and a worn brown leather jacket. The breeze picked up and whisked cool air over her cheeks while it tangled with the curls brushing his forehead.

Her heartbeat echoed in her ears.

She wanted to reach up and smooth those curls back, but she kept her mittened fingers clasped on the back of the bench. "Hey, thanks for coming."

"It was the bribe of hot chocolate that did it."

"Figures." She pulled a thermos out of her tote bag and dug out two insulated cups. Then she patted the spot next to her on the metal bench warmed by the midafternoon sunshine. "Have a seat, and I'll share my idea."

Oliver dropped down next to her and stretched out his legs, crossing them at the ankles, the white tips of his black Converses pointed toward the water. He folded his hands and rested them on his flat stomach.

Pulling her attention away, she poured hot chocolate into one of the mugs, silently celebrating she hadn't spilled any, and handed it to him. After filling her cup, she capped the thermos and set it on the other side of her.

Then she retrieved a container of chocolate chip cookies Mom had made and lifted the lid. "Cookie?"

"You bake these?" He raised an eyebrow as he reached for one.

"Not if you want something edible. Mom made them yesterday. I think she's been baking up a storm before she loses the space in the ranch kitchen." She took one and set the container on the bench between them. She dunked it into her cocoa, then took a bite. "So, I was thinking . . . yesterday's story time was pretty fun. Anytime you want a break, let me know, and I'll do it again." She paused and waved a hand over the park. "What if we did a family-friendly event here called Stories Under the Stars or something like that? We could provide books for families to purchase, and they could spread out here and read together."

He popped the rest of his cookie in his mouth. Once he finished chewing and swallowing, he looked at her. "What will be the appeal?"

"It could offer another sense of community. Or even family time. We could put together book baskets with books, snacks, and even a blanket for families to purchase. For those who don't want to buy the baskets, we could still offer the books."

"It would help promote children's literacy and quality family time together." He remained silent a moment, then glanced at her. "I like it."

"You do? I mean, that's great." She bit into her cookie before something else stupid came out of her mouth.

"I need to be more open and cooperative since we both have a lot riding on the outcome." Oliver leaned forward and cupped his mug. "Dani told me about the lights they strung through the trees for last year's Summer Sunset concert when Asher and Sadie sang."

Eliza lifted the container and held it out to him again. "I saw pictures."

He took another cookie. "You didn't come?"

"I was at a conference in Pittsburgh with my aunt. We wanted to come, but she'd agreed to be the keynote before the dates for the concert were in place. Are you thinking of threading those lights for the Stories Under the Stars event?"

"I think the kids would like it."

"You know a lot about kids without having any of your own."

As soon as the words tumbled out, Eliza wanted to snatch them back . . . then crawl under the bench and hide as humiliation washed over her. How could she have been so thoughtless?

Oliver ran a hand over his jaw, lowered his gaze to the ground, then looked at her. "That's not by choice." He rubbed his hands together, then sat against the bench. "I was . . . uh . . . married."

Even though that wasn't news to her, she remained quiet, not wanting to squelch him from opening up. She glanced at his left hand. No wedding band. Or tan line.

When had he taken them off?

"I met Melody in college, and then we landed internships with the same publisher. We got married a couple years later. My wife was six months pregnant with our daughter, and they were killed in a small plane crash." Oliver glanced at her, then looked away, but not before she caught the sheen in his eyes.

What did she even say to that? Her vision blurred as her throat thickened.

Eliza had just swallowed the last of her cookie, and crumbs caught in her dry throat.

She risked a look at him.

His eyes focused in the direction of the children playing, his jaw tightened, but other than that, his neutral expression gave nothing away.

"I'm sorry, Oliver. When was that?"

"Three years ago. My wife loved to travel and always wanted to learn how to fly. A mild heart condition prevented her from joining the Air Force, so she chose her second love—editing. But, being the awesome husband that I was, I wanted to help her check something off her bucket list. One of my buddies owned a small private plane and offered to take her up. So I surprised her with flying lessons for her birthday, expecting her to wait until after our baby was born to begin. However, her OB gave her a clean bill of health, and she took her first lesson. After that, she was hooked. The morning of her third lesson, she woke up not feeling well. I begged her to stay home, but she refused. Her plane went down, killing my friend, my wife, and our baby." His voice caught on the last word as a muscle jerked in his lower cheek.

Eliza's breath caught in her chest. She fumbled around in her brain for the right words, but couldn't find any.

"Oh, Oliver. I have no words. But I'm so, so sorry for your losses." She laid a hand on his arm. "Wasn't your fault, you know."

"Didn't say it was my fault." He cupped his hands around his mouth.

"But you've been thinking it." She kept her voice soft and without judgment.

His eyebrows pulled together. "Now you're a mind reader too?"

Eliza lifted a shoulder, ignoring the sarcasm. "Your tone. If you hadn't been such a generous husband, then she wouldn't have been able to take the lessons. And she'd still be alive today. You're blaming yourself for something outside of your control."

He remained silent a moment. "Something like that." Then Oliver pushed to his feet. "I have things to do back at the shop."

"You're closed today."

"Perfect time to catch up on paperwork."

"Need a hand?"

"It's your day off."

"I'm not doing anything."

Maybe not at that moment, but her long to-do list, including packing up her room at the ranch, tumbled through her head.

He started to walk away, then turned back to her, his eyes roving over her face. "Hey, what are you doing Wednesday night?"

Eliza shrugged. "Not sure yet. Why?"

He looked off in the distance, shoved his hands in his back pockets, then turned his attention back to her. "There's a family dinner at Island Pizzeria Wednesday night. Want to go with me?"

"Like a . . . date?" She raised her eyebrows.

He scowled. "Not really."

Of course not. Silly her. What was she thinking?

"More like two friends going to the same event and sitting at the same table. Just my parents, my siblings, my nephew, and Liam will be there." Oliver scraped a hand over his face. "Honestly, I'd rather skip it, but I need to be there for Dani. And I promised to make sure her wedding goes smoothly. My family's . . . a bit challenging, but with you there, they're less likely to argue in front of someone who isn't family. If you'd rather not, I get it."

"If it's a family thing, maybe I shouldn't be there."

"I'd like you to be."

His words, spoken low, were threaded with something she couldn't quite name. Vulnerability, maybe?

She flashed him a smile. "Sure, I'll be your 'not date.'"

He let out a small breath, and his shoulders relaxed. "Food will be good, but ignore anything my brothers say about me. They make things up because they're jealous."

Eliza held up her hands and shook her head. "Oh no. Sorry, I can't make a promise like that. I'm all in for any tea they're willing to spill. I will listen with an ear of discernment, though."

"That's mighty big of you." His face twisted. "Maybe this isn't a good idea."

"Ha ha. You need me, and you know it."

"Yeah, like I need a paper cut." His mouth slid up in a half smile that did something funny to her insides. "Thanks." His gaze lingered a moment, then he walked away, heading toward the bookstore.

Oliver wore his stubbornness as a mask to hide his emotional wounds.

He trusted her and shared about his late wife, which answered so many questions.

Getting to know this different side of him was just becoming interesting. And she was looking forward to his family event more than she wanted to admit.

Nine

I F ONLY SHE'D HAD MORE NOTICE, THEN ELIZA would've been more prepared to give her aunt a better answer.

She could apply that logic to other areas of her life as well—her parents selling the ranch, coordinating the festival, and now this surprise opportunity to teach a workshop.

But that last one was for tomorrow.

Tomorrow? Seriously?

She placed volunteer packets on the rows of wooden folding chairs in the community room at the Jonathon Island Public Library as she talked with her aunt. "I just don't see how it would be possible, Auntie. The festival is next week, and there's still a lot to do. Oliver and I can't be in all the places at once, so we're recruiting volunteers. I have a meeting starting to see who is interested in helping, then I'm scheduled to work at the bookstore. Plus, I agreed to go with Oliver tonight to a family thing." Eliza sighed as she talked to her aunt through her AirPod. "But it would be a great networking opportunity."

"It's your choice to make, Eliza." Aunt Sally's voice softened in Eliza's ear.

"Problem is, I'm not sure what to do." She glanced at the clock on the peach wall of the light-blue clapboard building that sat at the end of Main near the boardwalk.

Eight more minutes before her meeting . . . if anyone showed up . . .

She tried not to allow the empty seats to deflate her enthusiasm.

"I can understand that, and I'm sorry for not giving more notice. But when one of the workshop presenters had a family emergency and needed to leave the retreat, we had a hole to fill. I told Candace I'd call and see if you were free to teach a class on social media marketing. These writers would eat it up."

"I'd be all over that with more notice. I don't have anything prepared, and I've already given my word to Oliver." She stood in front of the tall windows that overlooked the boardwalk and allowed the sunbeam shining through the windows to warm her. Remembering the look on his face when he invited her as his "not date" brought a smile to her face.

She didn't want to let him down. Her word mattered.

"Well, then that settles it. Go with Oliver. A person's word is everything. I've learned that in this business."

"I know." Eliza palmed the vintage globe on a wooden stand next to one of the floor-to-ceiling bookcases. "I hate missing out on this opportunity too."

"You'll have more opportunities, hon. Trust me."

After a few more minutes, they ended the call. Eliza closed her fingers around her phone, her heart tugging in two directions. And not just over the retreat.

Oliver was her boss.

She'd gotten burned before falling for someone she worked with and couldn't risk the same kind of heartbreak. But lately, managing her growing attraction to him felt like walking a tightrope. If she wasn't careful, she'd fall—hard—and risk not just her pride but her job. She loved working at the bookstore, and coordinating the festival stretched her but in a good way.

"What are you so deep in thought about?"

Eliza's head shot up. Finding Oliver in the doorway, she pasted on a smile. "Just pondering the complexities of life . . . and possibly cinnamon rolls."

She waved a hand toward the closed blue-and-white Good Day Coffee box of her favorite treat she'd bought to entice those who showed up to volunteer.

"I'm serious." He leveled her with one of his classic "you're being annoying" looks as he set his insulated mug on the table, shrugged out of his jacket, and draped it over one of the empty chairs.

He wore his usual black pants, but this time, his shirt was gray.

Letting out a long sigh, she straightened the basket that held paper plates, napkins, and plastic forks. "My aunt just called."

"Everything okay?" He moved toward her, the scuffed wooden floor creaking with each step.

"For the most part." She shared her conversation with her aunt.

Oliver slid his hands into his pockets and took a step back. "Hey, if you need to go teach, I get it."

Eliza shook her head. "You're not getting rid of me that easily."

He grinned.

That grin.

The one that transformed his whole face and sent her heart slamming against her rib cage.

"So we'll go to dinner with my family tonight. Then you can take the day off tomorrow and catch the first ferry to the mainland first thing in the morning. See if it's possible to teach during the mid-morning or afternoon session. If you miss the ferry tomorrow night, come in late on Friday."

"You make it sound so easy."

He scoffed. "It's not that complicated."

"Maybe not for you, but they want me to present tomorrow, and I don't have anything ready."

"Work on it today." He waved a hand across the empty room. "Doesn't look like your meeting's going to be much of a success. I'm surprised Dani didn't have volunteers lined up before she turned the festival over to us."

"Thanks for the vote of confidence." Shooting him a dirty look, she picked up her phone. "Your sister meant to, but it was one of those things that fell through the cracks while trying to plan her wedding and get a start on the festival prep. I told her we'd take care of it."

She texted her aunt.

Eliza
____

We can make that work. I'll call after my meeting. See you tomorrow.

A moment later, her phone buzzed with Aunt Sally responding with a line of smiley face emojis.

Eliza smiled. "Thanks, Oliver."

"Anytime." He rubbed the bridge of his nose, then pointed to the clock. "It's five after. How much longer are you going to wait?"

Eliza wrapped her arms around her waist. "I don't get it. When I posted in the Jonathon Island Facebook group, several people expressed interest. Plus, I posted signs on the door of the store, the community bulletin board at Good Day Coffee, and at the Tourism Bureau. I'll wait ten more minutes. If no one shows, then I'll leave."

The words were no sooner out of her mouth when Henrietta Hudson, Doris Poe, and Annabelle Kennedy came through the open door. Longtime friends, the seventysomething women were laughing, their joy a bit infectious.

"Sorry we're late, love." Henrietta brushed her white hair off her forehead and straightened her purple sweater over her narrow hips.

"We stopped to talk to Allean at the front desk. One thing led to another, then Doris"—Henrietta nudged her friend—"looked at the clock and realized we were late."

Dressed in a gold and teal bohemian-style tunic and flowy pants, Annabelle waved a hand over the room. "Where is everyone?"

Eliza lifted her arms, then dropped them again. "Looks like you three are it."

"Well, we'll see about that." Henrietta lifted her chin toward her friends. "Girls, get out your phones and get people down here." Henrietta reached into her purse and pulled out her smartphone. "I'll text Pastor Arnie and Tara. Doris, get a hold of Ginny and Fred Miller. The antique shop is closed today. Annabelle, get Augo down here."

Grinning, Eliza leaned in close to Oliver. "Maybe Dani should've asked Henrietta to oversee the festival."

The corner of his mouth lifted. "She knows how to get things done."

Fifteen minutes later, nearly a dozen people filed into the community room, shed their outerwear, and took seats toward the front of the room.

Eliza offered cinnamon rolls and coffee. While they enjoyed the snack, she launched into the presentation she'd rehearsed at least three times in front of the mirror. "Let's start with the basics. Novel Connections will kick off with the return of the horses on Thursday morning, followed by a horse-themed scavenger hunt for kids, and a book signing at the Island Bookstore featuring Sally Jo Wilson and B.L. Parker."

Henrietta rubbed her hands together. "I just read Sally's latest and let me tell you—I could not put it down."

Eliza smiled at the older woman. "I'll be sure to let her know. After the book signing, we'll do an informal mingle at the Island Pizzeria. On Friday, we'll start with breakfast at Good Day Coffee, followed by an informal author meet and greet with Victor Holt—"

"Excuse me, Eliza." Augo Kennedy, Annabelle's brother, cut in, hand in the air.

"Sure, Augo. What's up?"

"Why are we doing more festivals again? Didn't we have plenty last year?"

Eliza exchanged looks with Oliver, and he held his hands in front of him as if to say it was on her to answer.

Fine.

"The festivals raise awareness for the island, reminding people that we're here and we're open for business." She waved toward the window that overlooked Main Street. "Look how much business has picked up since Dani Sullivan started on her island revitalization project. I hear business is increasing at the Island House Inn too."

Augo stroked his white mustache and nodded. "Yes, sure is."

"Plus, not only do we want people to fall in love with our beloved island, but we want to help new businesses like the reopened Island Bookstore get established again and grow. We'll share our love of books, reading, and community. Any other questions before I move on?"

Several hands shot in the air. Eliza spent the next forty minutes answering questions and getting input about where the volunteers wanted to serve. By the time her hour was up, Eliza's discouragement had flipped as the volunteers finished the cinnamon rolls and coffee, understood their assignments, and agreed to meet again next Tuesday.

Maybe, just maybe, they could pull this off after all.

She'd hoped a few people would show. Then, when they did arrive, she could barely keep up with their questions.

But she did it. And they left with answers.

Once the last person filed out of the room, Oliver walked toward her doing a slow clap, a genuine smile on his face. "Well done. You turned that around."

Eliza laughed. "More like Henrietta. I was a little concerned it was going to be a train wreck."

"But it wasn't. Now we have twelve volunteers. By this evening, I'm sure that number will double, thanks to Henrietta. I'd say your first volunteer meeting was a success."

His praise flowed over her like a warm shower on a cold day. Rolling her shoulders, she soaked in his words as she gathered her things.

After turning off the lights, she and Oliver walked out of the community room together, his arm brushing against hers as they exchanged more ideas to make next week's meeting go better.

They'd just stepped inside the bookstore when the door opened again, the bells jangling.

Doug Manning poked his head around the corner of the door. "Hey, guys. I don't know what you've been doing lately, but business has been picking up. Personally, I'm quite thankful. Just wanted to say I appreciate it. Looking forward to the festival."

As he ducked back outside, Oliver flipped the sign from Closed to Open and turned to her. "It's because of you, you know."

Eliza blinked. "Me?"

He nodded. "Yes. Your social media campaigns are drawing more awareness to the island. Sure, a lot of people came for last year's festivals and plan to return, but you're reaching a new audience—bookstagrammers, readers, people who've never even heard of the island until now." He jerked a thumb over his shoulder. "On my way to the library, I ran into one of the servers from Parker Fish & Chips. She said business has been steadily increasing. A couple shops on Main Street are even talking about hiring seasonal workers early if this keeps up."

Hands on her hips, Eliza flashed him a saucy grin. "So you're saying I'm responsible for an economic boom? Maybe my ideas aren't so bad after all."

He made a face. "Okay, okay. Fine. I'm man enough to admit when I was wrong. I wasn't fully on board at the beginning, but you're definitely the real deal. And I appreciate that."

"Thanks, Oliver." She swallowed. "I love what I do."

"It shows." He nodded toward the window display she'd designed featuring books by undervalued authors. "Not sure what all you did for your aunt, but you definitely have a gift of reaching people. You're helping invisible authors feel seen by sharing their stories."

She considered his words.

"I've thought about taking on more authors." She glanced at the display she'd enjoyed putting together. "But the festival's been consuming a lot of my time. Almost like another job, you know? Even if it's temporary. But with my job here and the experience I'm gaining by helping with the festival, I'm beginning to think I can do something more . . . once I figure out what that is exactly. But thank you. For everything."

Oliver rolled his hand and bowed slightly. "Glad I could be of service by giving you a job."

He did more than that, but she didn't dare tell him. As it was, her brain tended to short-circuit when he was around.

But hearing him recognize her abilities was enough. She didn't know why his opinion mattered so much, but it did. And the idea that her work was helping local businesses? Well, that filled a piece of her heart that she didn't know was missing.

Once the festival was over, she'd take some time to figure out what was next for her. But one thing was clear—she didn't want to give up her job at the bookstore.

Because it would mean seeing less of Oliver. And she definitely didn't want that.

Sitting through a family dinner was the last thing Oliver wanted to do that evening. But he'd show up for Dani.

She deserved to be celebrated, and if that meant swapping old stories with his siblings over pizza and garlic knots, then that's what he'd do.

Eliza's presence would help deflect those annoying questions he had no desire to answer.

He held the door to Island Pizzeria and allowed her to pass, taking a moment to breathe in the fruity scent of her shampoo. Her long, dark hair was tucked in the collar of her belted white coat, and it took everything in his power not to free it.

He had to remind himself this was a "not-date."

But that didn't mean he couldn't appreciate how she looked in her jeans and light-blue sweater.

He followed her into the joint owned by Antonio and Juliet Lombardi who reopened the place last year. Scents of oregano, melted cheese, and marinara hung in the air. Along with the memories of Friday night dinners with his family while growing up.

Red-and-white checked vinyl cloths covered square tables turned at different angles on the vintage black-and-white checked floor. Black-and-white photos of generations of Lombardis lined the red and yellow walls. Retro Tiffany-style lights hung over the tables.

Laughter echoed from the back corner where Dani, Liam, Mom, Tyler, Zachary, Kate, Ashley, Benny, James, and Dad had claimed three tables and pushed them together.

So he and Eliza were the last ones to arrive. Nothing like making an entrance.

Mom sat so close to the wall like she wanted to disappear through it, but his ten-year-old nephew Benny kept her engaged.

Dad sat at the opposite end, eyeing the door like he was planning his escape.

Should be a super fun night.

Oliver lifted a hand in acknowledgment then guided Eliza through the maze.

Over her shoulder, Eliza raised an eyebrow. "You don't have to stay long, you know."

"What makes you think I don't want to stay?"

"The pressure of your fingers digging into my back."

"Oh, sorry." Oliver released her and shoved his fingers in his pants front pocket.

They reached the table, and Oliver passed out the dutiful hugs to his mom and sisters, then shook hands with his dad, bumped fists with his brothers and Liam, and ruffled Benny's hair. He pulled out a chair for Eliza. "You all remember Eliza, right? Eliza, remember my family?"

"Of course." She smiled at them as she took her seat. "It's good to see all of you again."

His father, Daniel Sullivan, tugged on the collar of his crewneck sweater and reached for his glass of water. Was he wishing for something stronger? As far as Oliver knew, Dad hadn't touched alcohol since the incident at the Grand, but if anything could make him relapse, it would be seeing Mom again. His designer haircut showed off his tan—probably from daily rounds of golf at his hotel's course in Florida.

James, Oliver's oldest brother, sat next to him. From behind, the two were nearly clones, except James's hair remained dark while Dad's had started to show streaks of silver.

Zachary and Tyler, Oliver's younger brothers, sat across from each other. While Zachary kept his dark hair short, which was better for working in the kitchen, Tyler's sun-bleached blond hair nearly brushed his shoulders.

Oliver flicked his brother's hair. "Dude, time for a cut, don't you think?"

"Hardly." Ty smoothed a hand over his head. "You're just jealous yours doesn't look this good."

Ashley smiled at Oliver as he sat across from her. Her light blonde hair was gathered in a messy bun. Next to her, ten-year-old Benny, Oliver's only nephew, shot him a grin. "Hey, Uncle Ollie."

"Ben-ja-min. How's it going, my man?" Oliver held out his fist.

The kid bopped it and shrugged. "Good."

Kate kicked him under the table and subtly pointed at his shirt, rolling her eyes. "Really?"

Oliver shrugged and tugged on the hem, reading the words upside down—*Sorry I'm late. I didn't want to come.* "Fitting."

His mom, Becky Jonathon Sullivan MacBride, wore a pink sweater under her white denim jacket. Her auburn hair hung in loose waves around her face. Hard to believe she'd just turned sixty.

At least with his parents on opposite ends of the tables, they wouldn't be bickering. There'd been enough tension in the family over the past decade.

Their server came by and took their drink orders. While he waited for his iced tea, he browsed the menu even though he planned to get his usual—deep dish with ham and chicken.

Ashley reached across the table and tapped Eliza's menu. "Good to see you again, Eliza. Heard you're working at the bookstore with Ollie."

"Yes. And we're coordinating Novel Connections, the book-lovers' festival, together."

Ty smirked. "Knowing Ollie as I do, I'm sure you're the heavy lifter in this project."

Oliver playfully slugged his brother in the shoulder. "What's that supposed to mean?"

"Dad, Ollie hit me." Ty rubbed his arm.

Dad's lips lifted as he shot a glance down the table. "Behave, you two."

"Dude, you couldn't coordinate a picnic, remember?"

"One time." He turned to Eliza. "He's referring to a disastrous picnic when I was eight and he was six. And I forgot the sandwiches."

"I was a growing boy. I needed nourishment. Ollie picked up a cricket and offered it to me for lunch."

Eliza laughed, a musical sound that speared him in the chest. She placed a hand on his arm. "Oliver's come around. You'd be impressed with what he's accomplished."

"We have no doubt about Oliver's accomplishments." James leaned in front of Ty. "He's been quite the success story. Problem is, we also know he's not exactly the most . . . social person."

"You don't think so?" Eliza raised her brows. "He deals with people every day. You should see him at the shop. Always helping readers find the right books. And his Saturday afternoon story time is a lot of fun. I think you guys underestimate your brother."

Zach's and Tyler's eyebrows shot up, while James let out a low whistle. "Ollie, sounds like you've got yourself quite the cheerleader."

Oliver's face and neck warmed. The way she stood up for him stirred something inside him. Something he wasn't ready to name. How long had it been since someone had his back like she did?

Not since Melody.

Ty leaned in close to Oliver's ear. "You talk to Dad yet?"

"Not yet. Why?"

Ty reached for a garlic knot from the napkin-lined basket in the middle of the table. "Just wondered. Heard he and James are staying for a bit after the wedding so James can learn the ropes of managing the Grand Sullivan."

"Good for him. As long as he and Mom don't do anything to ruin Dani and Liam's day . . ."

"Don't worry—we'll keep them both in line. Dani deserves this." Ty popped the rest of the knot in his mouth.

"By the way, you bring your boat?"

"You know it. Now that the lake has thawed, I figured it was time to come back to the island in style. Want to get some time on the water with me?"

Oliver glanced at Eliza. "Once we wrap up this festival."

Ty held out a fist. "You got it."

"Excuse me." Their server reached in front of Oliver and set his full glass of iced tea on the table. Then she pulled out her ticket pad and a pen. "Is everyone ready to order?"

She went around the table and took everyone's orders.

"How are things going with the festival prep?" Ashley bounced her straw on the table until it poked out of the paper wrapper.

Eliza glanced at him. "We still have a lot of details to finish. Hard to believe it's next week."

Dad slid his chair back and stood, holding his glass. "Before we dig into Antonio's amazing pies, I just want to say congratulations to our beautiful Dani. You took on the impossible task of bringing this island back to life. Without you, we wouldn't be gathered here tonight. And Liam, from what I've seen, you're a pretty okay guy. Take good care of our daughter . . . because we wouldn't want to cause you pain."

Laughing, everyone raised their glasses. As Oliver took a drink of his tea, his eyes connected with Dani's watery ones, and he winked.

Liam pushed to his feet, his hand settling on Dani's shoulder. "Thank you, Sullivans, for bringing me into your family. Every day spent with Dani is a joy and an adventure. I look forward to getting married, settling into our home, and starting a family someday. And I don't have to worry about any of you." Gesturing with his glass, he pointed to each of them. "Because Dani could probably take me down on her own."

"You know it." Dani reached for his hand and planted a kiss on his palm.

Oliver raised his glass. "To Dani and Liam. May the blessings of each day be the blessings you need most."

"Hear! Hear!" His family clinked glasses.

Dad pushed to his feet once again. "I have another announcement. I didn't plan to share this news tonight because I didn't want to steal Dani and Liam's thunder. But Dani's the one who suggested I do so since we're all gathered under one roof for the first time in a very long time."

Oliver exchanged glances with Tyler, who gave him a slight shrug.

Smiling widely, Dad rested a hand on James's shoulder. "As you know, James has been working with me at the hotel in Florida. Since Dani and Liam have done such a superb job with the Grand rebuild, it's going to need a full-time manager. Tourism is picking up, and the hotel is coming together faster than expected, so James is going to take over as manager in May. Let's raise our glasses to James and wish him all the best."

The family cheered just as their server arrived with their meals.

Ashley slid a small slice of Hawaiian pizza she shared with Benny and Mom onto her red stoneware plate, then looked at Oliver. "Remember that Thanksgiving when we played hide-and-seek in the suite after dinner? No one could find you, and you ended up falling asleep behind the dryer with a book in your hand."

"What can I say? The turkey tryptophan got to me. Besides, not my fault you guys were terrible seekers."

"Yes, give Ollie a book and you'd lose him for days."

Books didn't let him down. But he didn't voice that thought. Not when things were going better than expected.

"Remember the time Zach tried to make a pizza on Dad's new gas grill?" James elbowed his brother.

Zach covered his face with his hand. "I'll never live that down, will I? Give me a break—I was nine. At least now I know you can't put unbaked dough on a grill grate."

James gestured with the slice in his hand and nearly dropped pepperoni in Zach's lap. "It caught on fire, and Mom came out with a fire extinguisher."

Oliver looked at Eliza. "He had to work the rest of the summer to earn money so he could buy replacement components for the grill."

Laughing, Ashley and Kate talked over each other as they continued the story.

Oliver glanced at his mom and found her laughing along with his siblings. But Dad . . . well, he didn't even crack a smile. He kept his attention on his shrimp Alfredo.

"Remember the summer Dad taught us how to roll dough and make pizza in the kitchen after hours?" Ashley wagged a finger at Zach. "The right way. On pans. That was before—" Then, as if realizing what she was about to say, Ashley got quiet and reached for her glass of tea. "Well, that was a long time ago."

The laughter died down as Oliver's siblings focused on eating. He took a bite of pizza, then set it on his plate, not feeling particularly hungry as memories of happier times had been pushed away by flashbacks of their changing family dynamics. Dad pulling away. The fighting. Mom's affair.

For all of them.

Eliza nudged his foot beneath the table. He met her gaze. Strong and steady with softness in her eyes.

She lost a brother she loved deeply while he was surrounded by family he didn't always want to be around.

He needed to change his attitude.

For a moment, he allowed himself to remember the good parts. The games of hide-and-seek. Family dinners, even the disastrous ones. Mom's laughter. Dad's ability to tell stories, mostly stretched truths, of course. Back when the Sullivans were together. Before everything changed.

Oliver lifted his nearly empty glass. "To family."

"To family." Everyone raised their glasses, and Oliver made it a point to make eye contact with each of them. As he looked at Mom, she blew him a kiss and mouthed, *Thank you.*

An hour later, he and Eliza left the restaurant and headed toward Blueberry Boulevard. The night air wrapped around them as the bright moon lit their path.

"That was lovely, Oliver. The blessing for Dani and Liam. The toast to your family. All of it. I know you may not see it or even feel it, but you're very blessed."

"I realize that now. So many choices have fractured our family. I wasn't sure if we could come back from them, but what Dani has done made a difference."

"You can all make a difference." Eliza stopped and pointed in the direction of the Grand. "I was in college when it caught fire. Home for the summer and teaching riding lessons at the Grand."

"I was home that summer too. I had just proposed to Melody. She'd taken a job as a counselor at a summer camp, so I came back here and lived with a few guys on a houseboat. Mom had gotten engaged to Ryan MacBride even though her divorce from Dad wasn't final. The night she got married, well, Dad just lost it. He got drunk and ended up catching the hotel on fire."

"My parents never thought it was deliberate."

"Your parents always looked for the best in people. But Dad loved that place. He wouldn't deliberately destroy it. The fire was an accident."

"But devastating nonetheless."

"Exactly. The seasonal workers had no place to live, so they left. And once the workers left, the businesses didn't have enough help and shut down, one by one. Then the pandemic hit, and the island practically became a ghost town. What Dani and Liam have done is nothing short of a miracle."

"Miracles do happen."

"To select people, maybe."

"You sound like a skeptic."

"Not a skeptic—a realist. I prayed for a miracle after my wife's accident, but God didn't see fit to answer. I lost her—and our unborn daughter."

They passed under one of the old-fashioned streetlights. Eliza remained quiet for a moment as her eyes shifted up at the sky, then back at him. "I'm sorry, Oliver. That's so hard."

He lifted a shoulder. "It's in the past."

She stopped walking and pressed a hand to his chest. "Even though it's in the past, they were a part of your life. You can't just dismiss them. They deserve that place in your heart."

"You're right. And they do. Hold a place in my heart, I mean. When I lost them, it nearly crushed me."

"But it didn't. You're stronger than you may think. And apparently a great hider, judging from the story I heard tonight."

"That was a good day." A smile tugged at his lips. "I know events are in place for the festival, but Ashley's story made me think of something."

"What's that?"

"What if we do a literary escape room? One of our suspense authors, maybe even Graham Lee, could help readers find their way out of a fictional plot line."

She cocked her head as her eyes widened and her mouth formed an O. "Oliver Sullivan, are you actually proposing something for the festival?"

"What if I am?" He lifted his chin.

"But you haven't had days to process or analyze." Her voice held a teasing tone as she nudged him with her shoulder.

"Maybe I'm changing." Hands in his pockets, he kicked a stone off the sidewalk. "I appreciate your insight and ability to brainstorm solutions quickly. Sometimes I get caught up in indecision . . . not wanting to make another grave mistake. I don't want to be seen as a failure."

Eliza cupped Oliver's cheek, the warmth of her fingers searing his skin. This time, he had no desire to move.

"Oliver Sullivan, you are many things, but a failure is not one of them."

The side of his mouth lifted in a grin. "It could be fun."

"You're right. Let's do it."

He mimicked her movements, complete with the O-shaped mouth. "Eliza Quinn, are you actually agreeing with me?"

"I'd agree with you more often if you were right." She laughed, and the sound coming from her mouth smacked him in the chest.

A breeze blew over them, brushing strands of Eliza's hair across her cheek. Before he took time to think, Oliver reached out and caught the hair with the tip of his finger, then smoothed it behind her ear. He ran his thumb along the curve of her neck and placed his hands gently on her shoulders.

Her eyes widened, and her lips parted. This time, she remained quiet.

A voice screamed in his head. *Danger! Danger!*

Swallowing hard, he took a step closer and framed Eliza's face with both hands. His thumbs caressed the silky smoothness of her cheekbones. Lowering his mouth, he captured her lips with his. One hand slid over her shoulder, down her arm, and rested at her waist. The other slipped around and cupped the back of her neck as he drew her closer.

Her arms slid around his neck, and her fingers tangled in his hair.

She tasted of sugar, vanilla, and sweetness from the crème brûlée they'd ordered for dessert. She smelled of springtime and brought sunshine and hope to his dark world, showing him it was possible to live again.

After what seemed like forever, Oliver forced himself to pull back. He wrapped his arms around her and drew her to his chest. No doubt she could feel the thud of his heart against her cheek.

She'd been the first woman he'd wanted to kiss since Melody. But he didn't want to think about his past.

For now, he wanted to savor the moment and allow himself the unexpected venture of wondering just what could be . . .

Eliza released a small laugh, then drew back and looked up at him, her eyes bright. "Well, *that* was unexpected."

Oliver closed his eyes and tilted his head back as he let out a sigh. "So much for not mixing business with pleasure. You're my employee, and I'm—"

She pressed a finger to his lips. "Don't you dare say you're sorry. That kiss needs no apology."

"Is that so?" Raising an eyebrow, he wrapped his hand around her fingers. "I'm your boss, and it's not professional to engage in a relationship with you. I don't want to do anything to jeopardize our working relationship."

Eliza pressed her hands against his chest and looked at him with wide eyes swimming with a touch of uncertainty, maybe even some vulnerability. "I like you. I do. I love working at the bookstore and partnering with you for the festival. But I'm also looking for more. I don't want to be some guy's casual fling and then be tossed aside when someone more important or something better comes along."

Oliver frowned. "Whatever made you think I was like that?"

Eliza pulled away, causing him to miss the warmth they shared. "Very few people know this, but I was engaged a few years ago. His name was Tim, and we met at a writers' event that I attended with my aunt. We dated for six months while I helped him with several social media projects together, and I fell hard. He proposed, and I said yes. Then I learned he cheated on me with a friend I'd made in Pittsburgh. When I confronted him, he was such a jerk. He called off our engagement and ended up with her."

A muscle jumped in the side of Oliver's jaw. "I'm so sorry he hurt you, Eliza. Guys like him deserve to be pounded into the ground." He took a step closer and lifted her chin. "I'm not a casual kind of guy. I loved one woman in my life, and I lost her." He swallowed again. "So we're clear—I like you too." Then he laughed. "We sound like we're in middle school."

"Kisses have a way of complicating things."

"There's something I didn't share about the whole Constance King situation. We were at a conference and met for dinner one night, supposedly to discuss her story and her future with our company. She was a little flirty, and I tried to dismiss it. I walked her back to her room, which was on a separate floor from mine. As I said goodbye, she kissed me . . . and I returned the kiss. Even though I didn't initiate it, it wasn't professional to allow myself to be put in a compromising position." Oliver dragged a hand over his face.

"But you stopped it."

"My business partner happened to be walking past her room at that moment since his was at the other end of the hall and made a smart remark. I realized I jeopardized our working relationship and turned her down gently, which embarrassed and hurt her. She decided it would be better to work with Dennis from that moment on, which gave him a greater opportunity to take advantage of her. When I confronted him about his mishandling of her movie rights, he basically said I was no better than he was."

"But what he did was illegal. He stole money from her."

"Yes, but I can't afford to make the same mistake with someone I've employed. Let's get through the festival, and then we can talk about us."

She looked over his shoulder, then returned her attention back to him and gave him a soft smile that melted what was left of his heart. "I'd like that."

Those three words gave Oliver something he hadn't felt in a long time.

Hope.

Ten

WHO KNEW THE QUIET BOOKSTORE OWNER was quite a kisser?

After last night, things were definitely changing between her and Oliver, and she wasn't sure how to handle it, especially in light of his confession about Constance King.

And what did that mean for her? Or them? And her job?

But she couldn't think about that right now.

She needed to focus on the rest of her workshop and spend time with the authors who had come to Candace's author retreat and gathered to hear Eliza speak.

Despite not wanting to leave him when he walked her back to the ranch, she'd managed to complete her presentation and fall asleep at a decent hour and made it to the first ferry going to the mainland this morning.

She'd borrowed her parents' car from the long-term lot where residents kept their vehicles, and drove the two and a half hours to the lakeside lodge near Traverse City.

Standing to the right of the lit fireplace in the main lodge where the retreat was being held, Eliza skimmed over the couple dozen writers curled up on vintage furniture with handmade quilts as they alternated between drinking hot beverages and taking notes.

Beside her, the fireplace popped and crackled, lending a calming vibe to an already laid-back event.

One she wouldn't have minded being a part of from day one.

She glanced down at her notes, then progressed to the next slide on her computer that projected to the portable screen above the fireplace.

For the remaining fifteen minutes of the class, she discussed practical strategies for adding social media marketing details to their author platforms while trying to manage their writing time. "Thank you for listening. If you have any questions, I'm more than happy to answer them."

She pulled a stack of thank-you cards out of her tote bag that she'd prepared for the retreat and handed them to Candace's assistant to pass out to the authors.

Each A2-sized card featured a watercolor image of a vintage typewriter she'd purchased from artist Mia Franklin. Inside, she included her new business cards with the same logo and an invitation to the Novel Connections festival. She opened one of the envelopes and explained what was inside.

"We have several events featuring authors and opportunities for readers to connect with them. So far, attendance reservations have exceeded our expectations. If you'd like to be part of this, it's not too late to sign up. Please see me before I leave, and I'll make sure you get all the details."

Applause echoed around the room, and Eliza couldn't stop the grin that spread across her face.

This felt right.

Affirming.

Like she was exactly where she was supposed to be.

If the retreat had been during a different time, she would've attended with her aunt just as she had in the past. But with the festival and her job at the bookstore, she couldn't afford to take the time.

Plus, she wouldn't have traded last night with Oliver and his family for anything.

The writers stretched and gathered their things, then trickled toward the dining room for lunch.

Scents of seasoned chicken filtered from the kitchen, causing Eliza's stomach to growl. She'd been too nervous before her presentation to have more than a chai latte while the ferry took her to Port Joseph.

She shut down her computer and disconnected it from the audiovisual equipment provided by the lodge.

Dressed in gray yoga pants and a navy pullover hoodie advertising her daughter Kimberly's college, Aunt Sally joined Eliza by the fireplace, her Julia Roberts smile wide. Her auburn hair had been twisted and clipped at the back of her head. "El, that was fantastic. You knocked it out of the park." Then she waved at Candace, who stopped and talked with one of the authors lingering in the doorway. "I'm having lunch with Candace. Care to join us?"

"I'd love that." Eliza slung her heavy tote bag over her shoulder, then hooked arms with her aunt, who stood a head shorter, and headed out of the room. They joined Candace at one of the half dozen round tables scattered around the large dining room.

Eliza reached for her water and drained half the glass, soothing her parched throat. She'd forgotten to grab a bottle of water before teaching her workshop.

Another fireplace heated the dining area. Eliza glanced out the window that overlooked Lake Michigan. Snow fluttered from a gray sky and drifted on the windowsill. A breeze rippled the water.

Candace cleared her throat, jerking Eliza's attention back to the table.

Candace folded her hands on the table and gave Eliza a direct look. "Eliza, dear, I feel I must rescind my previous offer."

Eliza set her glass on the table and frowned. "Your offer?"

"Remember when we met at Good Day Coffee and I offered to bring you on as an assistant so you could learn more about becoming an agent?"

"Oh. Yes. I remember." Eliza folded her hands in her lap.

Candace brushed a crumb off the front of her blue sweater. "I've had a change of heart. You're not meant to be an agent."

Eliza blinked and glanced at her aunt, who shook her head, lifted her hands, and mouthed, "Don't look at me."

A server arrived at their table with a coffee carafe. While Candace and Aunt Sally pushed their cups closer to the server, Eliza requested hot tea.

She turned back to Candace. "Why do you say that?"

Candace laughed softly. "I watched you during your class. You lit up while sharing marketing strategies with those authors, and answered their questions with clarity and focus. You had the whole room in the palm of your hand. You'd be wasting your talents trying to become an agent."

The server returned with a steaming cup of hot water and a small basket with assorted teas.

Heat crawled up Eliza's neck and settled in her cheeks at her older friend's words. She chose Lady Earl Grey and added the tea bag to her water. "Thank you, I appreciate that. I really enjoyed it. More than I expected, honestly. I wasn't sure how my workshop would go over."

"They ate it up, girl." Candace leaned forward and grabbed Eliza's hand. "That's where you shine. And that's where I think you belong. Instead of becoming an agent, you need to promote authors. Become an author marketing consultant." Then she leaned back and gestured to Aunt Sally. "Look what you've done for your aunt these past five years. You have what it takes to step out on your own."

Although she expressed her desire to help authors shine, doing it full-time just didn't feel real.

Until now.

She reached for her cup. Maybe a slug of tea would dislodge the words stuck in her throat.

Because stepping out of the comfort zone she'd built around herself filled Eliza with a fear she couldn't quite shake. She had so many questions about her future and the potential path she could forge. And today's workshop helped validate what she truly loved.

Eliza lifted her face to the ceiling, closed her eyes, and whispered a prayer from her heart.

Lord, is this my will or Yours? Help me to go in the right direction.

Aunt Sally squeezed her hand. "You came to me after Jared died. You were grieving. While your parents clung to each other, you needed someone to be there for you. I'm very thankful for the past five years. Kimberly's not you, and she's not meant to be. She'll find her own way. Now it's time for you, honey."

"Time for what?"

"Time for you to step into your calling." She reached into her bag at her feet, pulled out an envelope, and tapped it on the table in front of Eliza. "I wanted to give this to you the day you left for JI, but I decided to wait and see if you'd come back or not. Now I'd like you to accept this. Consider it a bonus for a job done exceptionally well."

Candace pulled her chair next to Eliza's and clasped her other hand. "I've seen what you've done to promote my authors—through the bookstore, the festival, and even on your personal social media accounts. Some of them have already seen boosts in traffic and sales. And the festival hasn't even started yet. I'd like to work with you to create your business plan and offer your services to my authors—and others I know."

Eliza's fingers shook as she looked at the envelope in her aunt's hand. Her vision blurred, and her throat thickened. "Thank you. Both of you. I'm overwhelmed and don't know what else to say."

Candace patted her hand. "No need to say anything."

Eliza focused on Aunt Sally with misty eyes. "I love working with you, you know."

"I've loved it too. You know I don't like change." Aunt Sally lifted a hand and slid a lock of Eliza's hair behind her ear. "With Candace retiring, I need to make some changes too. You could return to Pittsburgh, move back in with Kimberly and me, and start your business there. I can introduce you to even more writers, and you could meet with people in person. The city's large enough to help you get started."

Eliza twisted her fingers and lowered her eyes to her lap, swallowing past the lump in her throat. "I appreciate the offer. Thank you. And I appreciate both of you. I'm sure I'll have a thousand questions, but I need to get through the festival first."

"Well, you're not getting rid of me just yet." Aunt Sally tapped the envelope again. "Kimberly and I will be on island next week. We're looking forward to the festival. And we can discuss your moving back to the 'Burgh. But more than that, I'm looking forward to seeing you take your rightful place in the industry."

The rest of the afternoon passed in a blur as Eliza stayed for the remainder of the retreat. Bronte Parker wanted to talk about a new publicity campaign. That evening, with her brain and heart full to overflowing, she took the nearly empty last ferry back to the island, her head still spinning from the day's events.

Scratch that—the past couple of days had made an impact.

Memorable in so many ways.

Darkness shrouded her as she stepped off the ferry and trekked back to the ranch. With the cold nipping at her face, she picked up her pace. Stars glimmered from an inky black sky. The bright moon lighted her path toward Sugar Maple Lane.

Eliza shoved her hands in her coat pockets and curled her fingers around her phone.

Twice she reached for her phone to call Oliver. Twice she stopped herself.

She didn't want to be *that* girl who needed reassurance or read more into a kiss than he intended.

He needed to make the next move.

The ranch house came into view as she turned onto Sugar Maple Lane. Everything was dark except for the glow of the porch light and one lamp shining just inside the entryway.

Thirty-one years old—and her parents still left the light on for her. The thought brought a tiny smile to her lips—and a dull ache to her chest.

She slipped off her shoes and tiptoed barefoot across the wooden floor, careful not to let the old planks creak beneath her as she climbed the stairs.

With her dad still waking up around four thirty or five every morning, her parents headed to bed by nine each night.

She opened her bedroom door with a quiet click, stepped inside, and flicked on the overhead light. Stacks of boxes lined the wall next to her dresser as her life had been packed away. The space looked more like a storage unit than her childhood retreat.

A package lay on her neatly made bed with a sticky note attached to it. She lifted it and read her mother's familiar handwriting.

Oliver dropped this off for you.

Huh. Why had he come by, knowing she wouldn't be here? Why not wait until she showed back up at the shop tomorrow?

Shrugging away the questions, she reached for the handled kraft paper bag stamped with the bookstore logo and reached inside. She pulled out a small, light-blue square box and an envelope.

Sitting on the edge of her bed, she slid a finger under the flap and pulled out a card that showed a watercolor beach at sunset, recognizing it as Mia Franklin's work from her gallery.

She read Oliver's precise, slightly slanted handwriting.

Saw this in the window at Maritime Treasures and it reminded me of yesterday. Thanks for being my not-date. Thanks for being <u>you</u>. Oliver

He'd underlined *you* three times.

No "Love, Oliver." Nothing romantic, but she didn't mind. They weren't there yet.

But *could* they be heading in that direction?

He was the kind of man who took things slow. And she was willing to wait.

Eliza lifted the cardboard lid from the light-blue box and gasped.

A delicate silver necklace with a blue stone lay on a bed of white satin. She lifted the pendant carefully and ran her fingertip over the smooth matte surface. Tiny black speckles marked the stone's turquoise finish—imperfections that made it beautiful.

She removed a chipboard card and read about the significance of the stone. Called a Leland blue, it was actually a piece of slag glass—a by-product of Michigan's 1800s iron-smelting industry—turned into a treasure by time, water, and weathering.

Something once discarded—now cherished.

After yesterday, she liked how her relationship with Oliver was improving. And growing. But what would happen after the Novel Connections festival ended?

Aunt Sally had given her a bonus that could put her future in motion, along with sharing her connections if Eliza moved back to Pittsburgh. Plus, getting a new business off the ground took time, energy, and focus.

Would she have the space to build a relationship while building a new career? Sure, if she stayed on island. But not if she changed her address.

Did she even want to leave the island?

She fingered the stone once more.

Especially now?

Those questions—and a thousand more—swirled in her mind as she slipped into pajamas and slid under her comforter.

She'd think about it tomorrow. Tonight, she needed rest.

The changes between last night and this one proved her heart was wide open.

And her future was waiting . . . whatever that might be.

Oliver hadn't been this excited professionally since discovering Logan Kingsley's unpublished manuscript years ago when he worked at Palmer & Jones.

And now, the thrill of finding a new diamond in the rough coursed through him.

Resting his palms on either side of his laptop, Oliver leaned on his arms as he scanned the open document again.

When Logan asked him to read a manuscript from his writing friend, Oliver hadn't really expected much.

Unpublished writers often showed promise, but in most cases, their work wasn't ready yet. In his years of publishing, he'd sent out a lot more rejection emails than contract offers. His least favorite part of the job.

But this woman? She was different. She showed more than promise. She had a unique voice that Oliver hadn't seen in a long time. In fact, he was a little envious of the editor who would be credited for discovering this fresh talent.

And that's what Oliver missed about the job—the thrill of the potential packaged with well-crafted words.

With soft jazz playing through the shop's sound system and the scent of his favorite blend from Good Day Coffee on the counter next to him, Oliver was glad he'd come into the shop to read before jumping into his day.

He reached for his phone and typed out a text.

Oliver

> Just read your friend's manuscript. Thanks for sending it. She's got talent. It's good. More than good. I'll make some notes and get it back to her. Your friend should polish, then try submitting again. Little jealous of the editor who gets to launch her.

A moment later, three dots appeared at the bottom of the texting window, then Logan's reply popped up.

Logan

> Phew! So glad to hear that.
> Thought it had promise too.
> Thanks for reading, man. Hope all
> is well. See you in a few days.

The handle on the front door jiggled, followed by a light knocking on the glass.

Oliver's head snapped up as his heart slammed into his ribs.

Eliza.

No, she would've used her key.

His twin sister Kate stood outside with her face pressed to the glass.

Stifling his disappointment, Oliver strode to the door, flipped the deadbolt, then threw it open. "Congratulations, you're the grand prize winner who gets to clean the face smudges off the door."

"Hello to you too, little brother."

"By eight minutes." He closed the door, blocking the icy wind that whistled between the buildings.

"Still makes me older." Kate breezed past him, uncurling her fluffy scarf from around her neck. Then she wrapped him in one of her constricting hugs.

"What are you doing here?"

"I'm not allowed to visit my little brother?"

"Not here as in the store, but why are you on island? I thought you were heading back to Benton Harbor this morning. Don't you have a business to run?"

"I was hoping we could grab some lunch."

Oliver checked the time on his phone. 11:45. "Depends. Eliza hasn't shown up yet. If she doesn't come in, then I need to stay here."

Kate lifted an eyebrow. "Is that normal for her?"

"Quite the opposite. She was out of town yesterday. Maybe she missed the ferry. I texted, but no response yet."

Was she ghosting him?

Maybe kissing her was a mistake. Didn't feel like one at the time, though.

Kate tilted her head, her tone gentle. "Maybe her phone died."

"Maybe." But the doubt lingered. This just wasn't like Eliza.

Kate shifted her weight and tugged on the sleeves of her navy-and-white striped sweater. A nervous tell.

Oliver narrowed his eyes. "Hey. What's going on?"

She flicked her hair over her shoulder and looked away, but not before he caught the sheen in her eyes.

He cupped his sister's face. "Kate. Another panic attack? Are you slowing down like your doctor recommended?"

She blinked rapidly, but a single tear slipped down her cheek.

He pulled her into a hug.

"Ollie . . ." Her voice broke. "I don't know what to do."

"About what?"

She stepped back and wiped under her eyes. "The panic attacks are happening more often, and I don't know why. My photography business is going well. I even brought on an assistant, Gabby, thinking that would help." She pressed a closed fist against her chest. "But some days, I just can't catch my breath."

Oliver frowned. "You need to take time off like your doctor suggested. Otherwise, instead of landing at urgent care, you're going to wind up in the hospital."

"I can't afford to slow down." Wrapping her arms around her waist, she paced in front of the counter. "I have clients who need me, but I also need to be here for Dani."

"You can't help them if you're not taking care of yourself."

"What do I do, Obi-Wan?"

The pain in her eyes nearly gutted him. He paused before he responded. Despite his sister's boast that she was the older one, she seemed to turn to him the most when she needed help. Which wasn't often. Kate didn't admit defeat easily. If she was asking, then she was hurting more than she let on. In fact, he hadn't seen her like this since being ditched at the altar a number of years ago.

His eyes roved around the shop and landed on the flyer on the front door advertising the festival. He looked at her. "Would it help if I hired you to take photos during the festival? I'll pay your current rate. It'll be fun and very low stress. The festival's only a few days, and you don't have to be at every event. Wouldn't be a ton of cash."

"With what money? You've got most of your funds tied up in this place." She waved a hand around the room.

"Don't worry about the money."

She crossed her arms and glared at him. "I don't need pity jobs, Ollie."

"It's not a pity job. You're a talented photographer. You could help us increase exposure for the bookstore, but I don't want to add more pressure on you. A few candid shots without the pressure of dealing with a lot of clients."

She hesitated, then gestured toward the Victor Holt display. "Is Victor Holt really coming to the festival?"

"Yes. Victor Holt, B.L. Parker, Sally Jo Wilson, Graham Lee, and as many others as we can fit in. When I agreed to take on the festival, I didn't expect it to grow as much as it has, but Eliza . . ."

"Eliza has always been a powerhouse." Kate moved between the shelves.

"Yeah, now I need to figure out the logistics of the foot traffic."

Kate stopped in front of the storage room and opened the door. "What if you move the book signing in here?"

"Ugh. That room's a disaster." He moved behind her, taking in the stacks of boxes, old displays, shelves needing repair. Dingy white paint peeled off the walls. Dust settled on old fixtures.

"The signing's in less than a week. I don't know if I have the time to get it ready."

Arms folded over her chest, Kate raised her eyebrows and gave him the same look he'd received from their mom growing up. Not that he'd tell that to Kate when her relationship with their mother was tenuous at best. "And, of course, it didn't dawn on you to ask for help."

Oliver scratched the back of his head. "Who would I ask? Everyone's busy."

Kate pulled up the sleeves of her sweater. "Well, I'm here now. I can lend a hand."

"Well, I won't turn down free labor."

"Who says it would be free?" She flashed a grin.

Oliver shoved his hands in his front pockets and moved into the room, an idea forming. "If we can move the boxes and ditch the old displays, you think we'd have time to scrub, repaint, and add some sort of decor in here?" Then he held up a hand. "Without involving Dani."

"Yes, absolutely." She pushed past him and headed for the register. She opened the drawer below it and pulled out a notepad and a pen. "Let's make a list." She glanced at his computer, then frowned. Looking up at him, she pointed to the screen. "Ollie, are you writing a book?"

Oliver moved to the counter, closed the laptop, then shoved it on the shelf under the register. "When would I have time? I'm doing a little freelance editing for a friend."

She didn't need to know Logan Kingsley had requested his services.

"Freelance? I thought you left editing behind."

"I did. This was just a one-time favor." He couldn't stop the smile from spreading across his face as he thought of the story he'd finished editing less than an hour ago.

She tilted her head as she surveyed him. "But you enjoyed it."

Not a question but a statement.

He nodded. "More than I expected. Reading this story felt like settling into a pair of shoes that fit really well."

Kate laughed and grabbed his arm. "Okay, Grandpa."

He shook off her hand. "Hey, don't be a punk. I just meant it felt good to read again. To find a story that excited me like it used to. You know—that spark. I thought it was gone . . ."

Kate nudged him with her shoulder. "I'm just teasing. I think it's great. Thinking of going back to editing?"

"Dennis tanked any chance of that happening. After we dissolved the business, he shredded my name to anyone who would listen."

"He's an idiot. You don't need him."

"I didn't say I needed him. I said he ruined my reputation. No publisher will touch me." Oliver swept a hand over the room. "Jonah's counting on me to keep this business going while he finishes out his tour in Germany. Once he's back on island for good, we'll discuss how we're going to manage the store together."

"So . . . why can't you do both? Manage the bookstore *and*

freelance? Be your own boss. Set your hours. Take on your own clients."

He lifted an eyebrow. "And end up in the urgent care when the stress of running my own business burns me out?"

She lifted the corner of her lip in a sneer. "Very funny. But I'm serious. You had a career in publishing. And now . . . you're selling the books you helped get started. Feels like a step back."

"Why does everyone feel the need to keep reminding me of my own failures?"

Her words had touched a nerve. Not because she was wrong. He'd told himself the same thing. And others, including Patrick Kelley.

"Without this store, I wouldn't be helping with the festival. And sales are starting to pick up. Gives me hope that I can have a thriving business again."

"And Eliza?" Kate's eyes sparked. "She brings more than hope. I saw how you looked at her at the pizzeria."

"I looked at her because it'd be rude to walk around with my eyes closed."

She rolled her eyes. "You know what I mean. You haven't looked at anyone like that since Melody."

Hearing his late wife's name sent a pang to his chest.

He'd never have another Mel. She was one of a kind. And he wasn't looking to replace her. But he could invite someone new into his life.

"Eliza's my employee, and we have less than a week until the festival. That's where my focus needs to be." Then why couldn't he stop thinking about that kiss?

"And after that?"

He shrugged. "We'll have to see."

Kate reached for his hand. "Just don't overthink it. Don't talk yourself out of something beautiful. Eliza brings you out of your shell. And for that, I'll always be grateful. But if you want a relationship with her, you're going to have to let your heart off its leash. Are you willing to do that?"

Was he?

That would mean stop analyzing every situation, let his heart be free, and embrace the unknown. Maybe with a dark-haired dynamo.

"I'm afraid of falling in love and having my heart broken again." The words felt as if they'd been painfully ripped from his chest.

"Of course you are. No one wants to experience that again. If you want to learn to love again, you need to stop overthinking it and allow things to play out according to God's plan."

The front door opened, and a customer walked in. He'd forgotten to lock the door after letting Kate in. He flipped the Closed sign to Open.

Kate reached for her coat. "Since it doesn't look like you can make it for lunch, I'm going to find Dani and see if she needs help with anything. Think about what I said. Text me when you're done, and I'll come back tonight and help with the storage room." She gave him a quick hug, then blew out the door.

Her words lingered the rest of the morning.

What would it take to become a freelance editor? Could he juggle that and the bookstore? And still make room for Eliza?

Because if it came down to choosing between a second shot at editing—or a second chance with Eliza . . .

He knew which one he wanted, and that came with another set of complications. They'd agreed to wait until after the festival was over to talk about what was happening between them. Then he'd have to make a decision that would affect both of them—allow her to remain as an employee and keep his distance, or let her go and see where their relationship went.

If not handled well, one of them could end up hurt all over again.

Eleven

I F OLIVER HAD KNOWN WHAT A HASSLE IT WAS going to be to get his furniture into his apartment, he would've gone with beanbag chairs.

Soon after Kate had left earlier in the day, Hunter came in with Eliza and proclaimed his apartment ready for furniture. Since Eliza arrived shortly after noon, reminding him of their previous conversation where he said she could come in a little later, she offered to cover the store. He rescheduled cleaning out the storage room with Kate, then made arrangements to empty his storage unit in Port Joseph and get his furniture moved into his place.

Now, several hours later, sweat dripped down his back as his muscles screamed. He felt as if he'd gone a few rounds with the heavy bag, but he hadn't even laced up his boxing gloves.

Instead, he wore leather work gloves as he and Hunter maneuvered his couch up the back stairs behind the bookstore and into Oliver's apartment without getting drenched.

"Who buys an oversized couch anyway?" Hunter grunted as he lifted his end higher.

"Someone who didn't expect to move." Oliver shifted his hands and pinched his fingers between the wall and the awkward piece of furniture wrapped in a green moving blanket and bungee cords.

Sucking in a breath as pain shot up his arm, he pulled his hand free and left behind a layer or two of skin on the inside of his glove.

He managed to turn the couch forty-five degrees and release it from where it had gotten wedged rounding the corner. "Okay, I'm good now. I'll walk backward if you can steady it from flipping again."

Oliver bent his knees, fought for a better grip, then grunted as he lifted the couch higher. Balancing as best he could, he started down the hall.

At his door, he lowered it carefully and caught his breath. He eyed the doorway and then looked at the couch. "We're going to have to turn it on its side and pivot the top around the doorframe, then swing the rest of it through."

Hunter wiped sweat off his forehead and shot him a mock salute. "Yes, Ross."

Oliver grinned at the *Friends* reference. He blew out a breath, bent at his knees once more, then lifted the couch onto its side. Without wedging himself between the couch and the door, he pulled the top around the doorframe while Hunter pushed from his end.

"Tilt it a little toward me so there's more clearance."

"Sure thing, boss."

The arm of the couch scraped a layer of paint off the doorframe, but Oliver would fix that later.

They managed to get it through and back on all four legs without too much damage.

Hunter dropped on one end and flung an arm over his head. "A little brute force, and we did it."

Oliver strode to the fridge and opened it, grabbing two Mountain Dews. He moved to the couch, handed one to Hunter, and dropped on the other end.

Hunter cracked his can open and guzzled. Then he sighed and wiped his mouth. "Thanks, I needed it."

Oliver ran the cold can across his forehead. "What happened to Waylen lending a hand?"

"He got called into work." Hunter lifted the edge of his shirt and wiped his face. "Probably volunteered to get out of moving."

"Thanks for showing up, man. I appreciate it."

"Sure thing. I got you."

Oliver's eyes roved over the stacks of boxes lining the walls, the chair that matched the couch, his widescreen TV, his bed frame, mattress, and box springs stacked against the opposite wall, and totes full of clothes.

He wasn't looking forward to unpacking.

"Man, I don't want to move again."

Hunter raised his can. "I'll drink to that. I don't want to move you again. If you do decide to ditch this place, leave the couch for the next tenant."

Oliver took another drink and chuckled. His head fell against the back of the couch that sat just inside the door. He closed his eyes and released a sigh. "I'm beat."

"Yeah, but the hard work's done." Hunter rolled his head to the side and looked at him. "You okay? Other than feeling like someone used you as a heavy bag?"

"I'm fine." Oliver drained his pop, pushed to his feet, and set the empty can on the counter. He moved to the window, rolled his shoulder, then looked at the rain racing down the glass. "Can I ask you something?"

"Anything. You know that."

"How'd you know it was safe to go after Daisy?"

Hunter let out a loud laugh that bounced off the bare walls.

"Safe? Dude, falling in love's the riskiest thing I've ever done. And being one of those bad Barrett boys, you know. Daisy and I had our ups and downs, but somehow, we made it through. And now we're getting married."

"You make it sound easy—too easy."

"Are you kidding? Hardest thing I've ever done. We had to start at the ground floor and rebuild what was broken. That and trust that God was in it—*is* in it. And He won't walk away." Hunter joined Oliver at the window. "If we both lean into Him, He'll help us through any future heartache the world might throw at us. Every day, we need to choose to fight for—and not against—each other."

Both stood there, hands in their pockets, as they watched the rain. Finally, Hunter smacked Oliver's shoulder with the back of his hand. "Let's get your bed set up so you have a decent place to crash."

Oliver crossed the room, grabbed the pieces of the queen metal bed frame, and carried them into his bedroom. "Kate said I over-think."

He'd repainted the walls the same off-white as the other room. Easier that way. He set the frame on the floor, careful not to scratch the laminate.

"Is she wrong?" Hunter knelt and helped him tighten the bolts in place.

"If I don't plan, don't calculate every detail, then it feels reckless. I can't afford reckless. Who's going to have my back when I make a mistake?"

"How about God?" Pushing to his feet, Hunter folded his arms over his chest and arrowed Oliver with a direct look.

"Now you sound like Kate again. She said overthinking is my way of trying to stay in control rather than trusting God. That I need to step back and God . . . well, let God be God. To see what

He has planned. But where was God when my wife was killed? Where was God when my business failed?"

Hunter followed him back to the living room and reached for one side of the box springs while Oliver grabbed the other. "I'd say He was right beside you the whole time. Here's the thing—you don't need to have everything figured out for God. No need to analyze your relationship with Him or calculate the risks. Just go to Him and ask for direction and guidance. He'll often give it, but if He chooses to remain silent, you can rest in the knowledge that He's still there. He's unchanging and promised never to leave you nor forsake you."

"Deuteronomy 31:8. Mel's favorite verse." Oliver lifted his end and walked backward toward the frame. They set the springs in place.

"God's timing is perfect. He'll show you the next step."

Oliver returned for the mattress. Instead of lifting, he folded his arms on the corner and exhaled as his friend's words bounced around in his head. "I used to believe that until everything fell apart."

Hunter lifted his end of the mattress, forcing Oliver to move. They carried it into the bedroom and set it on top of the springs. Hunter shoved it in place with his knee. "I'm not going to pretend I've been there, but I do know how it feels when a parent walks away. I know what it's like to feel alone in my pain. But I wasn't alone. And neither are you. God put people in my path to help me see the truth. Who knows? He may have even dropped me in your path today because, frankly, I haven't talked this much in who knows how long."

"I hear you." Oliver chuckled as he dropped onto the end of the bare mattress.

Outside, the Little Stone Bible Church bells rang, signaling the top of the hour. Oliver pushed to his feet and held out a hand. "Thanks for everything, man. I mean it. I appreciate it."

Hunter grabbed his hand and shook it, then pulled him into a man hug, complete with a back slap. "Sure thing. When you decide to move again, be sure and call Waylen instead." He laughed as he headed for the door.

As it clicked closed, Oliver returned to the living room and surveyed everything that still needed a place. His eyes roamed over the off-white walls.

He chose the color because it was nondescript and went with anything. But now, the color felt dull and basic.

What about something brighter that would still go with his beige microfiber couch? What was that soft yellow Dani and Kate had tried to convince him to buy? Was that even a guy color?

Before he could talk himself out of it, he found his coat and phone and headed out the door.

Hopefully, Smith's Hardware was still open, because he had a busy evening ahead of him.

If Eliza came up with any more ideas for the festival, they were going to need another week to pull them off.

But this one was good. Although she needed to run it by Oliver first, she wanted her family on board to make it happen.

After church, she spent the rest of the afternoon working on festival prep and packing up her room. She headed downstairs and found her parents trying to figure out when they were going to do their annual picnic now that they were moving into town.

As she headed for the stables to help with the horses, the idea to combine the picnic with the horses' return came to her.

Chilly air breezed through the open stable doors as the evening sun sank lower into the lake, sending streaks of gold, scarlet, and hot pink across the sky. Light streaming through the windows caught the flecks of dust floating in the air. Another gust of wind carried in the scents of pine and woodsmoke and the whisper of a memory.

"Mom, remember how we used to make a whole day of the horses returning to the island?" Eliza glanced at Mom, then ran a hand over Gus's muscled back, the gray dappled Percheron standing patiently as she cross-tied the muscular workhorse by clipping lead straps to both sides of his halter. Not only for his protection as she groomed him, but also for her own.

Even though Gus was as gentle as they came, safety was the ranch's number one priority. Besides, after her parents moved, she wouldn't have too many opportunities to groom her favorite horses.

"Yes, of course. Everyone met at the docks and helped us usher the horses to the stables. Then we'd have a large get-together here." Mom swept the rest of the hay, grain, and dirt from the aisle and out the door. She brushed her hair out of her eyes and leaned on her broom. "This year, though, the horses are returning at the beginning of the festival."

"Even better. We have the horse scavenger hunt for the kids, so we'll come up with some things for the adults. With yard games and plenty of food, I think people will love it." Eliza grabbed the hoof pick out of the grooming basket and ran a hand down the stallion's leg. Gus lifted his foot, and she removed small stones from the horse's shod hoof.

"El, honey. You have plenty of activities without crowding more into your schedule."

"We'll keep it low-key, I promise. Nothing super fancy. More like a potluck picnic. We can ask locals to bring a dish. You know they'd be on board."

She repeated the same process for the other three hooves, then traded the hoof pick for a currycomb to loosen and release the dirt from the horse's coat. "I want everything to work out."

"You and Oliver have put so much planning, time, and energy into this festival. Everything's going to be fine."

"I want more than fine. It needs to be perfect." She rested a hand on Gus's back.

"That's putting a lot of unnecessary pressure on yourselves. You can do everything right, and things can still go wrong. Or you can do everything wrong, and things can still go right. No matter what, honey, God loves you and blesses your efforts. Pray and ask for peace in the process . . . and for the outcome."

Mom's advice tumbled over in Eliza's head as she whispered to Gus in a calm, soothing voice while using the dandy brush to remove the bits of hay and dirt brought to the surface by the comb.

With each rhythmic pass, her anxiety about the festival eased. She'd been too busy lately to spend much time with the horses, and she missed it. Even the menial, yet essential, tasks such as hoof care helped erase her worries.

Mom returned the long-handled broom to the hook on the wall, then brushed off the front of her jeans. "Listen, honey, your dad and I wanted to do a final picnic before we moved to the cottage anyway, so we'll just move it up a little sooner. I'll talk to your dad, then call the church and borrow some tables." She moved to the open door and waved a hand over the yard. "We'll set up out here like we used to. Your dad can light fires in the portable pits. People can gather around them and stay warm. You have enough on your plate, so Dad and I will handle everything here."

"You're the best." Eliza dropped the brush in the bucket at her feet and hurried over to Mom, throwing her arms around her neck.

"You can always count on us, El. You know that."

"Yes, I can." Eliza returned to Gus and unclipped the lead straps. She rested her cheek against his strong neck. Gus's ears flickered as he rubbed his muzzle over her chin. She walked him back to his stall, closed the door, then leaned her back against the weathered wood.

Closing her eyes, visions of picnics on the ranch property from years ago scrolled through her head.

Islanders who were like family gathered around tables laden with homemade food while kids raced around the yard, playing tag. Her brother Jared strummed his guitar and led singing late in the evening around the fire as wood popped and crackled, sending sparks toward a star-studded sky.

Idyllic times before their lives had been turned upside down.

She missed those ordinary moments that now became extraordinary. Had she known the last one would've been the last one, she would've savored it a bit more.

Those were the memories that kept her warm at night when grief tiptoed into her dreams.

That was what she wanted to recreate for people coming on island—the sense of community. She wanted them to leave with the memory of something real, of something that mattered.

Because it could be gone in an instant.

She pushed away from the stall door, shook off the encroaching melancholy. "Think we need some music too?"

"Did someone just say music? I could strum a chord or two if persuaded."

Eliza whirled around and found Asher, her cousin who was more like an older brother, striding through the side door carrying a bag of grain over his right shoulder.

A backward baseball hat covered his short dark hair. Bits of hay and dust from the bag clung to his beard.

Dirt clung to his faded jeans, and sweat ringed the collar of his tattered gray, stained sweatshirt. He smelled of horses, fresh air, and hard work.

"You'd do that?"

"Sure. I can stream from my phone like the best of them, Busy Lizzie." He shot her a cocky grin.

"Don't call me that." She smacked him playfully on the chest. "And I'm serious."

"So am I." He dropped the grain on the floor, then sliced open the top. He emptied it into the storage bucket, then scooped some into Gus's and Ginger's feeders. Straightening, he winked at Eliza. "For you, though, I'll actually sing."

Eliza threw her arms around his neck. "Thank you. You're the best cousin ever."

"I'll be sure to tell Abi when I talk to her later this week." He winked as he referred to his younger sister.

"You're such a brat. I don't know how Sadie puts up with you." She released him and stowed the grooming gear.

Eliza's phone chimed. She pulled it out of her jeans back pocket and found her aunt's number on the screen. She stepped outside the barn and answered. "Hey, Aunt Sally."

"Hey, El. Hope I'm not catching you at a bad time. I know you have a lot going on."

"I'm doing chores with Mom. What's up?"

Aunt Sally paused. Too long.

Eliza's stomach tightened.

Uh-oh. What now?

"Remember that talk show you got me on before Kimberly took over?"

"*Mornings with Lucille*? Yes, I believe we scheduled that about six months ago."

"Right. Problem is, the studio just called and needs to reschedule. They've slotted me in for Thursday instead of Wednesday."

"This Thursday? As in the day the festival kicks off?" Eliza tried to keep the panic out of her voice. "What time?"

"Ten a.m."

"But . . ." Eliza lifted her eyes to the sky and scanned the darkening clouds as she did mental calculations. "I thought you were coming in Wednesday night so you could be here for the horses' return on Thursday morning. And how will you finish your interview and get a flight to be here in time for the book signing, which begins at five, by the way? Much later than that and you might not be able to get a ferry back to the island. They're running at a limited capacity until the season opens. I guess I could hire someone to pick you up in Port Joseph and bring you across the lake, if necessary." Eliza couldn't stop the rambling thoughts that were coming at her faster than a pack of wild horses.

"Oh, hon, I'm so sorry to create last-minute problems. I should just call them back and cancel."

It wasn't like Aunt Sally to apologize for creating problems. Eliza wanted to shout *Yes, do that. You promised me first!*

But that wouldn't win her any points. Aunt Sally had been looking forward to this show for months.

Why did it have to happen now?

Eliza swallowed her disappointment and the urge to stomp her foot like a toddler. She forced a smile into place, even though no one was around to see it. "Do the interview, then text me when you're finished. I'll figure out the rest. We'll get you here."

She didn't add that they *needed* her here. After all, her aunt was one of the big draws for the festival. If she didn't make it to the signing, Eliza didn't know what to do.

She needed to come up with a Plan B quickly.

Because that's what she did.

Eliza ended the call, then released a long breath that scraped the sides of her ribs. She thumbed through her contacts and stabbed Oliver's name. Putting it on speaker, she headed for the pasture and walked the fence line.

"Oliver Sullivan."

"Why so formal?"

"What?"

"Why do you answer your phone that way? It's me."

"Eliza?"

"Yes. Don't you have me listed in your contacts? My name would've come up when your phone rang."

"I didn't even pay attention. It was ringing, so I answered." He released a groan. "What's up?"

"Why are you groaning? Are you okay? Or is talking to me that painful?"

"I'm moving boxes. Kate's helping me clean out the storage room at the shop."

"Storage room? Why?"

"We decided it would create a better flow for the book signing Thursday night. We're going to repaint and have it ready to put the author tables in there."

"You and Kate? I could've come in and helped."

"You put enough hours in this place. You don't need to give up your Sunday too. Especially with everything on your plate."

She swallowed her disappointment in not being included. "Do you have a moment to talk?"

"Sure, what's up?"

She shared her idea about the picnic at the ranch after the horses returned and then the call with her aunt.

He paused a moment.

Eliza glanced at her phone to ensure she still had bars.

Then his rich voice sounded in her ear. "First, I like the idea—I used to love the big deal that your parents made about the horses returning. And the thing with your aunt—don't worry about it. Everything will work out as it's supposed to."

Had she called the right Oliver Sullivan? Well, she knew only one, but his response seemed to be out of character for him. In fact, he sounded a bit more like . . . the Ollie Sullivan she used to know.

"Have you been kidnapped and replaced by a pod person? Do I need to video chat so you can blink twice if you're in danger?"

"You're hilarious."

"I don't feel hilarious. Unless you count hilariously freaking out at the moment. How can I not worry about it? I've done nothing but worry about things since I agreed to help with the festival. Do you think this is a piece of cake for me? Do you realize how many nights I've stayed up late putting pieces into place so this festival is a success? *Of course* I worry about it." Voice cracking and chest heaving, Eliza stopped walking and blew out another soul-scraping breath to slow her racing heart as she gripped her phone. Resting her elbow on a fence post, she cupped a hand over her eyes. "I'm sorry. I'm not taking it out on you. You're only trying to help. It's just . . . well, everything needs to be perfect."

"Eliza." The smooth cadence of her name coming through the phone sent a shiver down her spine.

"What?"

"It doesn't need to be perfect."

The six words spoken low and slow caused her to pause.

She closed her eyes and breathed deeply, taking in the scents of the ranch—the smells from the barn, the squishy earth beneath her feet, and the lingering trace of a fireplace somewhere. Then she opened her eyes and released the breath. "Why aren't you freaking out? Overthinking this?"

Wasn't that his MO?

She waited a beat for his answer, then he sighed. "Because I said yes when you burst into my store and demanded I hire you. I'm trying to change my perspective. What will worrying bring us? Let's focus on what we can do and what we have to work with. You're doing a great job at the store and with this festival. Everything will fall into place as it's supposed to."

Oliver *was* changing.

And those changes were causing her feelings toward him to deepen. Maybe he did like her for who she was and not for what she could do.

Could she afford to fall for him?

He was still her boss.

And there was her aunt's suggestion to move back to Pittsburgh to consider. If she really wanted to launch a full-time career as a marketing consultant, living in a big city with easier access to airports and an abundance of authors would go a long way to getting her there.

More than living on a tiny, isolated island.

A sudden rush of tears blurred her vision. She must be more tired than she thought for his response to dredge up a well of emotion.

"Thanks, Oliver. That means a lot."

He cleared his throat. "Another problem. Just received a text that Bronte's books are delayed and won't arrive in time for the festival."

Dashing away the wetness clouding her vision, Eliza swallowed the yelp that nearly escaped her mouth, then shook her head. "So Sally Jo Wilson may be a no-show, and B. L. Parker will be there but with no books."

She kicked a clump of grass, but her foot slipped in the evening dew and slammed against the fence post. Pain shot up her big toe, and she bit her lip to swallow a scream.

"We'll figure something out." For the second time, Oliver seemed to be having an out-of-body experience, but he was right. "Get some sleep, Eliza. We'll tackle the problem tomorrow. Together."

They would.

Because they had no other choice.

Twelve

IT WAS AMAZING WHAT A GOOD NIGHT'S SLEEP and warm food could do to turn a person's attitude around, giving Eliza a fresh sense of purpose.

Despite last night's wave of problems, she did as Oliver suggested and managed to get seven solid hours of sleep, waking up when the sun shone through her second-story window.

She had forgotten to pull the blinds by the time she'd headed upstairs last night. All she wanted was to pull the covers over her head and bury herself in a cocoon of blankets that would send her into an exhaustive slumber.

Now, with the air warmer than it had been in weeks, Eliza pulled her hair into a braid that fell over her left shoulder and slipped on a long-sleeved, flowered dress with pockets and paired it with burgundy leggings and her favorite jean jacket.

She headed down Sugar Maple Lane, where bare limbs were starting to bud, and turned onto Blueberry Boulevard. She side-stepped a child's chalk art design and breathed in scents of the lake wafting across the island. Church bells from Little Stone Bible Church chimed on the eleventh hour, and Eliza picked up her pace.

Part of her wanted to veer off toward the Driftwood Hills neighborhood, knock on Candace Bishop's blue door, and give the woman a great big hug. But she didn't have time. Not today.

Not with the festival only a few days away and everything hanging in the balance.

Unlike last night, today she had a solid plan.

She turned onto Main Street, the business hub of the island, where pastel storefronts lined the cobblestone streets. She passed the bookstore—still dark—and waved to her dad guiding a carriage with Gus and Ginger at the helm. Once they passed, she crossed the street and hurried to Martha's on Main.

The scents of fresh-brewed coffee, grilled burgers, and greasy fries wrapped around her as she stepped inside. Giving her eyes a second to adjust to the dim, cozy lighting, Eliza scanned the restaurant. She spotted Oliver in a back dark-hardwood booth, head bent, tapping something into his phone. The light from his screen cast a shadow across his face.

Clattering dishes and conversations competed with Martha's favorite oldies rock playing through the restaurant's sound system. Eliza strode past the "Check your guns, politics, and religion at the door" sign and the wooden bar with green-topped stools and wove through the square tables separating the bar from the booths. She slid onto the green vinyl bench across from him. "Hello."

He looked up, his eyes softening as he smiled. "Someone sounds better today than she did last night."

"Someone got some good sleep for a change." She folded her hands in front of her. "I'm sorry for last night."

Turning his phone screen side down on the table, he studied her for a moment, then the crease in his forehead relaxed, and a smirk tugged at the corner of his mouth. "Hey, we're partners in this. No apologies necessary. Let's focus on fixing last night's problems today."

"Speaking of today . . ." She pulled her phone out of her dress pocket. "I talked to Candace Bishop this morning."

He leaned back and laid his arm on the back of the booth. "About what?"

Eliza tapped open her Notes app. "She said there's a printer in Port Joseph who could do a short print run of Bronte's books for us. I called Lexi, Bronte's agent, who talked to the publisher and explained the situation. They're willing to send the files directly to the printer, covering all costs and deducting everything from the invoice included with the delayed shipment. While we won't have the promised hardbacks, I think readers will be fine with a free paperback copy. It's a short run, but it may be just enough to get us through the signing."

"That's great." He shot her a smile that warmed his eyes.

Buoyed by the hope that coursed through her, she scanned the rest of her notes and glanced at him. "I called the printer, and they promised to have everything ready by this afternoon. The only catch is—we have to go and pick them up before they close at five."

Oliver leaned forward and settled his arms on the table. "See? I told you things would work out."

"Yes, because I spent two hours on the phone making it happen." She fought the urge to stick out her tongue.

He smiled. Warmth flickered behind the usual wall in his eyes. "Thank you. We'll close early and head over."

She leaned back, allowing those two little words that packed a punch to settle over her.

"I have some news of my own." Oliver thumped his face-down phone. "I just got off the phone with Cody Hart. He's willing to meet your aunt in Port Joseph and bring her back to the island in his private boat if she misses the ferry. The boat's small, but it'll solve our problem. All she has to do is text him. He's rearranging his schedule to be available."

For the second time that day, Eliza wanted to throw her arms around someone. But she knew better than to launch herself across the table at Oliver, not when the diner was half full of curious locals. And he was her boss.

Instead, she grinned. "Thanks. That's one thing I can cross off my list."

"Glad I could help." He handed her a menu. "Let's get some lunch. I'm hungry. I skipped breakfast so I could keep painting."

She held up a hand and shook her head. "Sorry, but I can't stay. I'll open the bookstore sooner since we're closing early. As soon as we get back from Port Joseph, Sadie and Mom are helping me put the final touches on the horse scavenger hunt. I wanted to give you an update so we can stay on track."

Oliver reached across the table, plucked her phone from her hand, and closed both his hands around hers. "You can take time out of your very busy schedule to eat a hamburger. You need fuel to keep going."

Her shoulders slumped as the adrenaline of the morning subsided and the awareness of Oliver's touch warmed her fingers. "Maybe you're right."

"Maybe?"

"Yes, maybe." Pulling her hands out of his—reluctantly—she opened the menu. A burger did sound really good.

Vera Graves, her sixtysomething retired Sunday school teacher, approached their table. Her glasses hung from a chain, and a pencil was stuck through her silver bun.

"Hey, guys. What can I get you?"

He smiled at Vera, reminding Eliza of that former Ollie Sullivan charm. "Hi, Vera. How are you doing?"

"Can't complain." She looked at Eliza. "What can I get you, honey?"

"I'll have a cheeseburger and fries."

"Anything to drink?"

"Ice water is good."

"Ollie?"

Eliza bit her lip as Oliver visibly cringed.

"I'll have the same." He reached for Eliza's menu, stacked them together, and slid them to the edge of the table.

Vera picked them up and nodded. "Be right back with your drinks."

Eliza tilted her head. "So, what's the big deal about your nickname? It's been a part of you for as long as I've known you."

Oliver rolled his eyes. "Ollie's fine for a little kid. Or even a dog. But not a grown man approaching forty."

"It's cute."

"I'm thirty-six. I don't want to be cute."

"What do you want to be?"

He hesitated, then muttered, "Respected."

The word hung between them like a surprise, heavier than she expected. Judging by the look on his face, Oliver hadn't meant to say it out loud.

Eliza swallowed a snarky comment and reached for his hand, giving it a gentle squeeze. "Oliver, you are respected. People on this island love you."

"You're kidding, right?" He scoffed. "People have long memories on this island. They love to talk about the Sullivans and the disaster we leave in our wake."

"Not you. What happened was in the past. And you weren't responsible for your dad's actions."

He looked down at the table and dug at a scratch. "I'm not worried about this place."

She frowned. "What are you worried about?"

Vera returned carrying a small round tray, and set two glasses of water on chipboard coasters. Droplets slid down the sides of the glasses as she dropped two straws on the table and turned away.

Eliza reached for a straw.

Oliver slid his straw into his glass, then wrapped the paper around his finger, his gaze drifting over her shoulder. "I just don't want my past mistakes to follow me and overshadow the festival. I meant what I said last night—I am trying to change, but it doesn't happen overnight."

"What past mistakes?"

"Trusting the wrong person. And that incident with Constance."

The vulnerability threaded through his whispered words stole her voice. She didn't know all of Oliver's backstory, at least not yet, but he'd shared enough to know he put a lot of pressure on himself to succeed.

And more than anything, she wanted that for him too.

"We've had a few unexpected setbacks, but we've also worked hard to kick off the year with a fun festival that's guaranteed to bring tourists back on island. And quite honestly, I think they're going to be so thrilled with what you've done, they won't care. Readers don't know the industry politics. They just want their books. Writers might've heard rumors, but that's all they are—rumors." She leaned in, her gaze tangling with his, and her voice firm. "Focus on presenting your best self and having a great time. And as you told me last night—everything will work out."

And Eliza had to believe that. Because she didn't want to think what could happen if it didn't.

After they finished lunch at Martha's, Oliver made the impulsive decision not to open the store. Instead, he and Eliza headed for the ferry and planned to pick up the books from the printer in Port Joseph, but they weren't ready yet. Needing to kill some time, and again, without taking time to analyze it, Oliver headed north and took Eliza to one of her favorite places . . . that he'd just learned about on the ferry.

The smile on Eliza's face was exactly what Oliver needed to prove he'd made the right decision.

"Thank you for bringing me here." She threw out her arms and smiled so wide it practically lit up the cloudy sky. "Even if it feels like we're playing hooky."

"I'm the boss. I can close the bookstore any time I want."

After descending the steps to the platform at the brink of the Upper Tahquamenon Falls in the Upper Peninsula, Oliver pulled in a lungful of musty air, breathing in the scents of pine and damp earth as they viewed the powerful fifty-foot waterfall. Mist dampened their faces as they listened to the roar of the water.

Leaning closer to her, he pointed at the two-hundred-foot stretch of rushing amber-gold water. "You know why they're called the 'Root Beer Falls,' right?"

"Because the tannins from the hemlocks, spruce, and cedar leach into the water." Gripping the wooden railing, she nodded toward the trees populating the state park and surrounding the water. "They're darker now than in the summer. And they're gorgeous in the fall when the leaves turn."

Before they left the island, Eliza returned home and changed from the cute dress and jean jacket she'd been wearing into a green turtleneck sweater, brown leather jacket, dark wash jeans, and brown ankle boots. She'd pulled her hair back into a ponytail, exposing small gold hoops in her earlobes.

Oliver took out his phone and framed Eliza leaning forward and gazing toward the water. She turned just as he took the picture, and the result nearly stole his breath. The angle of her profile, the peace in her brown eyes, and her hair blowing around her face created an unexpected longing he wasn't sure how to process. He wanted to draw her against his chest, but instead, he stowed his phone and curled his fingers into a fist to keep from reaching for her.

He cleared his throat and jerked his head toward the stairs that brought them to the platform. "Want to check out the Lower Falls?"

Eliza lifted a shoulder and moved away from the railing. "The Lower Falls aren't as impressive in height, but they're still quite beautiful. It's like a four-mile hike, though." She glanced down at her ankle boots. "I'm not really prepared for the hilly, rooted terrain. Besides, as much as I could spend the day here, we have a lot to finish for the festival."

"So you want to call it?" A part of him didn't want to leave. Ever.

She glanced at the falls once again, then shook her head. "Want to? No. But . . ." She lifted a shoulder. "I don't know . . . maybe we could come back again. Another day when we have more time."

Another day.

The thought of the two of them doing something together in the future twisted his gut.

He wanted to spend time with her. More than just spend time together. He wanted to touch her. Hold her. Kiss her again.

But she was still his employee. And that issue had waged a war in his chest.

Oliver pulled out his car keys and swung them around his finger. "Let's head back."

They climbed back up the ninety-plus steps that took them from the platform to the paved trail connected to the parking lot.

He opened the passenger door to his silver sedan and held it while Eliza slid inside. Once he backed out of the parking space, Eliza leaned her head back and sighed.

"You okay?"

She looked at him with warm eyes and a smile. "I'm more than okay. When you asked about my favorite place to visit while we took the ferry over to Port Joseph and I mentioned this place . . ." She gestured toward the state park. "I didn't expect to visit today." Then she lowered her gaze to her fingers. "Or ever again."

One look at Eliza's face, and Oliver parked in another space. He shifted in his seat, one arm resting across the top of the steering wheel. "Why do you say that?"

She peered out the window a moment, then looked at him with watery eyes. "Mind if we walk a little?"

"Not at all." Oliver turned off the ignition, then exited the driver's side. He jogged around the front and opened her door. He spied a sign for a paved trail off the parking lot. "We can walk this way."

"Sorry. I just said we needed to get back, and now I'm delaying us even more."

Oliver held up a hand and smiled. "It's fine. I promise."

They started down the trail under a canopy of bare branches. Snow littered the ground between the trees where the sun hadn't melted the remains of winter. Short furled ferns lined the path.

Eliza thrust her hands in her jacket pockets. "Before Jared left to go on tour with Phoenix, he came home for a couple weeks. Two days before he had to meet up with Asher's band, he and I took a day trip and came here. My parents used to bring us here during the summer, and it quickly became a favorite spot. So we decided to go for the first time by ourselves. We packed water and snacks, hiked the trails, and talked about our futures."

"Sounds like it was a great day."

"It was. Being the lyricist and lead guitarist for Phoenix, he loved going on tour with the band. Their new record, *Dark Side of Midnight*, had been such a hit. Jared had become good friends with Sadie's older sister Lauren, and she started touring with them, hoping to break in doing backup vocals."

"I'd forgotten Sadie had a sister, but now that you mention it, I do remember them coming on island to visit Hank and Henrietta during the summers."

"Sadie and I have bonded over losing our siblings, unfortunately."

"I've heard rumors, and I read some stuff when the story broke late last summer when Asher was discovered on Jonathon Island, but I didn't know what really happened."

"Two weeks after Jared and I spent the day here, Mom and Dad received the devastating news that Phoenix's tour bus crashed during a terrible storm, rolled, and caught fire. Everyone died in the accident. Except Asher, who has permanent scarring from the flames." She stopped in the middle of the trail and faced him, a tear drifting down her cheek. "That's why this place holds a special place in my heart. I haven't been back since losing my brother."

"I'm sorry, Eliza." Oliver took a step toward her, cupped her elbows, then lifted a thumb and dried the tear off her face. "I'm sorry for your loss. I know how that changes you. I'm sorry for bringing you here without asking first. If I had known, I would've taken you somewhere else while we waited to pick up Bronte's books."

She shook her head and gripped his arms. "No. Don't apologize. Today has been wonderful. Absolutely lovely." She lowered her lashes, bit the edge of her lip, then looked up at him. "Outside of my brother, there's no one else I'd rather be here with than you." She stood on tiptoe and brushed a kiss across his cheek. "So thank you."

Oliver ground his jaw as his heart slammed against his ribs. He needed to take a step back. Put some distance between them. Instead, though, he pulled her gently against his chest and wrapped his arms around her.

She fit perfectly in his arms with the top of her head nestled just below his chin.

More than anything, he wanted to cradle her face in his hands and kiss her, but he settled for holding her close. Anything more blurred the lines he'd been trying to untangle in his head.

She pulled back and looked up at him, her arms moving to his waist. "I've been a little lost since coming back on island, trying to figure out my place and what I want to do. I'm really feeling like I'm beginning to find my footing again. And that's thanks to you."

"Me? What did I do?"

She cupped his cheek and ran her thumb over his jaw. He stifled a shiver. "You hired me. You put up with me and my crazy ideas for the festival. Working at the bookstore and coordinating the festival has given me purpose again. I feel like they're opening a door to a future I hadn't expected."

Despite the screaming in his head, Oliver reached for Eliza's hand, threaded his fingers through hers, and squeezed. "You are a gift, Eliza Quinn, and this festival is going to be a success because of you."

She returned the hand squeeze. "Because of us. Partners, remember?"

Partners. Right.

Without releasing her hand, he guided them back to his parked car. Sunshine split through the clouds and flooded the interior with light and warmth.

Oliver savored every moment with Eliza because after today, this would be the last time they spent time together outside of the bookstore or doing any festival planning.

No matter how much his heart begged him to, he couldn't fire her now and lose an invaluable employee—one who was finding her purpose after feeling lost.

He'd keep her on and take an emotional step back, no matter how much he was falling for her, because he couldn't cross that line as long as she was his employee.

As they returned to Port Joseph, they discussed what needed

to be finished for the festival, then fell into a comfortable silence except for the jazz music playing through the car stereo.

He parked in the long-term lot used by a lot of the residents who kept cars on the mainland, transferred the boxes of books to the dock so they could be loaded, then boarded the ferry with Eliza.

They settled into their seats, listened to the announcements he knew practically by heart, then he closed his eyes as his head leaned against the seat back.

"Tired?" Eliza nudged his shoulder.

He opened one eye and peered at her. "In a good way."

He glanced at Eliza, who lifted her face to the evening sun.

Did she realize just how beautiful she was?

Oliver had to nearly sit on his hands to keep from tucking the hair that had tangled in the wind behind her ears.

That was one of the things he loved about her—she didn't freak out about small things like windblown hair.

Whoa. Wait a minute. *Loved* about her?

Did he leave his brains back in Tahquamenon Falls?

He wasn't *in love* with Eliza. Couldn't be.

Even though he'd known her most of his life, they'd only been reconnected for the past couple of weeks.

That wasn't enough time to fall in love.

It wasn't like this was the movies or anything that ended in ninety minutes. This was real life. And in real life, a sane person didn't fall in love in less than three weeks.

The ferry pulled into the harbor. Oliver stood back as Eliza went ahead of him, leaving her fragrance in her wake. On the dock, they waited for their boxes as they were unloaded, and he carried them to Dani's golf cart he'd asked to borrow.

Once they were loaded, Eliza slid into the passenger side while he moved behind the wheel. "I'll drop these off at the store, then run you up to the ranch."

At the bookstore, Oliver pulled around back, fished out his

keys, and unlocked the door. He hit the lights, but nothing happened. "Mind checking to see if the other businesses on the street have power?"

Eliza climbed out of the golf cart and cut between the bookstore and Doug's Market. A few moments later she reappeared. "Lights are on inside the market and down the block."

Frowning, Oliver headed upstairs and checked for power in his apartment.

Nothing.

He knocked on Bronte's door, and she opened it. "Hey, Oliver. What's up?"

"Hey, B. You have power?"

Leaning against the doorjamb, she shook her head. "It went out about an hour ago. I'm reading by a battery-powered light Jonah gave me." She grinned. "If it doesn't come back on, I'll crash at Holland's house."

"I'll call Hunter and see if he can check things out." Heading back downstairs, Oliver tapped on Hunter Barrett's number, but the call went to voicemail. Same with Cody Hart. He met Eliza outside the back door to the bookstore.

"Bronte doesn't have power either. Neither Hunter nor Cody picked up." Oliver glanced at the time on his phone. "Sorry for the delay. I'll drop you off at the ranch, then figure out how to get the power fixed."

"Oliver, take a breath." Eliza grabbed his arms. "Let's unload the books just inside the door, return the cart, then walk to the ranch together. Mom made chili, so you can get something to eat, then call Liam."

"But you're supposed to be there in ten minutes. I don't want to hold you up."

"It's fine. I'll text and let them know we're going to be late."

They unloaded the books, and Oliver relocked the door. Trying to remain calm, he drove the golf cart back to the Tourism Bureau and parked it in Dani's spot.

He pulled out his phone and tapped a text.

____________________Oliver

Where do you want the cart keys?
Ask Liam to give me a call.

A moment later, his phone rang. "Hey, sis. Where do you want me to drop the keys?"

"Put them in the flowerpot at the edge of the door."

"Seriously? You know that's the first place people look for a B and E."

"No one is going to break and enter on the island, Ollie. Besides, we have security cameras."

"Look at you, upgrading technology."

"It was Liam's idea. He didn't like the thought of me working in the building after hours, so we compromised when he wasn't able to be with me."

"Is he around?"

"Just a minute."

"What's up, Oliver?"

"Power's out in my building. I tried calling Hunter and Cody, but no one's answering. Know of anyone else I could ask for help?"

"Let me make some calls and see what I can do."

"Thanks."

Oliver ended the call and shared the information with Eliza. "Let's head to the ranch."

An hour later, with his stomach full from Angela Quinn's homemade chili and cornbread, Oliver still hadn't heard back from Liam. He tried not to be distracted by his quiet phone and focused on what Eliza had put together for the scavenger hunt.

The Quinn kitchen radiated warmth from twilight coming

through the trio of windows to the light cabinets, exposed beams, and dark flooring.

Printed book covers, laminated paper horseshoes, and cartoon horses replaced the dinner dishes on the nicked and scarred oval kitchen table, every scratch having a story, no doubt.

Eliza picked up one of the book covers. "These are the copies you made of the covers of the books we've been featuring at the store, and Sadie helped me laminate them." She reached for one of the plastic stakes in a pile in the middle of the table. "We need to attach covers to these numbered stakes and place them around town. Those participating in the scavenger hunt will write the number next to the business where they found the horse book. They'll turn in their sheets and be entered into a drawing for one of the business prize baskets."

"I like it." Oliver attached one of the pictures to a stake with a clear zip strip and cut the ends. "Is this right?"

"Yes, perfect." She finished trimming another laminated horseshoe and held it out to him. "These horseshoes have fun facts about the horses in the featured stories. We'll place them around the store for families to find. They can turn them in for gift cards to the Fudge Shop on the Corner."

Eliza picked up two pictures of Gus and Ginger. "Their pictures will be cut into puzzle pieces placed in sponsoring businesses with clues. The first family to return their completed puzzle to the bookstore will receive one of the prize baskets."

Oliver pushed to his feet and looked out the windows behind the table that overlooked the pasture. "I'm sure your family has an incredible view of the sunrise from this spot."

"Yes, one of the many things I'm going to miss when we move off the ranch."

Oliver gripped the back of his neck and shook his head.

"Something wrong?"

He lifted his eyes and connected with Eliza's. "Just the opposite. I'm amazed by all you've done in a short amount of time."

She lifted a shoulder. "Mom, Sadie, Joanne, and Henrietta helped too."

Mrs. Quinn and Sadie came through the side door into the kitchen, bringing in the cool air and scents from the pasture, their cheeks pink and eyes bright.

Eliza pushed back her chair. "How was your walk?"

Sadie pulled off her hat and smoothed down her wavy dark hair. "Refreshing, especially after doing computer work all day." She gestured toward the table. "All finished?"

"Yes, thanks to Oliver."

Oliver eyed the table, then took in the three women standing together. He let out a little laugh. "Well, I really owe you guys big time for this."

Mrs. Quinn made a face and waved away his words. "You owe us nothing. We were happy to help."

Eliza held up a hand. "Hey, hey, hey. Slow down a minute. Let's see what he's offering up before we dismiss it."

As Sadie and Mrs. Quinn laughed, Oliver took a step toward them, his eyes fixed on Eliza. "Seriously, you've done a great job. I'm sorry for doubting you."

"Did anyone hear that?" Eliza pointed to each of them.

Mrs. Quinn gave her daughter a mock glare. "Eliza, no need to be sassy."

"But then he would be so disappointed." She laughed, that same sound that sent his heart skidding across his ribs.

She did keep him on his toes.

The door opened again. Asher and Mr. Quinn stepped inside. "Stephen Hastings of Hastings Farms just called. Everything's in place for the first horses to arrive on island on time."

"It's going to be a great week." Eliza thrust her fists in the air, then flung her arms around her family. "Thank you, guys, for every-thing. We couldn't have pulled this festival off without your help."

Feeling the odd man out, Oliver hung back and pocketed his hands.

He should've been the one who stepped up and helped Eliza with all of this. She shouldn't have needed to rely on her family and neighbors to get the work done.

He'd allowed his attitude to get in the way of what could've been fun preparations for the festival.

His phone vibrated. He pulled it out and found his sister calling. "Hey, Dani."

"Ollie, I used your emergency key and let Liam and one of his hotel workers in to check your electrical system. He can tell you what they found."

"Thanks."

"Hey, Oliver," Liam's voice came on. "One of the hotel elec-tricians looked at your box. The main fuse blew, so he replaced it and restored power to the bookstore. He suggested upgrading the wiring and replacing the fuse box with a circuit breaker panel."

Dollar signs flashed before Oliver's eyes. One more reason the festival needed to be a success. "Thanks. I'll talk to Jonah."

They had to get through the weekend first. He glanced at Eliza talking with her family. And then he could tackle the next prob-lem.

Thirteen

AFTER SPENDING LAST NIGHT AT THE RANCH with Eliza and her family, Oliver owed her more than he could ever repay. But he'd begin by offering her coffee and her favorite caramel-frosted cinnamon rolls.

He opened the door to Good Day Coffee and breathed in the scents of coffee and sugar lingering in the air.

Jill Kelley slid a tray into the bakery case and smiled. "Morning, Ollie. Ready for the festival? Looks like we're going to have great weather."

"I don't know about ready, but the festival will be here anyway. I'm thankful for the forecasted warmer temperatures." Then he spied Eliza sitting at one of the tables in front of the window that looked out over Main Street. "Did Eliza get anything yet?"

"No, she said she was waiting for you."

"Perfect. Give me two of those caramel-covered cinnamon rolls that she loves so much." Then he paused. "Wait. Hold that thought. Let me get her drink order first."

Jill reached for a paper cup and waved it at him. "Oh, I know that one. She drinks chai lattes."

"Great. Add one of those to the order. And I'll take a coffee. Black."

She marked Eliza's name on the side of the cup with permanent marker. "Coming right up. In fact, I'll bring it over to you."

"Thanks, Jill." Oliver paid for their order and slipped a couple of bills into the tip jar by the register.

He headed across the room and pulled out the chair opposite Eliza. "Good morning."

She looked up from the book she'd been reading and flashed him a white smile. "Good morning, Oliver. I didn't hear you come in."

He nodded to the book. "Good book?"

She lifted it so he could see the cover done in a light blue and silver with a woman wearing a fur hood and walking on a snow-covered road.

The Face of Winter.

"I haven't heard of that one." He cocked his head and gave her a mock frown. "Did you cheat on me and order online?"

Shaking her head, she laughed. "Of course not. This is women's fiction written by Silvia Raine. She's one of Candace's clients whom I met at last week's retreat. She sent an ARC—an advanced reader copy—because she wants me to create a publicity tour for her debut novel."

"Great. I'll order copies for the store."

"That's what I told her."

"Pretty confident, aren't you?"

"Absolutely. Told her I could pull a few strings."

He drummed his fingers on the table. "Yeah, about that."

"My confidence? Or the strings?"

He shook his head and searched his brain for the right words. "I—I feel bad about the festival."

Eliza closed the book and tucked it into her tote bag at her feet. Then she looked at him with a serious expression. "What about the festival? Did something happen?"

"No. Just my own stupidity. After last night, I realized just how much you've been doing … and I haven't. I've been a knucklehead about the festival since Dani asked me to take it over. I've done nothing but give you a hard time while you're working all your off-hours pulling it together. And I'm really sorry."

Eliza's face softened, and she reached across the table and laid her hand over his. "Oliver, you can be a knucklehead, but you don't have to apologize. You made it clear from the very beginning that this wasn't in your wheelhouse. And to be perfectly honest, I've been having a blast. Plus, you've been doing things like clearing out the storage room and repainting it for the book signing. And hello—who brought in Victor Holt? Huh?"

He snagged one of her fingers and rubbed his thumb over her knuckle. Then he looked up at her. "You're pretty amazing, you know that?"

Her cheeks pinked, and she shook her head and withdrew her hand. "I'm not amazing. I jumped in because I wanted you …" She blew out a breath and looked at him. "I offered to help because I wanted you to like me."

Her last words were spoken so softly. Did he hear her correctly?

"Like you? Well, that's just crazy."

"It's crazy to like me?" Her head jerked up, hurt mirroring in her eyes.

"No." Oliver laughed. "It's crazy to think you had to earn my appreciation. I've always liked you, Eliza. You were a good kid."

"I'm not a kid anymore, Oliver." Her expression shifted and something warmed in his belly.

Oh, he knew that.

"What I'm saying is, I've always liked you. And I really appreciate everything you've brought to this partnership. You're an invaluable employee, and I hope you stick around for a very long time."

That meant he needed to do what was best for Eliza and douse the rising feelings he had for her.

A shadow flickered across her face. "Oliver, I have to tell you—"

"Here are your drinks." Jill arrived with their drinks and plated cinnamon rolls. "Sorry for the delay. Had a problem with the frother."

"Oh!" Eliza's eyes lit up. "I didn't place my order." She glanced at Oliver. "I was waiting for you. Then we started talking . . ."

"I ordered when I came in. Jill told me what you liked."

Eliza smiled at them. "Well, thank you. Both of you."

As Jill returned to the counter, Oliver dug his fork into the soft, yeasty cinnamon roll and breathed in the sweet scent of sugar and vanilla. His mouth watered as he took the first bite. "I get why you like these so much."

"They're pretty awesome, aren't they?"

"Yes. I could eat these every day. But then I wouldn't fit through the aisles in the bookstore." He patted his stomach.

"I don't think you have anything to worry about." Eliza eyed him, then dropped her head, but not before he caught the flush that bloomed across her cheeks.

He let out a laugh.

Her head jerked up. "You need to do that more often."

"Eat cinnamon rolls?"

"No, laugh."

"Am I a grumpy curmudgeon to you?"

"I think that's a redundant description, isn't it, Mr. Editor?"

Someone pounded on the glass next to him, startling him. Bronte gestured to him with tears streaking down her face.

He dropped his fork, shoved away from the table, nearly toppling his chair, and raced outside. He grabbed her arms. "Bronte, what's wrong?"

She covered her face with her hands as a sob escaped. "Holland just called. There's been an accident."

"Jonah's sister? Is she okay?" A chill snaked down Oliver's spine as his fingers tightened. "What kind of accident?"

"She's fine. It's Jonah."

The cinnamon roll congealed in Oliver's stomach. "What happened?"

"I don't know all the details, but there was an explosion on base, and Jonah's been injured."

Ice sluiced through his veins as his pulse tripped. "No."

Bronte's head bobbed as she sucked in her lips. "I'm heading to the airport. I'm trying to get a flight to Germany. My agent is getting me tickets while I get on the ferry and schedule an Uber to the airport." Then she looked at him with tear-stained cheeks. "I'm so sorry, Oliver, but I have to cancel the book signing."

Blinking rapidly, Oliver swallowed a lump in his throat as he pulled Bronte against his chest. "No. Don't give it another thought. We'll manage." Then he pulled back and framed her face in his hands. "Promise me you'll call me as soon as you learn something. Promise me."

She nodded and gave him another quick hug. "Yes. But I have to catch the ferry. It's leaving in ten minutes."

"Go."

She raced down the sidewalk toward the dock as the ferry horn sounded its departure warning.

He puffed out his cheeks and blew out a breath. Then he lifted his eyes toward the cloudless blue sky. "Lord . . ."

Even though the name came out in a sigh, Oliver couldn't form any more words to add to the prayer. He dropped on the iron outdoor bench in front of the coffee shop, elbows on his knees, and cradled his head in his hands.

"Oliver?" Eliza sat next to him and placed a hand on his upper back. "What's going on?"

He swallowed past the battle of emotions clambering to the surface. Then he leaned into her touch and shared about Jonah.

She sucked in a breath, wrapped her arms around him, and rested her cheek on the top of his head. "I'm so sorry."

"Bronte canceled her book signing, of course. I feel like a jerk. I'm upset about Jonah, but now we need to scramble and come up with another idea. Without Sally Jo and Bronte, we don't have a signing. Not a great way to kick off a festival. We need to offer the readers something."

She pulled back and framed his face in her hands. "Everything will work out as it's supposed to, remember?"

His words from last night echoed back to him.

However, instead of bringing relief and peace like he was sure she intended, anger surged inside him. He held up a hand. "Stop. I don't need platitudes right now. The book signing, the festival— those aren't important right now. A man's life hangs in the balance. Someone I care about."

He pushed to his feet and jammed his hands in his pockets. He looked at Eliza a moment, then swallowed words blistering his lips. Deep red stained her cheeks.

Nodding, she stood and jutted her chin. "You're right."

She headed for the door and opened it.

"Eliza . . ." Holding out a hand, he stepped toward her.

Looking at him with hurt in her eyes, she shook her head and stepped inside the coffee shop, the door closing behind her.

He released a sigh. He shouldn't be taking his frustrations out on her. Without another word, he headed to the bookstore.

But when he reached the shop, he kept walking. Crossed Blueberry Boulevard. Cut through the park and strode to the water's edge, where Lake Huron lapped against the shore.

He reached down and picked up a handful of cold, wet stones and bounced them in his hand. One by one, he hurled them into the water as far as he could with as much strength as his muscles would allow. Over and over until his hand was empty.

Breathing heavily, he dropped to the rocky shore and pulled his knees to his chest. The damp ground seeped through his khakis. Wind licked across the water and swirled around him, chilling him to the core.

With shaking hands covering his mouth, Oliver lifted his eyes to the sky. "God . . ."

The prayer would have to do.

Clearly, Eliza had overstepped.

Surrounding herself with chocolate and friends soothed her wounded heart after Oliver's abrupt—and humiliating—exit.

After he went off on her outside Good Day Coffee, Eliza cleared their table, pitching his coffee and cinnamon roll in the trash, then marched her mortified self up Main Street, chai latte in hand, and headed toward the Fudge Shop on the Corner to get the gift cards Lily and Declan Kelley offered for the festival.

Except the shop wasn't open yet.

When Eliza texted Lily, she invited her upstairs to her and Declan's small apartment that he'd transformed before they got married a couple months ago.

In addition to Lily, though, Eliza found Sadie, Mia, and Dani there working on wedding favors—luggage tags with *Love is a journey* stamped on them. One side of the identification card shared Dani and Liam's thanks for attending their wedding, and the other side offered a place for name and address. Dani and her friends were adding the cards to the tags, then putting them in small cellophane bags and tying them with light-green ribbons.

Cupping her chilled fingers around a warm mug of Lily's home-made hot chocolate Dani had given her, Eliza perched on the edge of the love seat next to Sadie while Dani occupied the matching chair. Lily—her wavy lavender-streaked blonde hair pulled back into a ponytail—sat cross-legged on the bright green rug next to Mia Franklin, Cody Hart's fiancée and Lily's future sister-in-law.

"So then he just walked away." Eliza stared into her half-finished mug and tried to fight the heat climbing her neck once again. "I don't know what I did."

"You didn't do anything." Dani clamped a hand around Eliza's wrist. "Think about it a moment—he just got news that someone he loves is hurt again."

Hurt again?

Oh, wait . . .

Eliza covered her face with one hand and set her mug on the table. She stifled a groan. "I'm a self-centered idiot."

Next to her, Sadie laughed and wrapped an arm around her shoulders. "Oh, El, self-centered is not a word anyone would use to describe you."

"His wife." Shaking her head, Eliza pressed a fist against her lips. "Jonah's injuries must have stirred up all the emotions after his wife's accident. And here I made it about me."

Mia dragged a hand through her dark hair. "After losing Troy, I learned grief isn't linear. Sometimes the strangest things will trigger a wave." She scooted forward and grabbed Eliza's hand. "But it's okay to feel wounded. You reached out, offering comfort, and his reaction was hurtful. I'm sure his walking away wasn't because of you."

Dani lifted her cup in her cousin's direction. "I agree with Mia. My brother's a private person. He probably wanted to be by himself."

"Why not just say that?" Eliza looked up at her friends.

Sadie bumped her shoulder. "Because men can be strange."

The rest of her friends raised their mugs. "Hear! Hear!"

Lily encircled the group with her finger. "We all have stories about our guys acting like idiots. And if Daisy and Bronte were here, I'm sure they'd agree. But this isn't a male-bashing session. Our men put up with our frustrating behaviors too."

Sadie raised her mug to her former roommate. "So tactfully said, Lil. Marriage is changing you."

Lily twisted the amethyst ring on her finger. "I'm learning how to be a partner with Declan—with our business, but more importantly with our marriage."

Partners.

Hadn't Eliza just claimed she and Oliver were partners yesterday? Sure, she was referring to the festival, but what if they could be more?

Maybe he'd seemed to pull back a little after their visit to the falls, but she brushed it off as being preoccupied with the loss of power at the bookstore.

She pushed to her feet and looked at each of them. "You're right. All of you. Thank you for letting me vent. I need to show him some grace . . . and get to work on finding a last-minute author for the book signing." She looked at Dani. "Have any ideas?"

Dani tapped her fingernails against her mug. "The Grand received several boxes of Victor Holt books yesterday that will be used for one of your events, I believe. Didn't you say he was coming in on Friday for his meet and greet? Maybe you can see if he can come in early and do the book signing."

Eliza's pulse tripped as her eyes widened. She leaned down and threw her arms around her friend. "You are a genius. No wonder you've been so successful in revitalizing the island."

Dani blushed. "It's been a team effort."

Eliza gathered her things and waved her goodbyes. At the bottom of Lily's apartment stairs, she pulled her phone out of her bag. If Candace wasn't tired of her yet, she would be by the end of the festival, but Eliza didn't know who else to ask without involving Oliver.

Although her head realized she hadn't done anything to upset him, his actions still stung. She needed to shake it off and focus on a solution for Thursday night's book signing.

Candace responded with the information Eliza needed. With Logan Kingsley's number now in her possession, Eliza tapped a message to him, not expecting an answer right away. But hopefully he would respond before the night was over.

Within minutes, her phone rang.

"Hello?"

"Eliza? This is Logan Kingsley. I just got your message."

"Logan! Thanks so much for calling me back. I reached out to an agent friend who gave me your number. By any chance, are you heading to the island soon?"

Logan laughed, a warm, friendly sound. "Actually, my girlfriend and I are on the ferry right now. We have rooms at the Grand and plan to attend the book signing."

"Fantastic! How would you like to be a signing author instead of an attendee? The two authors we had scheduled had unexpected circumstances, so as of this moment, we don't have an author. But if you were to show up . . ." Eliza held her breath.

"One second."

The phone muffled, and Eliza could hear voices but not the words.

"Eliza?"

"Yes?"

"Sure, I can do that. What time would you like me at the bookstore on Thursday?"

"How about four o'clock? That way you can get set up before we open the doors at five. The signing goes until seven, then there's an informal get-together at the Island Pizzeria across the street."

"Sounds good. We'll see you on Thursday. And thank you."

"No, thank *you*, Logan. I'll text you some details."

They ended the call, and Eliza squared her shoulders.

She'd show Oliver good things *did* come out of bad situations.

Now to hunt down the giveaway copies of Logan's books and check the inventory at the store.

Infused with new energy to complete what she started, she headed down the sidewalk when her phone rang. This time, her aunt's number flashed on the screen. "Aunt Sally, I have only a minute to talk."

"That's all I need. I wanted to check and see if you've given my offer any more consideration."

"Offer?"

"Move back to Pittsburgh and start your business here."

"Right. Right. Yes, that offer. To be honest, I've been so busy with the festival that I haven't had a lot of time to think about it. There's just a lot going on right now."

"I get that. I do. I also wanted to let you know I spoke with Matt Goodwin from Inspire Media and showed him the social media posts you've created and shared for the festival. He's pretty impressed and wants to talk to you. I gave him your number. I didn't think you'd mind."

Eliza stopped in the middle of the sidewalk, then dropped on the bench in front of Smith's Hardware. "Wait. You did what?"

Aunt Sally laughed. "I think you heard me. It's a great opportunity, El."

"Yeah, but . . ."

"But what? What's up with the hesitation?"

Eliza ran her thumb and fingertips over her forehead. "Honestly, I just have so much happening right now. I don't have time to think about it. I don't want to sound like a brat, but I need to get through this festival first."

"Yes, yes, of course. Let's get through that, and then we can have a nice sit-down and chat."

"Sounds good. I'll see you tomorrow."

"One way or another, I'll be there—even if I have to swim across the lake."

Eliza laughed. "I'd pay good money to see that."

"Listen, missy. I'll have you know I was a swimming champion in school."

"I know. I'm just teasing."

Martha Kelley rode past Eliza on her vintage beach bike and waved.

Eliza waved back and stood. "Listen, Aunt Sally, I really do have to go now."

"Okay, hon. Take care."

Aunt Sally ended the call, leaving Eliza a little stunned.

While working for Inspire Media would be an amazing opportunity, it might not be the right one for her. She had other things to consider, like her parents, especially with their upcoming move, her job at the bookstore, and her relationship with Oliver.

Whatever that might be.

She strode down the sidewalk and unlocked the front door to the bookstore. As she stepped inside, she turned the lights on and spotted Oliver weaving through the shelves.

He'd changed from his black polo and black pants into jeans and a gray T-shirt with *I'd challenge you to a battle of wits, but I see you are unarmed* in white script across the front.

Looking up, he stopped and shoved his hands in his front pockets. His eyes tangled with hers, then he ran a hand over the back of his head. "I'm sorry."

The two words, spoken low and slow, coursed through her.

He took a step toward her, lifted a hand, then dropped it. "I'm sorry about earlier at the coffee shop—and what I said. The news about Jonah threw me, and instead of leaning into your support, I lashed out."

Eliza clasped her hands in front of her. "I just shared the same words you'd spoken to me, if you remember."

"I recognize that. And if you remember, when I said them to you, you went off on me."

Oh, drat.

He was right.

She twisted her face. "So we're both knuckleheads with some issues."

"I was just . . . well, I didn't want to take how I was feeling out on you, so it was better to walk away. Wasn't right."

She dumped her stuff on the counter and moved toward him. She touched his arm, then pulled him in for a hug. "Just for the record, I didn't like what you said, but I do want to be there for you. You don't have to face this alone. I'm sorry about Jonah. Have you heard anything yet?"

His arms tightened around her. "It's way too soon, although the waiting is eating me up. I don't want to bug Jonah's parents. I'm sure George and Renee will let me know when they hear something." He shrugged. "Not much I can do anyway."

"We can pray."

With her arms still looped around his neck, she pressed her forehead against his and whispered a prayer she hoped would bring him peace. And remind him he didn't have to continue going through life by himself.

"Thank you." He whispered the words, then brushed his lips across her cheek at the same time she turned her face.

Her lips caught his.

She didn't plan it, but it felt right. Her arms tightened around his neck, and she pulled him to her.

Oliver shifted and closed the distance between them. His hands rested gently at her waist a moment, then his arms snaked slowly around her back as their kiss deepened.

He smelled of fresh air, and his lips tasted of cinnamon and sugar. Her fingers curled into the soft cotton of his T-shirt.

In that moment, everything just felt right.

He slowed the kiss until his lips caressed hers with the barest of touches. Still holding her close, he looked at her. "Well, I take it you've forgiven me."

"Or maybe I just like kissing you." She rested her face against his chest.

"Is that so?" His lips grazed over the curve of her jaw and down her neck.

Her breath caught as her eyes closed. It was too easy to stay where she was, in the shelter of his embrace, where everything felt right and good.

But in the silence of the bookstore, the clock above the register ticked, reminding her of what still needed to be done.

Forcing herself to take an unwanted step back, she looked up at him. "We have work to do."

"All work and no play makes Jack a dull boy."

Eliza pressed a hand against his muscled chest. "Well, your name's Oliver, not Jack, and we have a festival starting in two days. Work first, play later."

He raised a brow as his eyes darkened. "Promise?"

"I will always keep my word with you, Oliver." She brushed a wave of hair off his forehead.

"I'll hold you to it." His eyes anchored to hers, he lifted her hand and feathered a kiss across each of her knuckles.

Eliza didn't know what had changed for him. Was he willing to consider a relationship while she worked for him? They really needed to talk, but it would have to wait a few more days. They had too much to do.

Somehow, someway, she needed to force her feet to move, because she wanted nothing more than to be swept up in Oliver's strong arms again and feel his lips against hers.

But that wouldn't get the work done, and they needed this festival to succeed.

Both of their futures depended on it.

Fourteen

IT TOOK MORE THAN A DAY OF DIGGING, BUT Eliza and Oliver found the boxes of Victor Holt's books at the Grand that Dani had mentioned.

Even though the books would be gone very quickly, they'd ensure readers could get a signed copy shipped to them—even if Eliza had to pay for everything out of her own pocket. She was not going to let anything ruin the outcome of this festival.

Thankfully, her dad had been able to meet them at the Grand and help transport the books back to the store.

Oliver grabbed a couple boxes while Dad grabbed the other two. Eliza unlocked the door and held it while they carried them inside.

Although he was pushing sixty, her dad still had the strength and energy of someone a third his age . . . and showed no signs of slowing down anytime soon, no matter what he and Mom said.

For that, she was so thankful.

Oliver stacked the boxes on the floor by the register.

Eliza hugged her dad, then kissed his cheek. "Thanks, Dad. I couldn't have done it without you."

Dad tapped her on the chin. "Sure you could've, baby girl. But a father always likes to be needed, especially by one of his favorite people." He lifted a hand toward Oliver. "See you, Ollie." Then he headed out the door and closed it behind him.

"Remind me again how you talked Logan into doing the signing? I was a little distracted by trying to kiss you again earlier and may have missed what you said." Oliver reached for her hand and tugged her toward him.

Laughing, she pulled away from him and reached for the box cutter by the register. She sliced open a carton and pulled out Victor Holt's first published book, *The Keeper*.

She ran her fingers over the dark royal blue cover. "When Bronte backed out of the signing, I asked Candace for another favor . . . we really owe that woman. I was able to get in touch with Logan, and it turns out he's already on island. He arrived yesterday and is willing to be a part of tomorrow night's signing as well as the fan mingle at the pizzeria and everything else he signed up for during the festival." She waved a hand over the boxes. "We don't have enough of the same books for everyone, but we do have copies of his others. So the book signing won't be a bust after all."

She wiped a hand across her brow. "I'll carry these into the storage room and get them ready for the signing. Nice job on the glow-up, by the way. Repainting it really transformed the room."

Oliver's hand shot out and grabbed her wrist. "Wait."

She looked at his strong fingers curled around her arm, then up at him.

Oh, man. She was a goner every time he was within feet of her.

"Thank you for fixing the signing. I truly appreciate your amazing problem-solving skills."

She closed her eyes for half a second and allowed his words to melt over her. Then she flashed him a smile and gently removed his fingers from her skin. "Thank you. I appreciate that. Now you have got to stop touching me. We have a lot of things to do today."

"But I love touching you." He laughed, the sound warming her heart. "You've got spunk, Eliza. I'll give you that."

She made a face. "Why is it when a guy speaks up, he's a leader, but when a girl does it, she's got spunk?"

The front door opened, and Dani came in followed by Mia, Lily, and Sadie.

Dani walked over to her brother and gave him a hug. "Hey, Ollie."

He hugged his sister back and then slipped his arm around her waist. "What are you guys up to?"

"We're here to help." Lily threw out her arms. "Put us to work."

"What do you mean, help?"

Sadie scrunched up her face. "After you left Lily's, we decided to pitch in and do what we can to help with the book signing."

"Sadie . . ." Eliza reached for her friend. "Thank you."

Sadie shook her head. "Thanks isn't necessary. I know you guys have a lot to do, so we want to help. Put us to work."

Eliza hugged Sadie and whispered in her ear, "Thank you."

"Anytime. I'm here for you. Hope you know that. We who have lost siblings have to stick together."

Tears pricked the back of Eliza's eyes. "Say that three times fast." She laughed. "I don't think I could."

For the next several hours, the six of them changed out displays and set up tables for signing stations. Dani ran back and forth from the bookstore to the Tourism Bureau, making copies of the schedule of events to pass out to the signing attendees while Mia and Lily hung colorful banners and Sadie packed the reader tote bags with festival information. Oliver and Eliza helped customers find books and encouraged them to attend the signing.

Once everything was finally done, Eliza wrapped her friends in a group hug. "Thanks. Couldn't have done it without you."

Behind them, Oliver cleared his throat. "What about me?"

Dani laughed and broke away, waving him over. "Come here, big brother. You can be part of the hug too."

He wrapped his arms around the girls, and his fingers brushed Eliza's hand. He threaded his fingers through hers and gave a gentle squeeze. Then, over the tops of the others' heads, Oliver's eyes caught with hers, saying more than if he'd spoken words.

They broke apart, and the friends left, leaving Eliza and Oliver alone.

Eliza glanced at the clock on the wall behind the register. "Even though we're closing in half an hour, would you be able to handle things if I left early? I really need a shower. I feel like I'm covered in cockroach dust."

Oliver's brows knitted together. "What are you talking about? We don't have cockroaches on island."

"No, but cockroach dust gets in the cardboard."

Huh. He learned something new every day.

"How about we close up shop, and I walk you home?"

"You don't have to do that. It's way out of your way. Besides, you could use a break too."

"Spending time with you is relaxing." He looked at her with an expression that threatened to buckle her knees.

Eliza waited while Oliver locked the door, and then they headed up Main Street and turned left onto Blueberry Boulevard.

His hand reached for hers. As she closed her fingers around his, Eliza realized something that scared her more than anything else . . . she had fallen in love with Oliver Sullivan.

That was going to impact the rest of her life.

Oliver wasn't being honorable, and that needed to change. It wasn't fair to tell Eliza he needed to keep things professional, then continue kissing her like nothing had changed.

They needed to talk—sooner rather than later.

Otherwise, he needed to figure out how to manage a working relationship with her, especially since she loved working at the bookstore.

Problem was, Oliver was finally being honest with himself—he wanted more. He wanted Eliza in his life. And that scared him.

After walking her home and kissing her again at the door, he left Sugar Maple Lane and crossed back onto Blueberry Boulevard. As he stepped onto the corner of Main, his mom came out of Doug's Market, carrying two fabric shopping bags.

She wore jeans, a light-blue jacket over a white T-shirt, and white sneakers. Her auburn hair was in a ponytail pulled through the back of the Jonathon Island hat she wore. Oversized sunglasses shaded her eyes.

"Hey, Mom. What are you doing?"

She lifted the bags and smiled. "Ollie! Just the person I wanted to see. I grabbed a few bags of chocolate to set out at the bookstore. Although, maybe I should've gotten some of Lily's fudge instead. Also, I'm volunteering my services for your book signing."

"Are you serious?"

"Absolutely." Her smile widened. "If it goes as well as people are saying, you're going to be swamped, especially since Dani mentioned Victor Holt will be signing. How'd you manage that?"

"Wasn't me." He shrugged.

"What do you mean it wasn't you?"

Taking the bags, Oliver fished out his keys and unlocked the bookstore door. "Eliza made it happen after Bronte backed out."

Mom brushed past him, her expensive perfume swirling around him. "I ran into Bronte at Good Day Coffee the other day, and she seemed excited for the signing."

Oliver flipped on the lights and set the bags on the counter.

"Bronte doesn't get excited about public appearances. She agreed only because she learned Jonah would be on island and by her side." He relayed what little he knew about Jonah's injury.

"Oh, honey, I'm so sorry." Mom's eyes softened. "I didn't know. How scary for her—and Jonah. And you, of course. Do you know what's going on?"

Oliver lifted a shoulder. "Haven't heard a word. My texts to Bronte and Jonah have gone unanswered."

"Have you talked to George? Or Renee? Surely his parents would know what's going on." Mom pulled her phone out of her purse. "I can text Renee, if you want."

Oliver closed his fingers gently over Mom's hand. "I don't want to bother them. I'll hear something soon."

"Okay, honey. If you're sure." She retrieved the chocolate and ripped the bags open. "Do you have anything to put this candy in?"

Oliver headed to his office, rummaged through the cabinets, and found a few small plastic red bowls. Better than nothing. He returned to the front of the store and set them on the counter.

She filled the bowls and placed them around the room. "Where's Eliza?"

"Taking the rest of the day off to finish up last-minute festival prep."

Mom sat on the edge of the armless couch and crossed her legs. "How are things going between the two of you? I enjoyed seeing you two together at the pizzeria."

"Fine." Oliver dropped next to her and threaded his hands behind his head.

"Just fine?" She eyed him as if she could penetrate his head and read his thoughts. "You're in love with her."

Oliver leaned forward, balanced his elbows on his knees, and clasped his hands. "It's not that simple."

She rested a hand on his back. "Honey, love never is."

"I haven't even been interested in anyone since Melody. But Eliza . . ." He blew out a sharp breath.

"Want to talk about it?" Mom moved her hand from his back to his arm.

He eyed her and lifted a brow. "No offense, Mom, but you're not my first pick to discuss my love life."

She withdrew her hand and sat back against the couch. "Fair enough. I haven't exactly inspired trust in you kids these days."

"It's not that." Oliver pushed to his feet.

"You buried your heart for years, Ollie. Don't allow fear to cause you to miss out on something real." Mom stood and straightened the pillows. "You know what I mean. I loved Melody. When she and the baby died, we all grieved. But your life changed the most. It was a double loss. I grieved for all three of you. I lost my daughter-in-law and future grandbaby. But you . . ." She cupped Oliver's cheek, her eyes shimmering. "You lost your joy. But I've seen that come back. And I think that's because of Eliza."

Oliver scrubbed a hand over his face. "I need to work out some things in my head."

"Then talk it out. With Kate. Your brothers. Or even a counselor." Gripping her elbows, Mom pressed her lips together, then she looked at him. "One of my biggest regrets is the pain I caused this family. I can't change what I did, but I can be honest about how the healing changed me."

Shoving her hands in her back pockets, Mom faced the windows. "When Ryan left, I didn't know who I was anymore. I couldn't be Becky Sullivan. I didn't want to be Becky MacBride. I outgrew Becky Jonathon. I was just . . . broken. Your Uncle Seb and Aunt Elise helped me to find a Christian counselor in Port Joseph. That's when the healing began." Mom turned and met his eyes. "You don't have to carry all this by yourself. It's time to let others in."

"Thanks, Mom." Oliver wrapped his arms around her. "I'll think about it."

"Talk to Eliza. Tell her the truth—the good, the bad, the messy. That's how relationships are formed—by being honest with each other."

"And if she doesn't feel the same way?"

Mom leaned back and gripped his chin. "I've seen the way she looks at you, so I really doubt that's the case." She gave him another hug, then moved out of his arms and grabbed her purse. "What do you have to lose?"

Oliver stared at her retreating back as she pushed through the door.

What did he have to lose?

Not much. Just his self-respect. And the pieces of his heart once he was brave enough to offer them again.

Fifteen

For the first time since leaving Pittsburgh and returning on island, Eliza felt like she'd finally found her footing.

And today, for the first time in six years, the horses were returning and kicking off Novel Connections—the first of what she hoped would be an annual festival.

The morning air blew over her, sending a chill down her back. Although the sun was shining, and the weather was expected to climb, she continued to shiver.

Crowds gathered at the docks, surrounding the fences and wanting to be a part of the celebration. Locals bundled in jackets and clutched paper coffee cups while tourists, particularly readers who'd come in early, waited with phones out and cameras slung around their necks. Kids tried to climb the weathered white fence for better viewing.

The horse scavenger hunt was going to be a success.

Not only was the story time crew here with their families, but children who had come with their parents to be a part of the festival were excited to participate as well.

Then the picnic at the ranch followed by the book signing tonight . . . yeah, it was going to be a great day.

Dad moved next to her and slung a beefy arm over her shoulders. He pressed a kiss to the top of her head. "You done good, kid."

Tears pricking her eyes, she leaned into his embrace, allowing his warmth and strength to soak through her. "Thanks, Dad."

"They're coming! I see the ferry!" Finn Franklin pointed toward the dot on the horizon as the ferry churned the water through the straits, making its way toward the island.

The little boy bounced on the balls of his feet, his eyes wide and excited. Next to him, Maggie tried to climb the weathered fence. "Where? I don't see."

"There, sissy." Finn pointed in the direction of the ferry. "See it now?"

She shook her head, her blonde curls smacking her cheeks. Cody lifted her up on his shoulders. "There, peanut. Try that."

Maggie kept a firm hold on Cody's head, her arms wrapping around his ears and cheeks.

Eliza sipped her chai latte, hoping that creamy warmth would chase away the chill curling around her bones.

She scanned the crowd, hoping for a glimpse of Oliver. She'd expected him to show by now.

Then she spied him jogging toward the marina, his open jacket flaring behind him like a cape. He wove his way through the crowd and reached her side.

Catching his breath, he grabbed her hand and gave it a light squeeze. "Sorry I'm late. Just got off the phone with Bronte."

"Everything okay?" She searched his face. His windswept hair fell across his forehead, and she fought the urge to smooth it back.

His eyes lit up. "Yes, I'll tell you everything, but first we need to focus on the horses."

She threaded her fingers through his. As long as Jonah was fine, she could wait for details.

A horn blast echoed across the water, and her pulse picked up speed, her heart nearly vibrating out of her chest. She gripped Oliver's hand as the buzz of the growing crowd increased.

Soon, the ferry was more than just a dot. It cut through the morning fog like a beast, carrying eight strong draft horses returning to the island for their seasonal work.

For the first time since the pandemic shut down the island.

Eliza turned her back to the dock and faced the growing crowd. She handed her cup to Oliver, released his hand, and then raised both arms. "Excuse me. Can I have your attention, please?"

The rumbling of conversation died down. "My name is Eliza Quinn, and I wanted to welcome you to the historic return of the horses."

Clapping thundered across the dock, and Eliza fought against the sob rising in her chest. Swallowing several times and clearing her throat, she gestured for her family to join her. Her parents stood on her left while Asher and Sadie stood to her right.

She opened her mouth, but words escaped as the ferry drew closer and she caught sight of a familiar-looking muzzle. A tear drifted down her cheek as she looked at her parents.

Dad squeezed her shoulder, then gestured toward the approaching ferry. "Once the ferry docks, we need to stay back and give the handlers space to lead the horses off the ferry." He wrapped an arm around Mom. "Then my wife Angela and I will lead the ceremonial walk to the ranch. For the last time."

Eliza blinked back another rush of tears as her throat thickened upon hearing those last four words.

Dad moved behind Asher and Sadie and placed a hand on their shoulders. "My fine nephew Asher and his lovely bride Sadie will be taking over the Q3 Ranch. And while Angela and I will still own the carriage tour business, Asher and Sadie will now oversee the ranch and the well-being of the horses. Change is tough, but it's time for Ang and me to make room for new traditions." Dad's deep voice caught, then he cleared his throat. "Let's give it up for Asher and Sadie."

As the gathered crowd showed their appreciation, Oliver slid an arm around Eliza's waist and pressed a kiss to her temple. Then he lowered his mouth to her ear. "I know this is hard, and like your dad said—change is tough, but it can be good. And I'm here for you."

She turned and smiled up at him, then found Mom wiping her eyes. Eliza wasn't the only one having a moment.

With Sadie still by his side, Asher reached for Eliza's hand. He gave it a gentle squeeze, then faced the crowd. "I am beyond honored to be taking over the 3Q Ranch that was started by my grandparents years ago. Named for my dad Noble, my Aunt Sally Jo, and my Uncle Terry, the ranch has been a long-standing fixture on Jonathon Island for as long as I can remember. For me, it became a refuge and a place of healing." He waved a hand toward the gleaming black carriage sitting by the fence. "Some of you may remember my grandfather's first carriage. I restored it last fall. Because today is such a special occasion, Sadie and I would like to offer complimentary tours of the island today. After the picnic at the ranch, we'll be picking up at the livery at the end of Main Street on Blueberry Boulevard, touring for thirty minutes, then returning for the next tour. We'll go until the book signing begins tonight. No tickets are needed. It'll be first come, first served. You'll find the departure times at the livery. If you're not able to ride today, we'll be having carriage rides all season long, and we will look forward to seeing you again."

A teenager with dark hair pulled back into a ponytail pushed her way to the front, her eyes wide. "Are you really *that* Asher Quinn? The lead singer of Phoenix?"

Eliza didn't miss the tightening of Asher's jaw, but he kept a smile in place. "Yes, I am really that Asher Quinn. I lost my band and crew in a tragic accident nearly six years ago. Through the grace of God, I'm singing again, creating music with my beautiful wife." He drew Sadie closer to his side. "She writes the lyrics, and I write the music. And with God in the center, it's the perfect partnership. Look for our new album, *Share the Scars*, to be released soon."

Asher nodded to Eliza. Taking Sadie's hand, they disappeared into the crowd.

Even though her cousin had spent years on tour facing millions of people, he loved his quiet and anonymity on the island the most.

While the ferry docked and the workers took care of the horses, Dad stepped forward once again and shared a brief history of the horses returning on island. "For over a century, Jonathon Island has relied on horses for transportation. Until the pandemic, every spring the horses' return from their winters on Hastings Farm marked the traditional changing of seasons. Over the next few weeks, more than five hundred horses will be transported back on island, ready to be ridden by guests, pull carriages, transport goods, and serve as the island's taxi service. They represent the start of the tourist season and our commitment to preserving our car-free lifestyle."

One of the Hastings Farm hands, dressed in jeans, work boots, and a hunter-green jacket with Hastings Farms embroidered on the upper left pocket, guided the first horse down the ferry ramp and onto the cobblestone street and handed the reins to Dad.

He blinked several times as he stroked the horse's muzzle.

The black Percheron's ears flickered as he shook his head. Standing about seventeen hands high, his shiny coat glistened in the sunlight, evidence of being well cared for over the winter.

Stepping out of Oliver's embrace, Eliza moved up to the large animal and laid a hand alongside his neck. "Hey, beautiful boy. Welcome home. We missed you."

While living on island, she'd loved the summers, especially

when she worked at the Grand, teaching riding lessons and guiding trail rides.

Dani hurried over to her and threw her arms around Eliza's neck. "You did it. You actually did it." Tears welled up in her eyes and spilled down her cheeks. "I dreamed of this day for years. Thank you for everything. I can't believe the horses have finally come home."

Home.

Yes, that's what it was—a homecoming.

Clinging to her friend and watching through a watery blur, Eliza's heart swelled from the significance of this life-changing day.

Once the final horses had been off-loaded, Mom and Dad took lead of the team, one on either side of the first horse. Asher and Sadie reached for the harnesses on the second horse.

Eliza left Dani in Liam's capable arms and hurried over to Oliver. She grabbed his hands and took her place behind her cousin. She settled on one side of the next set while Oliver took the other side. The Hastings handlers managed the rest of the horses. Dad led the procession past the Grand and up the hill to the ranch.

Hoofbeats against cobblestones echoed with her heartbeat.

The horses' return was as Eliza had hoped—that sense of anticipation, that sense of normalcy returning to the island, that sense of belonging.

Locals lined the route and clapped and cheered as the horses clopped their way to the ranch. Several people, even cranky Martha Kelley, wiped their eyes.

The horses. The scavenger hunt. The picnic. The book signing. All of it would keep her busy before she collapsed into bed tonight.

She pulled out her phone and turned on the video. As she panned the streets, taking in the celebratory sounds and the rhythmic clopping of hooves, she realized something.

For more than a hundred years, the return of the horses wasn't just a tradition—it was a reunion.

But this year, it was more than that. Dani Sullivan's efforts to bring the island back to life were working.

Even though the air was still cool and trees and flowers were still budding, the return of the horses meant the island would come alive again.

One hoofbeat at a time.

Even though Oliver had watched the return of the horses back on island numerous times, their return hadn't affected him like it did today.

Their return offered hope to the locals. Hope for a revived future they thought was in the past.

And now, as more guests arrived at the ranch for the celebratory picnic, Eliza and her family welcomed them and directed them to the tables piled with assorted salads, cut fruit, deviled eggs, and nearly any dessert a person could want.

Games had been set up in the large backyard between the stone ranch house and the whitewashed stables. Sunlight split through the budding branches and glinted off the deep green metal roof. Gus and Ginger and the eight other horses watched from the fenced-in pastures as they grazed.

Henrietta threw a horseshoe at a stake and hooked it around the metal. Her arms shot in the air. "Ringer!"

"Way to go, Hetty! You show them how it's done." Asher winked at her as he took his turn to throw.

"Thanks, love." She blew him an air kiss.

Oliver manned the grill, keeping an eye on the rows of patties, hot dogs, and brats. Partly to give Terry Quinn time to mingle with the guests and partly from having to make unnecessary small talk.

Laughter mingled with the scent of burgers filling the air as

Eliza wove through the growing crowd and joined him at the large outdoor grilling station. She grabbed on to his arm. "You good?"

Dressed in jeans, a knitted sweater, her favorite ankle boots, and with her hair pulled up into a messy bun, Eliza took his breath away. Wasn't too hard to do these days every time she was around.

"Now that things have settled down a little, care to let me know what's going on with Jonah?"

"With all the excitement of the horses returning, it slipped my mind." He flipped several patties with the wide spatula. Grease sizzled as the fat hit the flames. "Bronte called this morning. She didn't make it to Germany. While on her way to the airport, she got a call from Jonah—he's in Bethesda, Maryland."

"Maryland? How'd he end up there?"

"From what I could gather, an oxygen canister sprang a leak and exploded near the OR where Jonah was performing surgery. He got thrown by the blast wave and broke his upper arm and clavicle. He ended up being rushed into emergency surgery in another part of the military hospital while they took care of the damage from the blast. Then he was air-lifted to Walter Reed."

"Wait a minute. I thought this just happened yesterday."

Oliver lifted a shoulder. "I thought so too, and Bronte said they got the call yesterday, but everything happened the day before, and Jonah wanted to get stateside before notifying anyone. Unfortunately, his commanding officer reached out to George and Renee, Jonah's parents, before Jonah could contact Bronte."

Eliza folded her hands over Oliver's left shoulder and leaned on him. "I'm so glad it wasn't worse. Have you talked to Jonah?"

"Not yet. Bronte promised he would call soon. If I don't hear from him by tonight, I'll call first thing in the morning." Oliver waved a spatula at the crowd. "Great turnout."

"No kidding. I hope this is a forecast of what's to come for the rest of the weekend."

Zoey Dawson raced across the grass and flung her arms round Eliza's waist. "Hi, Liza."

Eliza crouched and embraced the child. "Hi, sweet girl. I like your shirt."

Zoey pulled out the long-sleeved T-shirt covered in gray horses. "My mommy bought it." Then she peered up at Oliver and waved. "Hi, Oliver."

Oliver crouched next to Eliza. "Good morning, Miss Zoey. Read any good books lately?"

She shook her head so hard her strawberry blonde braids smacked her cheeks.

"Don't worry, we'll find the right book for you."

Ivy Dawson, the owner of the island's Hair Haven Salon and Zoey's mother, hurried over to them. "Zoey, honey, please don't run off like that."

"Sorry, Mommy. I was just saying hi to Liza and Oliver."

Ivy ran a manicured hand through her strawberry blonde hair, then rested it on Zoey's shoulder. "Thank you both for the picnic. Zoey's been so excited about the horse scavenger hunt, so we've been walking around town collecting clues and talking about the books you've been reading."

Oliver and Eliza stood, and Oliver raised an eyebrow as he looked between mother and daughter. "Every week I asked if she liked the stories, and she tells me no."

Ivy sighed and shook her head. "The last eighteen months have been rough. My husband died of cancer at the ripe old age of thirty-six. My aunt Tara"—she nodded toward Pastor Arnie Chamberlain and his wife Tara, who were talking with Eliza's parents, then redirected her attention back to Oliver—"told me about your sister's revitalization efforts. So, we moved from Boston, took advantage of the one-dollar houses, and set up my salon. Being able to drop Zoey off for story time has been a blessing. My late husband looked a little like you with the same wavy brown hair and blue eyes. I think she needed to know someone who even looked like her dad out there could still see her."

Eliza's throat tightened as her eyes misted for the hundredth time that day.

"Mommy, I'm hungry." Zoey tugged on Ivy's hand.

"Okay, sweetie, let's go get a plate." Ivy looked at them. "Thanks again for what you're doing. Keep it up. It's making a difference. I'll swing by the shop tonight and get the books you've been reading."

Ivy took Zoey's hand, and they headed toward the food table.

Oliver turned back to the grill, smoke spiraling up between the grates and stinging his eyes. He blinked several times.

"Oliver, you have made a lasting impact on that precious child." Eliza rested a hand between his shoulder blades, her voice cracking on the last syllable.

Oliver kept his focus on the burgers and turning the brats as Eliza's words sank into his head. His throat thickened, and he cleared it. "We'll find her the right story. One that makes her smile."

"No matter what she says, I think she's going to like any story you read because you see her. And Ivy's right—that's what's important right now. Making a difference in even one child's life means everything you're doing is worth the time and effort."

Even though the bookstore needed to make a profit to thrive, he didn't care if Ivy Dawson bought a single book in his store. In fact, when she came in tonight, he'd have a basket ready just for Zoey. And he'd remain committed to doing his Saturday afternoon story time, reading books by talented authors, and allowing any child who showed up to be seen, because Eliza was right—that was what mattered.

He rubbed a finger and thumb across his eyes and wiped the wetness on his jeans, then slid the burgers, hot dogs, and brats onto a platter and handed it to Eliza.

Dani came up to them, her arm tucked in Liam's elbow. "Great picnic, you two."

Eliza smiled and stepped away from him. "Thanks, but my family gets the credit—and the locals for supplying food. I hope you're enjoying yourself."

"Absolutely." She grabbed Oliver's bicep. "And you . . . you've really stepped up."

He slung an arm over Eliza's shoulder. "Only because I have an amazing partner."

Eliza's face colored. Maybe it was from being too close to the heat emanating off the grill. She looked up at him with eyes that turned his stomach to mush. "We did it together."

Together. Man, he was liking that word more and more.

Over Eliza's head, he spied Mia and Cody arriving. "There's Mia and Cody. We'll have to see how Finn and Maggie enjoyed the horse scavenger hunt."

"I'll go check." Carrying the platter to her mother, Eliza exchanged it for the nearly empty one, then headed toward them, only to be nearly run over by Finn and Maggie.

"Kids, slow down!" Mia's command landed on deaf ears.

Dani looked at Oliver with serious eyes and leaned close. "She likes you, Ollie. Don't screw it up."

He scowled at her. "Thanks for the confidence, sis."

Clutching Liam's arm, she shrugged. "Just telling you like it is." She waved to Mia, then tugged Liam in the direction of their cousin.

Mia waved to Oliver, then handed Eliza a foil-covered plate. "I made brownies."

Taking the plate, Eliza waved toward the picnic table. "Thank you. I'm sure they'll get devoured. Grab some food. Oliver's grilling burgers and brats. There's plenty for everyone."

While she walked with Mia toward the food table, Cody caught up with Hunter and Waylen, and the three of them ambled toward him.

Wearing jeans, work boots, and a Barrett Construction hoodie that matched his hat, Hunter handed Oliver a dripping can of Coke. "Figured you might be thirsty with the way you've been drooling over Eliza."

"The grill's not the only thing heating up over here." Waylen, on duty in his blue police uniform and his wild hair tamed, slugged Oliver's shoulder.

Oliver cracked the can. "You're both idiots, you know that, right?"

The brothers looked at each other and shrugged. "Pretty much."

Their words spoken in unison made Oliver laugh.

Then Hunter sobered. "Any news on Jonah?"

Oliver lifted a layer of fresh premade patties on wax paper from the cooler at his feet and flipped them onto the grill. He balled the paper up and tossed it in the trash bag Eliza had provided when he took over the station. He recounted his conversation with Bronte.

Hunter set his Coke on the table behind the grill. "Well, I'm not as patient as you are. Now that I know he's stateside, I'll send him a text."

"The kids loved the scavenger hunt, Ollie. You guys did a great job." Cody raised his can and nodded. He wore an olive-colored *I'd rather be fishing* T-shirt under his Carhartt jacket.

"That was all Eliza and her family. I attached the pictures to the stakes and set them up around town."

Mia called Cody's name and waved him to her.

"Later, guys. My girl needs me."

Oliver's eyes trailed after him as Cody made his way to Mia's side and kissed her cheek.

Waylen drifted toward the horseshoe pit and struck up a conversation with Asher and Henrietta, leaving only Hunter and Oliver at the grill.

"Well, Jonah hasn't responded yet."

"Who knows—maybe his phone didn't make it on the plane with him. Call Bronte."

Hunter rubbed his chin. "Hadn't thought of that. I'll wait." He drained his Coke and crushed the can. "Good to see you fitting in here, Ollie." He slapped Oliver on the back. "Glad to have you back."

Hunter headed over to the food table, pitched his can into the recycling bin, and then stood behind Daisy, his fiancée, and wrapped his arms around her waist.

She leaned against him and smiled up at him.

Oliver turned his attention back to the burgers, suddenly desiring someone else to take over the cooking. Hunter's parting comment tumbled around inside his head.

He'd been back for a while, so what did his friend mean by that?

Truth was, Oliver wanted to fit in. He wanted community. A place to belong. But that meant taking risks and opening up.

Before he did that with anyone else, he wanted to open up with Eliza.

But he still needed to fire her first to make that happen.

And the sooner, the better.

Sixteen

IN ALL HER YEARS ON THE ISLAND, ELIZA HAD never seen the Island Bookstore as packed as it was tonight.

Not even during Bob and Lucinda's busiest blowout sale they used to host once a year.

Good thing Tommy McIntyre wasn't here because the fire chief would've cited them for breaking some sort of fire code. They maxed out capacity thirty minutes ago, and they still had another hour and a half for the signing.

People stood shoulder to shoulder as the line for Victor Holt snaked through the store and out the door. While some readers expressed disappointment over not having Sally Jo Wilson or B.L. Parker available to sign their novels, Eliza managed the situation with discount coupons toward the purchase of other books in the store and promised signed bookplates from the authors.

Plus, they were especially thrilled when Asher and Sadie stopped by. Her cousin sang a few of his old songs and signed autographs.

Oliver moved to her side, where she'd stationed herself next to the door to welcome guests and provide them with a handout of the festival events.

He bent his mouth close to her ear. "Have I told you lately how gorgeous you look?"

She fingered the Leland blue stone necklace around her neck that paired well with the blue fit and flare crepe dress with cap sleeves and scoop neck she wore for tonight's event.

She turned her head and gave him a side-eye. "Not in the last twenty minutes or so. You're slipping."

"Well, we'll change that." He straightened and slid his hands in the front pockets of his charcoal-gray dress pants. His light gray dress shirt stretched across his shoulders every time he moved, and she had to keep her eyes averted to prevent going into heat stroke. The store was warm enough as it was.

Kate called to him from the register.

As he passed behind Eliza, his fingers skimmed her back. She turned and smiled.

Her phone buzzed in her pocket. She pulled it out, didn't recognize the number, and pocketed it again. She didn't have time to talk, and if it was important, the caller could leave a message.

The door opened again, pulling her attention away from Oliver, and she let out a gasp.

Bronte held it open as Jonah—Jonah!—moved past her, his right arm in a sling. The right side of his face held an impressive collection of cuts and bruises that trailed down his neck. Dressed in jeans, an untucked blue button-down, and a Detroit Lions hat covering his military-short dark hair, he fit right in with the growing crowd.

Bronte, on the other hand, wore a gorgeous black-and-white patterned wrap dress with black knee-high, heeled boots. A black satin beaded headband held her dark curly hair away from her face.

A smile spread across Oliver's face as he made his way to the door and hooked his friend in a side hug. "Man, I'm so glad to see you upright."

Jonah wrapped his left arm around Oliver's neck. "Me too, man. Me too." He lifted a shoulder, then winced and reached for his right arm. "Thankfully it wasn't more serious than a fractured clavicle and broken humerus in my dominant arm. I'm now on medical leave, and my CO signed off for me to recoup stateside. So I'll be here about six weeks or so."

"Sorry about the bum wing. Where are you staying?"

"I'm gonna crash at Holland's while my pretty nurse waits on me." Jonah reached for Bronte's hand and drew her to his side.

Bronte batted him on the chest. "I'll take care of you, but I'm not waiting on you hand and foot, mister. I have books to write. Besides, you need to move around, Doc."

"She's worse than my CO." Jonah lifted his chin toward the packed store. "Looks like business is booming. Great job."

"I have Eliza to thank for this." Oliver reached for her hand.

Jonah's eyes lit up as he came toward her, his left hand extended. "Eliza Quinn, it's great to see you again."

She gave him a gentle side hug. "You too, Jonah. I'm sorry to hear what happened."

"By the grace of God, it wasn't worse. I hear you've been lending a hand."

"Lending a hand?" Oliver let out a laugh that speared her chest. Moving behind her, he gripped her upper arms gently. "She's been the brains behind the whole festival. And she's been an asset at the store. Check out those displays."

The left side of Jonah's mouth lifted. "Yeah, Bronte and I commented on them when we arrived at the store. We both said there was no way Ollie did that." Jonah's warm eyes caught hers. "From what I remember, you never let anything stop you once you put your mind to it."

"Thanks, Jonah, that's very kind of you to say." Eliza turned to

Bronte. "I know this isn't the time nor the place, but if you have time next week, I'd like to discuss the publicity campaign for your upcoming release that we talked about at Candace's retreat."

Hand on her hip, Bronte frowned. "Girl, how did you have time to work on my stuff when you had all of this going on? Yes, let's get together once things settle down here. I'm so glad she invited me even though I'm not one of her authors." She reached out and touched Oliver's arm. "I'm so sorry for bailing on you." She lifted a shoulder and nodded toward the crowd. "If you want, I could still sign."

Oliver held out his hands. "Of course I want you to sign. We reclaimed the storage room and turned it into a usable space. It was just easier to put the authors in there and allow people to still mingle in the rest of the bookstore."

"Okay, great. Let me get set up, and then we can do this." She looked at Jonah. "You don't mind, do you, babe?"

"Of course not. I love seeing my woman in action."

Oliver looked at Eliza. "Would you mind showing Bronte where to go while I grab her books out of my office?"

"Not at all." Eliza turned to Kate, who was helping run the register, and handed her the flyers. "Would you mind handing these out to anyone who needs one?"

Kate waved her way. "Go. I've got this."

Eliza made her way through the crowd, then turned back to make sure Bronte was following her.

With her head ducked low, Bronte shouldered her way to Eliza's side and shivered. "Not sure if Oliver told you or not, but I'm not a fan of crowds."

She laid a hand on her friend's arm. "He mentioned it. I'm sorry. It is pretty tight. At least you can hide behind the table in here and use it as a buffer."

They entered the room where Bronte would be signing. Eliza

introduced her to Logan Kingsley, his girlfriend Devin, and the three young children in their care.

Dressed in jeans and a gray sweater over a white collared shirt, Logan extended his hand. "Pleasure to meet you, Bronte."

She took his hand. "Likewise."

Devin nearly tripped over Logan's chair leg as she shook Bronte's hand. "Oh my goodness, I can't believe I'm meeting B.L. Parker. I love your Pike Sisters series. I've watched the movie several times."

Bronte's cheeks turned a rosy shade. "Thanks so much. That means a lot. And I can't believe I just shook hands with Victor Holt. You've taken the fantasy world by storm."

Logan laughed, his blue eyes bright. "I don't know about that, but thank you. It's nice to hear."

Logan excused himself and helped Eliza move Bronte's cloth-covered table in place. Eliza grabbed a chair and gestured for Bronte to have a seat. "We bought special pens for signing the books—they won't bleed through the pages. I'll go grab them out of Oliver's office and see if he needs help with your books."

Eliza made her way out of the signing room and found a pocket of space next to one of the bookcases. She climbed on a round stool she used to access books on the higher shelves of the wall cases and lifted her arms. "Excuse me. May I have your attention? We are excited to share that B.L. Parker has arrived, and she will be signing books after all. As soon as I come back with her pens, we'll start a line to her table."

Eliza climbed off the stool and cringed against the squeals that echoed through the room, but that didn't stop the grin from sliding into place.

They'd done it.

They'd actually pulled off a successful signing. A great way to kick off the festival and revive the bookstore's presence on island.

She hurried down the hall and found a splinter of light spilling from the cracked office door. She reached for the knob, heard talking, and paused. She didn't want to interrupt and started to turn, but then she heard Oliver say her name.

"How's the working relationship going?" Jonah's voice trailed out into the hall.

"She's a godsend, man."

"Glad to hear it."

A grunt sounded from inside, and then Oliver's words were muffled. "... fire her."

Wait. *What?*

Eliza froze as Oliver's last words turned her blood to ice. Her eyes widened as she repeated the words to herself.

Fire her?

"... work with you instead?"

She missed the first part of what Jonah had said.

"... someone else in mind." Then the door clicked shut.

Was he serious?

He had someone else in mind to take her place?

But that didn't make sense. She'd worked her tail off at the store and for the festival.

Didn't he call her an asset not even ten minutes ago? And a godsend just now.

The door opened again, wider this time. "I need to get these books to Bronte, but thanks for listening, man."

"Anytime, Ollie. I'm here for you."

Not wanting to get caught eavesdropping, Eliza scrambled for an escape.

The restroom door opened, and a woman walked out. Eliza hurried to the door and caught it. She rushed inside, slammed the door, and pressed her back against it, chest heaving.

Tears filled her eyes, but she blinked rapidly. She could *not* fall apart now.

Her phone vibrated in her pocket. She fished it out and found the same unknown number that had called earlier. She let it go to voicemail. She wasn't about to take a call while holed up in the restroom.

She pressed an ear to the door, but she couldn't hear any male voices on the other side. She opened it slowly and found the hallway empty. She slid out and hurried to the office. She spied the pens they bought for the signing and grabbed them off her desk.

Her hip bumped her standing desk, knocking it into Oliver's. A picture frame next to his monitor fell over, and she picked it up.

Melody and Oliver wrapped in each other's arms.

The love on their faces so evident.

She bit her lips and put the frame back where it belonged.

Forcing a smile in place, she made her way to Bronte's table and handed her the pens. Jonah stood in front of her table, spine straight and shoulders back, as he worked with Oliver to direct readers to the right tables.

A redheaded woman in her mid-thirties and wearing skinny jeans, boots, a black flowy blouse, and rings on her fingers pushed through the crowd, hurried over to Oliver, and flung her arms around him so quickly that he teetered back. Releasing her, he caught himself, then allowed her to pull him into her embrace.

She said something, but Eliza couldn't catch her words or Oliver's response.

Turning toward Logan, the woman kept an arm around Oliver's waist, and he didn't move away from her. "You're so awesome, Ollie. Thank you so much. I couldn't have gotten this far without you and the time you spent with me. I'm so excited to work with you." She pressed a kiss to his cheek, leaving a very red imprint on his skin.

Ollie?

Who was this woman? And how well did she know Oliver to call him Ollie?

He said something low that made the woman laugh, and a stupid grin crossed Oliver's face.

He was actually enjoying her company.

His confession about Constance King snaked through her head. So not only was he planning to fire her, but reserved Oliver had been spending time with some other girl?

Logan rounded his table and stood between Oliver and the woman. "I'm glad I could connect you two. You're going to love working with Oliver."

"Oh, no doubt about that." The woman shot him a toothy grin and grabbed his chin. "I do already."

This time, Oliver caught her arms. He put distance between them and nodded. "Let's talk later, okay?"

"Absolutely. I'm all yours."

Who *was* she?

Eliza's stomach churned as her chest tightened.

Oliver caught her eye and smiled, but she couldn't muster up a smile in return. Not when his words still echoed inside her head.

He frowned and cocked his head as if to ask if she was okay.

Eliza's stomach lurched, and she pivoted away from them. She struggled to catch her breath, and a wave of dizziness crashed over her.

Feeling overheated, she made her way to the door and pushed past a couple coming inside. She hurried around the back of the building and sat in the shadows on the bottom step of the stairs leading to Bronte's and Oliver's apartments.

The cool night air closed around her, and she shivered against the draft sifting through the trees behind the building. The glow of the streetlights cast irregular shadows across the ground.

Laughter and conversation spiraled from the front of the store, but Eliza couldn't hear anything past the echo of Oliver's words in his office.

. . . fire her . . . someone else in mind.

Her phone vibrated again. She pulled it out, finding another missed call from the same unknown number. Talk about being a persistent caller.

This time, a notification showed a voicemail. She stabbed the button and listened.

"Hello, this is Matt Goodwin from Inspire Media calling for Eliza Quinn. I'd like to discuss an opportunity within my company that may be a good fit for your skills. I apologize for making several calls, but I'm in Port Joseph until Monday. Please call back at your earliest convenience."

Clutching her phone, she buried her head in her arms and battled the emotions warring in her chest.

If Oliver planned to fire her, then what did that mean for their future?

She couldn't date a guy who'd let her go after all she'd done to help the store, the festival, and him.

Was he just using her for the sake of the festival?

Never in a million years would she have compared him to her former fiancé, but if he was truly seeing the redhead on the side while kissing Eliza, then he belonged in the same stupid cheater club.

And if he could replace Eliza so easily as an employee, then what about in his heart too? What was the point of staying on island?

Now that her life was packed in boxes due to next week's move, it would be just as easy to ship them off island and get settled in a new place that she might be able to call home.

Because she wasn't about to find it here.

Not anymore.

Letting out a breath, she tapped on her phone screen, noted the five percent battery life, and tapped the unknown number in her recent calls. Hopefully she had enough juice to make just one call.

That was all she would need.

The phone rang in her ear, and a deep voice answered. "Hello?"

"Matt Goodwin? This is Eliza Quinn. If the opportunity is still available, I'd like to meet and talk. Preferably tomorrow morning, if you can make that happen."

With her heartbeat pounding in her ears, she ended the call, slipped in the back door, grabbed her purse and coat from behind the door, and left the same way she'd gone in.

She dropped her purse on the bottom step and slid her arms into her jacket. As she pulled her hair out of her collar, it caught on the clasp of her necklace. She tried to untangle her hair and felt a pop. The necklace started sliding down her neck.

She caught it before the chain fell down the front of her dress and clutched the Leland blue stone between her fingers. The delicate silver chain with the mottled stone puddled in the palm of her hand with a broken clasp.

She hadn't taken it off since he'd given it to her, keeping it tucked under her shirt . . . as close to her heart as possible. Now she didn't want to wear it again.

Her nose twitched as tears filled her eyes and spilled down her cheeks. She ran a thumb over the smooth surface. Part of her wavered between hurling it into the lake or tucking it into her coat pocket.

She cut through the grass and hurried up Blueberry Boulevard toward Sugar Maple Lane, the cool wind chilling the tears on her face. Fatigue wrapped around her bones.

Since Oliver planned to fire her, he could carry on the rest of the festival without her.

She was done.

Thirty minutes until the book signing ended, and the store was as full as it had been when they unlocked the doors.

Oliver couldn't be more pleased.

Readers snaked around into the kids' room, waiting to check

out. He moved back to the register and helped Kate ring out customers.

He scanned the crowd, searching for Eliza, but didn't see her. Or hear her laugh above the din of conversation.

In fact, he hadn't seen her since they got Bronte settled in place for signing her books.

While he handled a transaction with a customer trying to use a gift card, Oliver leaned over to Kate. "Have you seen Eliza?"

"Not since she handed me the flyers and went to help Bronte."

Strange.

Oliver bagged the woman's purchases and handed them to her. "Thank you and come again."

Jonah came out of the signing room and made his way to the register. He nodded toward the door. "Ollie, got a minute?"

"Sure." Oliver rounded the counter. "What's up?"

Jonah lifted his left arm and snapped his fingers twice. "Excuse me. May I have your attention, please?"

The buzz of conversation quieted.

Jonah looped his arm around Oliver's shoulders. "I'm Jonah White, and this is my business partner, Oliver Sullivan. We're so glad you could be here tonight and help us kick off this festival and be a part of the bookstore's grand reopening. Oliver's been at the helm while I've been in Germany, so join me in giving him a big round of applause for all that he's done to get the store open and running."

The tips of Oliver's ears felt as if they were on fire. Shaking his head, he lifted his hand, and the clapping died down. "Thanks, Jonah, for that very unnecessary thrust into the spotlight." Oliver clamped a hand on Jonah's good shoulder. "I'm Ollie Sullivan. And Jonah's taught me a lot about partnership. While he's been serving our country, I've been working with a very talented partner who brought a lot of light into the store and helped take this festival deeper and wider than I expected. Let's give it up for the amazing Eliza Quinn."

Oliver put his hands together as he scanned the crowd for Eliza's dark hair. Heat climbed up his neck as the clapping continued, but she didn't come forward. "Eliza? Anyone see Eliza?"

The applause died down as murmuring rippled through the remaining crowd.

His face hot with embarrassment, Oliver pulled out his phone and tapped out a text, his fingers hitting the keyboard a little harder than necessary.

Oliver

____

You okay? Where are you?

He waited for the three dots to appear, but nothing happened. Shoving his phone in his pocket, he blew out a breath and dragged a hand over his face. He shot a look at Jonah. "Sorry, man. It's not like Eliza to disappear like that."

"No worries. I hope she's okay."

"Me too."

The door opened, and his head jerked up.

A petite woman with auburn hair, dressed in a navy pant-suit with a colorful scarf and sunglasses holding back her hair, stepped inside. Spying him, she strolled toward him with arms outstretched. "Oliver Sullivan! What a delight. You're a sight for sore eyes."

"Sally Jo Wilson! How's it going?" Eliza's aunt's designer perfume swirled around him as he returned her hug, then stepped back. "I'm glad to see you made it to the island."

"Yes, thank you so much for sending Cody. Even though I missed the book signing, I'm able to do tomorrow's workshops." Sally looked around. "Where's Eliza?"

"Good question. She was here, but I'm not sure where she went."

"I tried calling to let her know I arrived but didn't get a response. This island and its cell service." She shook her head.

Sally's phone rang from the depths of her bag. "Oh, maybe that's her now." She fished it out and checked the screen, then shook her head. "Sorry, it's not, but I have to take this. I'll be right back."

She headed out the door, phone pressed to her ear.

Once the rest of the readers had made their way out of the shop and crossed the street to Island Pizzeria for the informal mingle, Oliver closed the door and leaned against it.

Logan, Devin, Bronte, and Jonah came out of the signing room, laughing about something.

Oliver held out his hand to Logan. "Thanks, Logan. For everything. We couldn't have pulled this off without you."

"I'm honored to be a part of it."

Oliver gave Bronte a hug. "I'm glad you and Jonah showed up. Thanks for taking good care of him."

"Always, Ollie. Always."

Oliver pulled out his keys and jerked his head to the restaurant across the street. "Let me grab my jacket, then we'll head to the pizzeria."

He strode through the bookstore. Abandoned paper cups and half-finished water bottles littered the tops of the chest-high bookshelves. Lingering scents of perfume mingled with stale coffee. His dress shoe slid on something, and he reached down to pick it up. An abandoned bookmark.

He'd have to come in first thing in the morning and make sure everything was cleaned up before the festival brunch.

While walking down the hall, he dug his phone out again and tapped out another text to Eliza.

Oliver
Heading to the pizzeria.
Want to join us?

He paused a moment, hoping to see three dots.

Nothing.

He tapped on her number and called. Her line rang in his ear, then went to voicemail. He opened his office door, flicked on the light, and tossed the bookmark on his desk. He reached for his jacket behind the door and realized his was the only one there.

Closing the door, he glanced at Eliza's desk. The top was as neat and tidy as it had been earlier in the day. And her tote bag wasn't sitting on her chair where she usually kept it.

She'd left without saying a word.

He slumped against the doorjamb as he tried to process the chill that slithered through him.

Why would she do that? Leave without a word? Especially in the middle of the book signing they'd worked so hard on to be a success.

Jonah's laughter rippled down the hall.

The busyness of the day ground his bones to mush.

Even though he needed to spend time with his friends, his heart wasn't into hanging out with more people.

Not now.

Not when the one person he wanted to see most wasn't by his side.

He didn't want to imagine the worst. But since they hadn't even argued, he fought the fear clawing at his chest. What could've happened to her?

Seventeen

L IKE A LIGHTHOUSE IN STORMY WATERS, THE outside light on the ranch house beckoned like a beacon.

As she drew closer, though, it wasn't just the porch light that lit up the driveway. Lights glowed from the second-floor windows above the porch.

Jared's room.

Eliza quickened her pace as fast as her stupid heels would allow. Before the signing, she'd hitched a ride with Dad, who was heading into town. She'd promised to call if she needed a ride, but after the disasters that just occurred, she didn't want to see or talk to anyone.

She just wanted to burrow under her covers and pretend the last ninety minutes hadn't happened.

Too late for that.

The images were burned into her brain, and she wouldn't forget Oliver's words of betrayal for as long as she had breath in her lungs.

She pushed through the door, raced across the nearly empty living room, and hurried up the steps. At the top of the staircase, she found Jared's room open, light spilling out into the hall, and laughter.

Laughter?

She ran down the hall and stood in her brother's doorway. The blue-and-white pinstriped wallpaper had been stripped of photos, Jared's music awards and ribbons, and his first guitar that had been above his bed since he was in high school.

The nightstand had been pushed to the other side of the room, next to a stack of taped boxes sitting by the door. And the guitar-shaped lamp, black digital alarm clock, and the framed photo that had sat on Jared's nightstand for years were missing.

Mom stood in front of his dresser, removing clothes and stacking them neatly in boxes on the stripped bed. Sadie sat on the floor and removed books from Jared's shelf.

"What are you doing?" Sobs clawing at her throat, Eliza strode into the room and stabbed the top of the empty nightstand. "Where's the picture?"

"What picture?" Mom's head jerked up, a stack of Jared's shirts in her hands.

"The one of Jared and me wearing cowboy hats and sitting on Gus and Ginger." She jabbed a finger toward the empty indentations in the carpet next to the bed. "It was on his nightstand."

Eliza moved to the boxes by the door and pulled back the tape. It contained trophies that used to sit on top of his dresser. She removed it and carried it back to the dresser, placing it on top.

"Eliza, what are you doing?"

"That's where it belongs." She pulled a stack of clothes from the box and carried them back to Jared's dresser.

Mom grabbed on to her arm. "Eliza, stop."

"No, Mom. It's not right. We can't just pack up his life and give it away like it doesn't matter."

"Doesn't matter? What are you talking about?" Tears filled Mom's eyes as she took the clothes back out of the dresser and placed them in the box. "Of course Jared's life mattered. But we are moving and need to pack up this room."

"*His* room, Mom. Not 'this room.'" Eliza's voice rose and bounced off the empty walls.

Sadie's eyes widened as she added more books to the box at her side. She pushed to her feet and hurried out of the room.

Still wearing her coat and with her purse smacking her in the side, Eliza dropped to the floor and scooped the books out of the box. A couple slipped under her arm as she cradled the rest to her chest.

Tears trailed down her cheeks. She lifted the books to her nose, breathing in her brother's scent that remained in his closed room long after he passed.

Mom sat next to Eliza and wrapped her arms around her. "Honey, what's going on?"

"His life is being packed away. Clothes given to someone else."

"El, honey. Jared is gone. As much as it breaks my heart all over again, we have to face the facts. He's in heaven and not coming back. If someone can be blessed by wearing his clothes or sleeping in his bed, then who are we to stand in the way of that? Jared will live forever in our hearts. We have our memories of him that we can take out anytime we want."

"It's just not fair."

"Of course it isn't fair. Life isn't always fair. I can't tell you how many times I've said the same thing. He was my firstborn and my only son. A day doesn't pass without me remembering him or missing him. So it's not fair for you to say I'm packing away his life like it doesn't matter. Because it does matter. He matters. And it breaks my heart to do this." Mom's voice broke as she covered her face with her hands.

"I'm sorry, Mom." Eliza wrapped her arms around her mother. "I'm so sorry."

They held each other and cried. Feeling drained and with a

headache brewing at the base of her skull, Eliza dried her eyes with the backs of her hands, smearing her makeup. She blew out a breath and braced her forehead.

Mom stood, rustled around in one of the boxes, returned to her spot next to Eliza on the floor, and handed her something. "Here. This was in the box I planned to give you. It had a couple of Jared's T-shirts you used to borrow, this photo, and a few other things."

Eliza looked up and reached for the framed photo she'd had a meltdown over just moments ago. She traced her brother's face with her finger.

"What's going on, honey? That was completely unexpected."

Heat warmed Eliza's cheeks as she replayed her outburst in her head. "I'm sorry."

"Honey, you don't need to apologize. I'm just confused. It's not like you."

Fresh tears burned Eliza's gritty eyes. "I'm getting fired."

"Fired? Where did you get that idea?"

"From Oliver. I heard him." She explained about going to the office for pens and overhearing his conversation with Jonah.

"Honey, are you sure you didn't misinterpret what he said?"

Eliza gritted her teeth. "No, Mom. I heard him very clearly."

"Oh, honey, I'm sorry. You really enjoyed your job."

"Much more than I expected. Doesn't matter now. It's over. Tomorrow morning I'm taking the ferry to Port Joseph and interviewing with Matt Goodwin of Inspire Media."

"Inspire Media? That's the first I've heard of this development."

"Aunt Sally set it up. It's someone she knows from Pittsburgh."

Mom dropped her eyes to her hands. "So you're moving back to Pittsburgh?"

Eliza lifted a shoulder. "I don't know what I'm doing yet. Other than you and Dad, there's not a lot keeping me on island without a job." She waved a hand around the room. "And once we move out of here, I need to find my own place."

"I told you—you can move to the cottage with Dad and me."

"That's not my home. It's yours and Dad's."

"I want it to be your home too."

"I don't even know where I belong anymore."

"You belong with the people who love you."

"Honestly, Mom, I thought I could find that with Oliver." She shared about the woman who seemed to be way too familiar with him at the book signing. "No matter how much I did for the bookstore or the festival, it wasn't enough. I'm losing my job, and I'm losing him. Brings back Tim flashbacks."

"Tim was a jerk, and to be honest, your dad and I are glad you didn't marry him. He didn't appreciate you." Mom sighed. "As for Oliver, I will say that does surprise me. He doesn't seem to be the type to lead someone on, especially if he's dating someone else. You need to talk to him and get this straightened out."

"No, I'm not talking to him." Eliza's nose ran, and she reached into her jacket pocket and pulled out a tissue. The necklace fell out onto the floor.

Mom picked it up and held it out to her. "What's this?"

"A necklace Oliver had given me. I was trying to untangle a piece of hair, and the clasp broke." Eliza curled her fingers around the necklace. "I'm not sure what else I could have done to prove my worth for Oliver to keep me around. He called me an asset, then told Jonah he's going to fire me. I just don't get it."

Mom cradled Eliza's face in her hands. "Listen to me carefully. You are smart and funny and beautiful. And you don't have to earn your place in someone's life. Your worth isn't dependent on what you can do or offer others. People love you for your heart."

"Yeah, uh, someone forgot to tell Tim. And now Oliver is having his doubts." Eliza sniffed and dragged the heel of her hand over her eyes.

"Tim was a smug little creep for what he did to you. Forget him. Oliver, on the other hand, is a good man. Something tells me there's more to the story. Feelings have a way of clouding our vision." She reached for the necklace threaded through Eliza's fingers. "May I?"

Eliza dropped it in her hand.

"That's a very pretty necklace. Do you know what this is?"

"Leland blue stone."

"Yes. Did you know it comes from a small fishing village along the shores of Lake Michigan?"

Eliza nodded as she rested her head on Mom's shoulder. "I read the card that was in the box."

"So then you know this is actually a by-product of the iron smelting process. Years of being in the water softened the slag, broke it into smaller pieces. The sharp edges were rounded off and worn away by the elements. Someone decided the discarded waste could be transformed into something beautiful and valued and be given a new purpose, even bringing joy to others." Mom handed her the necklace. "I'd say he cares for you very much to give you a lovely gift like that."

"It's not like it's a gemstone or anything like that."

"No, but what does it mean to you?"

Eliza rubbed her thumb over the stone once again, taking in the nonsymmetrical edges. It wasn't perfect. But neither was she. It had endured for decades. And she would too.

"Okay, so maybe I won't toss it in the lake."

Mom laughed. "I didn't realize you were considering that option." She laid a hand on Eliza's arm. "The necklace can be fixed, sweetie. So can your relationship with Oliver. Question is, do you want it bad enough to try?"

Eliza considered her words a moment. "What does it matter if he doesn't want me?"

"Talk to him. Tell him how you feel. Right now, your relationship is a little like that slag waste. It feels ugly. And raw. But when you truly love someone, you don't just walk away. You stay and fight for what you want. The refinement comes when those sharp edges are worn away and you can experience something beautiful. Together."

Eliza wrapped her arms around her mom. "Thanks, Mom."

"You're welcome, honey." Mom pushed to her feet and held out a hand to help Eliza up. "Get some sleep, my amazing, smart, and beautiful daughter. I'm sure you'll have clarity in the morning."

Eliza pressed a cheek to Mom's temple. "I love you. I hope you know that."

"Always, honey. Always."

Eliza gathered the framed photo, crossed the hall to her room, closed the door, and leaned against it. Then she moved to her nightstand, set the picture next to her lamp, and sat on the edge of the bed, fingering the stone.

Mom was right. She needed to talk to Oliver. She'd do that first thing in the morning. Their conversation would determine if she stayed on island or headed back to Pittsburgh.

Oliver had never felt as alone as he did tonight in his apartment.

He'd tried to stay engaged in the conversation with his friends at the pizzeria across the street, but he was too distracted by his silent phone. He'd sent another text and tried to call, but Eliza still hadn't responded. He'd even texted Dani and asked her to call. She responded that she got Eliza's voicemail and no response to her texts.

Needing some answers to quell the rising panic, he hoofed it up to the ranch, only to learn Eliza was in bed. Sadie had promised to let her know that he stopped by.

Apparently, Eliza didn't have his back as she'd claimed.

And that cut deep.

Now, he sat on the end of his beige couch with his feet propped up and stared at the TV that was still unplugged and sitting next to the stacks of boxes needing to be unpacked.

He'd been so terrified he could've lost her as he'd lost Melody. Now that he knew the truth, did he really want to put himself through that again?

Loving her was too much. Too risky.

With his elbow resting on the arm of his couch, Oliver braced his head. He was dog-tired but still too wired from the rush of adrenaline stemming from the successful signing.

Maybe he'd stream a movie on his laptop. Something that would lull him to sleep. He sat up and looked around for his computer.

Then he remembered he'd left it in his office.

He headed to the door and ran down the back steps in his socked feet. He fished his keys out of his pocket, unlocked the door, and headed for his desk. He swiped his laptop, and as he did, he knocked over the picture of him and Melody.

He set it on top of his laptop and carried both out the door. He locked up and headed back upstairs. Jonah was coming out of Bronte's apartment as Oliver stepped into the hallway.

"Hey, didn't realize you guys were back already."

"We're beat from the flight and everything." Jonah stifled a yawn that punctuated his words.

Oliver strode to his apartment and opened the door. "You probably don't want to come in, then?"

Jonah looked at him a moment, then nodded. "Sure, I can stay for a minute."

Oliver set his computer and photo on the side table, then headed to the fridge and pulled out two waters. He uncapped one and handed it to Jonah, then he uncapped the other and drank a third of the bottle.

Holding the water bottle, Jonah sidestepped the couch and moved to the middle of the room, turning in a slow circle. "Love what you did with the place."

"Thanks. You're welcome to crash here if you don't want to hoof it back to Holland's. I'll even let you have the bed, broken wing and all that." Oliver headed back to the couch.

"Thanks, man, but I promised Holland I'd be back, and my pain meds are at her place." Setting down his bottle, he picked up the picture of Oliver and Melody. "Man, she was something, wasn't she?"

"She was one of a kind." Oliver pulled a box over and rested his feet on top. "Kept knocking it over on my desk, so I brought it up here."

Jonah set the picture back on top of Oliver's computer and moved to the bookcase. He picked up Melody's copy of *Pride and Prejudice*. "Didn't know you were a Jane Austen fan."

"Melody challenged me to read it. I started it, but . . ."

"What stopped you? You're almost done. Why not read the last few pages and finish it?"

"She died." The two words sliced through him. Bracing his elbows on his knees, Oliver clasped his hands and lowered his head.

"I'm sorry, man. I know it's been rough, but it's time to finish, don't you think?" Still holding the book, Jonah moved to the chair and sat on the edge.

Oliver eyed the hardback with the embossed cover. "What's the point? She's not here to discuss it."

Jonah opened the book to where Oliver had left off. "Like this bookmark, you've been stuck in a chapter you didn't want to be in."

Oliver dragged a thumb and index finger over his gritty eyes.

Stuck.

That was one word for it.

Jonah replaced the bookmark and set the book on the cushion next to Oliver. "I don't think Melody would want you to stay in that place. Maybe it's time to see how the story ends."

"The guy gets the girl, and they lived happily ever after."

"And you didn't get your happy ending." Jonah picked up his

water bottle and took a swig. "After that oxygen canister exploded, we were thrust in darkness, struggling to catch our breath. Took a while for the air to clear and to be rescued. I haven't lost a spouse or a child, but I have lost buddies in the name of freedom. Lost patients on the table who should've lived long and healthy lives. Grief's a bit like being trapped in darkness, trying to feel your way out."

"It's suffocating."

"Yep, sure is. But you can take a breath. And step toward the light. Love is worth the potential heartache." Jonah exchanged his water bottle for the photo of Oliver holding Melody. "Could you imagine your life without Mel? Would your life be better if she'd never existed, or if you'd never fallen in love with her?"

Oliver shook his head.

"You're a better man for loving her. God can use our pain for good in our lives. Mel will always be a part of your story." Jonah placed a hand on Oliver's shoulder. "Finishing the book doesn't change that, but it will give you closure and allow you to start a new chapter."

Oliver blinked several times as he considered his friend's words and cast a side-eye at the book.

"One page at a time." Jonah pushed to his feet. "Did you hear from Eliza yet? I noticed you checking your phone several times at the pizzeria."

Oliver shook his head and leaned against the couch. "I have no idea what's going on with her."

"Talk to her in the morning, and work things out." He rubbed his right arm. "Pain meds are wearing off, so I'm going to head out. I'll see you tomorrow."

"Thanks, man. So glad you're okay." Oliver stood, held out a fist, and Jonah hit it.

He closed the door behind his friend, then dropped on the couch. He picked up the photo and stared at Melody's beautiful face. His throat tightened as his eyes filled. He traced her belly with his finger. "I loved you, you know. Both of you. I wanted to grow old with you, Mel. Why'd you have to take that lesson? We'd still be together if you'd just listened to me. But, as usual, I couldn't say no to you." His chest shuddered as a tear leaked out the corner of his eye. He ran a hand under his nose.

Closing his eyes, he leaned his head against the back of the couch and allowed the tears to drift down the sides of his face and pool in his ears.

He imagined they were back in the field where they'd had the picture taken. Standing with her back to the sun, Melody wore her cherry-printed dress with matching lipstick, the light behind her creating a halo around her. Instead of having a swollen belly, she held a baby wrapped in a pink blanket. Try as he might, he couldn't focus in on the baby. Her face remained blurry, but Oliver had no doubt Melody was holding their daughter. The daughter he didn't have an opportunity to hold, to love, to read to. Smiling brightly, Melody lifted her hand and waved, and then she turned and walked toward the setting sun.

"No! Come back!" Oliver's own shouts startled him, and he jerked from his place on the couch. A little bleary-eyed, he glanced around the room.

Had he fallen asleep?

Was it a dream?

He closed his eyes, hoping to recapture the beautiful vision, but all he saw was darkness.

Oliver dragged a hand over his face, picked up the book, and followed the marker to chapter fifty-four where he'd left off.

Melody's bookmark with her favorite verse—Deuteronomy 31:8:

The Lord himself goes before you and will be with you; he will never leave you nor forsake you. Do not be afraid; do not be discouraged.

How many times had she quoted that verse to him? That was the last thing he'd heard before she took off for her lesson.

Oh, Ollie. I'm going to be just fine. Remember—the Lord goes before me and will be with me. He won't leave me nor forsake me. I'm not afraid, so you shouldn't be either.

His sweet Melody was fearless because of her faith.

"But He wasn't with you, Mel. He took you instead of bringing you back to me. How can I trust a God who would do something like that?"

His eyes welled up again. The book slipped out of his hand, and he caught it. A piece of paper drifted to the floor. He picked it up and found a note written in his wife's beautiful script.

My sweet Ollie, for an editor, you are severely undereducated, but I love you all the same. Jane Austen is my favorite author, and she reminds me of you. You both have wit and see people for who they are and still love them. Enjoy this book so we can have educational conversations. You know I'm teasing. Oh, and I read this verse in my Bible reading this morning, and it reminded me of you: Psalm 45:1—Beautiful words stir my heart. I will recite a lovely poem about the king, for my tongue is like the pen of a skillful poet. Whatever you speak, my sweet Ollie, comes from your heart.

May God's love and His Word stir your heart. I love you forever. Mel

Clutching the note in his hand, Oliver's head fell against the top of the cushion.

I will never leave you nor forsake you. Do not be afraid. Do not be discouraged.

He pushed off the couch, strode to the door, and opened it. He headed down the hall and stepped out onto the stairs.

Darkness had fallen, tucking the island in for the night, but millions of stars glittered across the midnight sky.

The cool air whisking off the lake curled around him, sending a shiver through him, but Oliver remained rooted to the landing. He gripped the weathered wooden railing as he kept his face to the heavens.

"God, it hurts."

I will never leave you nor forsake you. Do not be afraid. Do not be discouraged.

"Why did You allow this to happen to me?"

I will never leave you nor forsake you. Do not be afraid. Do not be discouraged.

"How do I know You'll have my back?"

I will never leave you nor forsake you. Do not be afraid. Do not be discouraged.

Fingers tightening on the railing, Oliver hung his head, his chin trembling. "I'm sorry. Sorry for doubting You. Sorry for harboring pride that I know better than You. Pride for feeling responsible for Melody's death. Forgive me. Help me to trust You to have my back."

Wind stirred through the trees and blew across his face. Oliver breathed deeply, feeling more peace than he had in a long time.

He returned to his apartment and closed the door. Grabbing a pillow off his bed, he headed back to the couch and balled it under his head. He stretched out, picked up the book, opened to chapter fifty-four, and began to read.

> As soon as they were gone, Elizabeth walked out to recover her spirits; or in other words, to dwell without interruption on those subjects that must deaden them more.

Eighteen

OLIVER NEEDED COFFEE.

He'd woken up with a crick in his neck and *Pride and Prejudice* closed on his chest.

After three years, he'd finished the book.

And Jonah was right—it was time to begin a new chapter.

And that would start with heading up to the 3Q Ranch and finding out what was going on with Eliza.

Sunlight poured through the bare windows and flooded his apartment in light. He rolled off the couch, scrubbed his hands over his face, and picked up the book that had fallen on the floor.

He reached for the framed photo, carried both into his bedroom, and set them on the top shelf of his empty closet and closed the door.

After a hot shower that worked out the knots in his neck, a fresh shave, and dressing in jeans, an Island Bookstore hoodie, and his favorite Converses, he jogged down the back steps, rounded the building, and headed down the street toward Good Day Coffee.

With blue skies and plenty of sunshine, even the wind shuffling between the buildings felt warmer.

The Bookish Brunch was happening soon, so maybe he'd find Eliza there with her favorite chai and caramel-frosted cinnamon roll.

Just thinking about it made his mouth water.

Whistling, Oliver shoved one hand in his pocket and waved to the unfamiliar faces crowding the sidewalks.

Yes, the festival was going to be a success.

His phone chimed. He stopped in front of Smith's Hardware, fished it out, and found a text from Eliza.

Eliza

We need to talk.

Four words. That was it.

His heart stuttered. What did that mean?

Oliver

Where are you?

Three dots appeared, stopped, then reappeared.

"Oliver!"

He jerked his head up and found Mrs. Quinn jogging toward him. He bridged the distance in several long-legged strides and reached her. "Good morning."

Shaking her head, she waved away his words as she caught her breath. "We don't have time for that. You need to get down to the docks and stop my daughter from making a big mistake."

"Docks? What's she doing there?"

She gestured toward the direction of the mainland. "She's going to Port Joseph for a job interview."

"Job interview? But she has a job."

"Apparently, not for long, according to her." Mrs. Quinn's brows met as lines deepened in her forehead. "Normally I wouldn't interfere in her life, but I think she's making a mistake. The ferry leaves in five minutes, so you need to hurry."

"Thanks, Mrs. Q." Shoving his phone back in his pocket, Oliver pressed a kiss to her cheek, then raced down the street toward the docks.

Chest burning and arms pumping, he dodged people on bikes, a horse-drawn taxi, and someone chasing after their dog.

The final departure horn blasted, scaring a flock of seagulls. Noah Rampart, one of the ferry workers, untied one of the anchoring ropes. White AirPods in his ears, his head bobbed in time to whatever he was listening to.

Oliver cupped his hands around his mouth. "Noah!"

The ferry crept away from the dock. "No! Stop! Wait! Stop!"

Oliver kicked off a shoe and whipped it at the bow. It bounced in front of Noah, then dropped into the water and sank out of sight.

Noah's head jerked up. Frowning, he pulled out an AirPod and thrust out his arms. "Oliver? What are you doing, man? Have you lost your mind?"

Oliver waved his arms. "Stop the boat. I need to get on."

Shaking his head, Noah lifted his arms, then dropped them. "Too late!"

"I need to talk to Eliza."

Noah held his thumb and pinky to his ear. "Call her."

Oliver rushed to the end of the dock and tried to calculate just how far he'd have to jump to catch the edge of the ferry. If he missed, though, he wouldn't just look like a fool—he'd end up soaking wet and probably injured. The lake was probably a balmy fifty degrees.

The ferry chugged through the water, heading away from the island.

Jumping was no longer an option.

Blowing out a breath, he dragged both hands through his hair as heat scalded his throat and cheeks.

He was too late.

He turned to head back to the bookstore and found a crowd had gathered to watch his stupid antics.

Perfect. Absolutely perfect.

He pushed through the crowd, ignoring the looks of pity, twitters, and stupid comments.

So much for a fresh start.

Eliza had left without a word, ignoring her commitment to the festival and to him.

Whatever they had would now be nothing more than a memory.

But Oliver couldn't give in to that hopeless feeling. God promised to have his back, and Oliver needed to trust Him.

Now more than ever.

Eliza couldn't do it. She couldn't get on the ferry with too many unsaid things between her and Oliver.

After helping Mom finish packing up Jared's room, she'd crawled into bed and collapsed after the wave of emotions from the evening crashed over her.

She'd cried herself to sleep and woken up to sunlight streaming into her room. Realizing she hadn't charged her phone, she plugged it in and dragged herself off to the shower.

Last night, meeting with Matt Goodwin had seemed like the right idea. But after taking time with her appearance, she'd gone into the kitchen and found Mom sitting at the table, her Bible open in front of her.

Even though Mom tried to talk her out of getting on the ferry, Eliza was determined to follow through with the interview.

That was until she headed toward the marina and found the

multiple texts and calls from Oliver. And even a couple from Dani. Listening to Oliver's voicemails slowed her steps, then redirected her to the bookstore.

She'd expected to find him there, but when she unlocked the door, the place was empty. She dropped her things on the counter, grabbed a trash can, and started cleaning up the discarded cups and water bottles.

She took out the trash then washed her hands.

As she headed for the front of the store, the front door opened. Oliver stepped inside.

Her heart tumbled. She clasped her hands together. "Got a minute?"

Without responding, he strode across the room to her and gathered her to his chest, his arms constricting around her. "Thank God you're okay."

His breath warmed her neck.

She wanted nothing more than to stay in his arms, but they needed to settle things before she did something stupid like kiss him.

She pressed her hands against his chest and took a step back, forcing him to release her. Closing her eyes a moment, she filled her lungs with air, then blew it out slowly. She opened her eyes. "Are you firing me?"

Something flicked in his eyes as he pocketed his hands and squared his shoulders. "I considered it."

Those three words rippled through her. Clenching her jaw, she nodded, moved to the counter, and gathered her jacket and purse.

She'd missed the ferry for nothing.

His hand shot out and his fingers wrapped around her wrist. "Wait."

She looked at his fingers, and he loosened his grip. With a gentle tug, he pulled her toward him. "Do you want to know why?"

His voice, soft and tender, did little to help with the emotions she tried to hold back so she wouldn't fall apart in front of him. She shook her head. "I don't get it, Oliver. I've done nothing to deserve this kind of treatment. I've been a great employee. You even called me an asset. Then I heard you tell Jonah that I was a godsend."

"I had to fire you so I could do this." Oliver cupped her face in his hands and captured her lips with his as he pressed his forehead against hers. "I can't go around kissing my employees."

She grabbed his hands, quite sure he could hear her heart hammering against her rib cage. "You just did. Technically I'm not fired yet."

Oliver caressed his thumb across her cheek. "Eliza Quinn, you're fired."

"Good. Didn't like the job so much anyway." Smiling, she wrapped her arms around his neck and pulled him close.

"You burst into my store, threw open the curtains, and brought light into my life. And now I can't live without you."

"And I don't think you should." She laughed and looked at his feet. "Oliver, where's your shoe?"

He gripped the back of his neck as scarlet stole across his cheeks. "Um, I threw it at Noah."

"You what?"

He told her what happened, and she threw her head back and laughed. "You're a knucklehead."

"I'm your knucklehead, if you'll have me." He reached for her hand.

Then she sobered and put some distance between them. She couldn't think straight with Oliver so close. "Who was the redhead hanging on you last night at the signing?"

"Redhead." Then recognition seemed to dawn as he sighed. "She's a writing friend of Logan's who hired me to read through her manuscript."

"She looked like she wanted more than your editing skills."

Oliver raised an eyebrow and took a step toward her, a smile tugging on his lips. "Were you jealous?"

Eliza crossed her arms. "I was mad. I thought you were leading me on while hanging out with another woman."

The grin dropped from Oliver's face. "Thanks for the trust."

Eliza scoffed. "Trust. Seriously? Why didn't you tell me about her?"

"I would have if you hadn't disappeared. I would've introduced you to her . . . and her husband—who, I promise you, is much bigger than I am. Jolene was just expressing her appreciation." Oliver moved closer and trailed a finger down the side of her face. "Is that why you left?"

Eliza dropped her gaze to her feet. "I was stunned by what I'd heard you tell Jonah, then I saw that woman, remembered what you'd shared about Constance, and . . ." She lifted her arms and dropped them. "I felt replaceable and jumped to conclusions. I'm sorry. I'm sorry for leaving. And not trusting you. I guess I have my own issues with that as well."

He framed her face with his strong hands. "It's because of that situation with Constance that I determined I needed to fire you. I don't want anyone, including myself, compromising my integrity."

Eliza slid her hands into her pockets. Her fingers touched plastic. "Oh . . ." She pulled out a small plastic bag and held it in her hand. "I broke the necklace."

He took it from her, opened the bag, and emptied it into his hand. He looked at the broken clasp, then back at her. "Looks like it can be fixed. Question is, do you want it?"

"Actually, I considered throwing it in the lake."

"Why?"

She lifted a shoulder. "Because it reminded me too much of you. Even though I considered it as I walked home last night, I couldn't have gotten rid of it."

Oliver held the necklace up and caught the light pouring

through the front display window. It glinted off the stone. "When I saw it, I thought it was beautiful and unique . . . and it made me think of you."

"My mom reminded me that it's more than a pretty stone. It was a waste product transformed into something worthwhile, something that brings joy to others." She lifted her eyes to his. "Kind of like relationships. Rough around the edges. Sometimes broken. But with enough care, they're still beautiful and worth keeping. I'm sorry I left last night without telling you."

"I'm sorry you overheard me telling Jonah I had to fire you." He brushed her hair away from her face. "If you'd stayed a little longer, you would've heard me tell him that I'd fallen in love with you. I don't deserve you. Or even us. But I will do my best to protect what we have, if you'll let me. I think part of me had gotten so wrapped up in what could be with you that I got a little scared. I didn't just care about you. I realized I was feeling things I hadn't felt in years."

Feeling so much braver and more secure than she did when walking out the door last night, Eliza pressed a finger to Oliver's lips. "No more regrets. No more bringing up our past mistakes. It's time to move forward. I love you, Oliver Sullivan. I love your passion for story. I love the way you make me laugh. I love your integrity. I'll leave the bookstore so we can see where this relationship goes."

"Not necessary." He wagged a finger between them. "I realized our relationship is different. You're different. I can't allow past mistakes to cloud future decisions. I want you to stay if that's what you want. We'll be partners in the store and outside of it. I love you too, Eliza Quinn. I have some stuff to work through and don't want to hurt you again. I need to fix what's broken, starting with my faith."

"We'll do it together—one link at a time."

Oliver trailed a finger along the curve of Eliza's face. She closed her eyes as she leaned into his touch. She opened them and found a softness in his eyes that she hadn't seen in a while. Gone was the doubt. The pain. The guarded expression. What he shared with her looked real, raw, and . . . hopeful.

"I missed you too." Her voice came out in a whisper, almost as if she were afraid to break the fragile reconciliation between them.

The corner of his mouth lifted, and her pulse jumped.

Oliver set the necklace on the counter, then cradled her face in his hands. He lowered his head and kissed her. Slowly. Deliberately. His fingers slid through her hair, then curled around her back, drawing her close to him.

She gripped his shoulders as she anchored herself in his gentle strength.

He ended the kiss, then touched his forehead to hers. She spanned his chest with her hand, feeling the rapid beating of his heart against her palm.

"Who knew the bookstore owner was quite a kisser?"

He laughed softly, a warm sound that melted all of her doubts and washed away her fears. "If you need more proof, I'm up to the challenge."

"Yes, I think I do. I like kissing you, Ollie. Sorry—Oliver."

Oliver caressed her cheekbone with the pad of his thumb. "Eliza?"

"Yeah?"

"Call me Ollie."

She opened her mouth to reply, but he silenced her with another kiss, proving his skills once again. Thorough. Confident. And oh so convincing.

Epilogue

SOMEHOW, OLIVER NEEDED TO KEEP HIS ATtention on his baby sister, who stood in the gazebo at the Grand with her about-to-be husband as they recited their vows in front of most of the island.

Problem was, Eliza hadn't been kidding when she said her dress would knock his socks off.

When she arrived on the grounds of the Grand for Dani's wedding, he nearly swallowed his tongue.

The soft green dress clung to her waist, then flared into a high-low hem, as she called it, and fluttered around her very shapely legs every time she moved.

The color complemented her brown eyes, and her hair was piled high on top of her head in a mass of curls with some strands framing her face. Every time he looked at her, he forgot to breathe. All he could think about was kissing the soft curve of her neck.

Standing between James and Zachary as groomsmen, he tried to keep his expression neutral and his attention where it needed to be.

White chairs stretched in rows under the large white tent in front of the gazebo, nearly every one filled with family and friends. The whole island had turned out to celebrate their island sweetheart getting her deserved happily ever after.

Still, his gaze kept drifting, and his eyes connected with Eliza's, and her smile deepened.

As if his heart wasn't a puddle enough. Watching Dani and Liam had already tugged at all his emotions.

He forced himself to focus.

Despite the temperature being only in the low fifties, Dani wore a strapless white gown that emphasized her tall, willowy figure. Her hair was up—something she didn't often do. Her veil hung halfway down her back and was secured with some sort of tiara or clip.

Oliver's gaze shifted to his parents sitting on either side of the aisle. Dad sat with his back straight against the white chair, his light gray tailored suit fitting him well. Mom wore a pink lace dress with a sheer jacket, looking as elegant as always. Her auburn hair had been pulled back into a low knot at the base of her neck.

Pastor Arnie Chamberlain lifted his voice. "By the power vested in me by the state of Michigan, I now pronounce you husband and wife. You may kiss your bride."

Liam slid his arms around his new wife and drew her close while Oliver's infantile brothers whistled and the guests clapped.

"May I be the first to introduce you to Mr. and Mrs. Liam Stone!"

Liam took Dani's hand and led her down the gazebo steps across the petal-strewn fabric runner.

Oliver blinked back an unexpected sting of tears. A memory of his own wedding day surfaced, but he tucked it away. Today wasn't about taking a walk into the past.

It was about new beginnings.

Jonah had been right—his sweet Melody, who'd once held so

much of his heart and would always have a place in it, would want him to be happy.

Finishing the book and being able to turn his apartment into a home was the therapy he needed.

Now he'd focus on Eliza and growing his relationship with her, building that trust between them one day at a time.

He looked at her, his next chapter. And he wanted to write it slowly and deliberately with her.

A couple of hours later, chandeliers threw sparkles of light against the rose-patterned walls in the Rose Room. Laughter and the clinking of silverware against plates and glasses filled the air.

Once the dinner plates had been cleared, the DJ switched from soft dinner music to the bride and groom's first dance.

As soon as their song ended and the DJ switched to songs that would fill the dance floor, Oliver excused himself from the bridal table.

He wound his way through the linen-covered round tables and stopped where the Quinn and Hudson families sat, passing his parents seated together. Dad had his back to Mom while he talked with Doug Manning, and Mom talked with Aunt Elise.

Oliver shook his head at his sister's bravery in forcing them together.

The DJ started playing "Just the Way You Are," by Bruno Mars, and he held his hand out to Eliza. "May I have this dance?"

She set her napkin next to her plate and smiled at him. "Sure."

He guided her to the dance floor. Finally, after what seemed to be an eternity, he could hold her in his arms. "It's about time."

Her hand fit so perfectly in his as her arm slid around his waist. "Behave. This is Dani's special day."

Pulling her closer, he wrapped both arms around her and sang along with the song for her ears only.

She shivered lightly, which caused him to grin. He liked the effect he had on her.

As soon as the song ended, he took her hand and guided her through the open heavy doors, through the hotel lobby, and onto the Grand's expansive wraparound porch.

Evening sunlight spilled across the manicured lawn and turned the impressive gardens to gold. Gentle waves lapped against the rocky shore and competed with the music coming from the hotel. The lake darkened as the sun sank lower in the dusky sky.

"Making a run for it already?"

Oliver glanced over to his three brothers lounging against one of the tall white columns, jackets and ties loosened and hands in their pockets.

"Just getting some air."

With his hand still at Eliza's back, he ignored his brothers, who were talking to his cousin Ethan. He didn't need their heckling right now.

Eliza drew her wrap tighter, rubbing her arms against a breeze that drifted up from the water.

Oliver shrugged off his jacket and draped it around her. She gripped the buttons in one hand. "You don't have to do that. You'll be cold."

"Actually, I'm quite warm. The reception was getting stuffy with all the people in there."

"The sunshine feels great, but that wind is a little cool." Eliza drew his jacket around her. "It was a beautiful wedding. Dani is very popular."

"She *is* the island darling. She's done so much to bring it back to life." He waved a hand toward the hotel. "And what she and Liam have accomplished with the hotel is nothing short of a miracle."

As they reached the rocky shore, another couple walked toward them. Eliza lifted her hand. "Hey, guys."

Sadie held on to Asher's arm as they stepped carefully over the uneven rocks.

"Beautiful song, Ash. Great job." Eliza smiled at her cousin.

Asher looked down at Sadie and touched her chin. "Sadie wrote it. Wanted the words to be perfect for Dani and Liam."

Eliza's chin dropped. "Seriously? *You* wrote their song?"

Sadie's cheeks turned a shade of pink. "It was my gift to them. Ash put it to music, so it was a collaborative effort."

"Both of you did a remarkable job," Oliver said. "How's the new album coming?"

Sadie's smile widened. "Great. We're leaving for Nashville next week to record a new song."

"Wow, that's so great. Congratulations."

"Thanks. And congratulations to the both of you on a very successful festival. It's going to be the talk of the town." Asher gestured toward downtown.

Oliver exchanged looks with Eliza. "Yeah, until the next festival starts."

Sadie shivered and rubbed her arms. Asher shrugged out of his jacket and draped it across her shoulders. "Let's get you back inside where it's warmer."

They waved goodbye and headed back to the Grand.

Oliver jerked his thumb over his shoulder. "Do you want to head back inside too?"

Eliza glanced at the hotel, then back at him. "I don't mind walking a bit more if you don't."

He waved a hand in front of them. "Lead the way."

Eliza stumbled on a rock and Oliver's hand shot out to steady her. He slipped an arm around her waist and drew her to his side. "I wanted to talk to you about something."

"Sure, what's up?" Eliza snuggled in closer.

"Well, with finishing up the festival and rushing into Dani's wedding, we haven't had much time to talk about the future. Mainly your career."

She pulled back and looked up at him. "Don't you mean our future?"

The way she said *our* wrapped around his heart.

"I do." He touched her chin. "If you want to take the job with Inspire Media, I'll support you one hundred percent. I wouldn't be able to leave the island until Jonah finishes his tour, but I'd do what I could to make sure we continued to see each other on a regular basis."

Eliza laid a hand alongside his cheek. "I'm not taking that job, Ollie."

"You're not?"

"No. Matt's a nice guy and all, but when I called and said I couldn't meet with him yesterday, I didn't like the way he pressured me with his limited-time offer. I want to work for myself and set my own hours."

"Oh, thank God." Oliver reached for her again and twirled her around. "That makes my next thought much easier."

"Now I'm definitely intrigued."

"The storage room that we cleared out for the book signing? What if we turn it into a community space? For book clubs and literary-type events. Maybe add in some comfortable chairs and a small coffee bar. Not competing with Jill, by any means."

"I love it. What does Jonah think about it?"

Oliver rubbed his jaw. "I haven't asked him. Just got the idea this morning, but I don't think he'll care."

Jonah, in full military dress that matched his blue sling, holding hands with Bronte, who wore a long-sleeved royal blue dress, walked toward them.

"Now's your chance."

As they approached, Oliver lifted a chin. "Hey, guys. What's up?"

Jonah looked at Bronte like she was the only person on the beach, then he shifted his attention back to them. "So, we have something else to ask."

"Sure, what's that?"

"How would you like to be my best man?"

Oliver blinked. "Your what?"

Jonah grinned like a fool. "We're getting married tomorrow after church with just family. Bronte and I aren't crazy about the distance between us. Since we've been talking about marriage lately, we decided, why wait?"

Bronte rested her head against Jonah's shoulder. "My best friend's on the last ferry to the island and will arrive soon. She's going to be my maid of honor."

Happy for his friend, Oliver nodded and smiled. "I would be honored to be your best man."

Jonah let go of Bronte's hand and clapped Oliver on the back. "Thanks. I knew you'd be there for me."

"Always."

"One more thing." Jonah and Bronte exchanged looks. "I'm cutting my medical leave in the States short, and Bronte's going back to Germany with me for the remaining months of my tour. We'll take the rest of my leave and get her settled into base housing. Holland's going to store her things until we return."

Bronte turned to Eliza. "So my apartment's going to be available. It's yours if you want it."

Eliza's eyes lit up. "Seriously? It would be a short walk to work."

"Speaking of work . . ." Oliver looked at Eliza. "Eliza and I will be starting our own businesses. She's going to be an author marketing consultant, and I'm going to take on some freelance editing in addition to running the store."

"I love that place." Eliza pressed a hand to Oliver's cheek. "After all, it brought me to you."

"Whatever you want to do is fine with me. I trust you completely." Jonah reached for Bronte's hand. "Well, we've taken up enough of your time. See you tomorrow."

As they walked away, Eliza sighed. "That's so romantic."

"Walking on the beach?"

"Choosing love over distance." She looked at the water, then turned back to him. "Would you want that again? Marriage? Family? Someday, I mean?"

"Yes. Someday." He whisked her hair off her face, lifted her chin, and brushed his lips across hers. "I think this is the beginning of a beautiful story for us. Let's write it together, one page at a time."

"I'd love that." She rested her head against his chest.

With his arms still around Eliza and hope for their new beginning rising steadily in his heart, Oliver could finally trust the One writing every chapter of their future.

Bonus Epilogue

Thank you for reading *Find Me in the Story*. We hope you loved this story. Find out what happens next for Eliza and Oliver with a Bonus Epilogue, a special gift, available only to our newsletter subscribers.

This Bonus Epilogue will not be released on any retailer platform, so scan the QR code to get your free gift. You acknowledge you are becoming a Sunrise Publishing and Lisa Jordan subscriber. Unsubscribe from any newsletter at any time.

Thank You

Thank you so much for reading *Find Me in the Story*. We hope you enjoyed the story. If you did, would you be willing to do us a favor and leave a review? It doesn't have to be long—just a few words to help other readers know what they're getting. (But no spoilers! We don't want to wreck the fun!) Thank you again for reading!

We'd love to hear from you—not only about this story, but about any characters or stories you'd like to read in the future.

Contact us at www.sunrisepublishing.com/contact.

Jonathon Island

Return to Jonathon Island in book 2,
Find Me in the Blooms
by Alyssa Schwarz.

He ran the night before their wedding. She's been running ever since.

Wedding photographer Kate Sullivan has spent five years proving she's fine. Fine with the panic attacks. Fine being the overachieving sister everyone counts on. Fine that Lincoln St. James called off their wedding and disappeared.

She's not fine. But nobody needs to know that.

When her doctor orders a mandatory break, Kate retreats to charming Jonathon Island to help her family with the spring flower festival. Sun. Blossoms. No stress.

Then Lincoln walks back into her life.

The florist hired for the festival is the man who shattered her heart—and he's more gorgeous than ever. Worse? He's looking at her like he still loves her. Like he never stopped.

Lincoln knows he doesn't deserve a second chance. He panicked and ran, terrified of becoming his absent father. But Kate Sullivan was the best thing that ever happened to him, and he's spent five years regretting the night he let fear win.

Now, working side by side among blooming orchards and island magic, the feelings they buried come rushing back. But trust doesn't rebuild overnight—and some wounds run deeper than either of them knew.

Can a runaway groom prove he's finally ready to stay?

One

S PINSTER OLDER SISTERS WEREN'T SUPPOSED to watch their younger sisters ride off into the sunset with Prince Charming. Especially when they were the ones packing up said sister's apartment like the forgotten twin from Cinderella.

Kate Sullivan stood on her toes, her full five feet four inches barely enough to reach the box on the top shelf of the closet. She slowly worked the box forward until it tipped and sprinkled a cloud over her like pixie dust, igniting a coughing fit. Roma, the orange tabby, watched indifferently from her roost on the corner of the bed.

"Careful, wouldn't want to accidentally get too close," she said to the cat, who merely looked at her. "Cinderella's fairy godmother only needed a pumpkin and a few mice. One sprinkle of this stuff and you might end up turning into a stepladder. Or better yet, a tall man with muscles to intimidate these boxes right into the back of Dani's golf cart." A giggle slipped out at the thought as Kate lowered the box to the floor beside her camera case. The soft thud made it sound like it was filled with blankets.

"At least it's not more travel books." They'd need to purchase at least another bookshelf to accommodate her sister's collection. But from the way Liam doted on her, it was obvious he'd build Dani an entire library if that's what she wanted.

Kate stood and observed the sparsely decorated room. Only a few photos remained on the walls—Paris, London, Rome—along with one propped on the nightstand, showing the happy couple at the Grand Sullivan Hotel's groundbreaking last spring.

She was happy for Dani. Proud, actually, of the way she was breathing new life into this island. Their family too. Only a wedding could get their parents to exist in the same room without something burning to the ground. Kate had secretly hoped hers would be the one to reunite everyone, but calling things off the night of the rehearsal dinner had hardly had a positive effect on such a strained family dynamic.

Faint music played from somewhere in the living room. After a moment of searching the couch cushions for her phone, she stood victoriously and tapped the screen. "Hey, Gabby. What's up?" Loud voices filled the background for a few seconds before Gabby finally spoke.

"Kate, hi!" She practically yelled over the other noise. "I know you're probably with your family right now, but I have a few questions on the Clarkson-Smith engagement photoshoot. Do you have a minute? I wouldn't ask, but they want these done as soon as possible, and they want the best. Which is you, by the way. In case there was any question."

Kate chuckled. "For you, anything." It was the least she could do for dumping things on her at the last minute. Not that the doctor had given Kate much of a choice, but leaving her business partner to deal with the early-wedding-season rush alone wasn't her idea of a stress-free vacation.

She waited for her laptop to power up and then navigated to the business's online Photoshop account. "Okay, I'm in," she said, already opening the RAW files. Set against an overcast sky, the muted colors hardly gave off that dreamy, romantic vibe they were known for.

Gabby stayed on the line as Kate softened the highlights and shifted the tone curve to bring a luminous glow back to the couple's smiling faces. A few more tweaks—bumping the peach undertone, brightening the mid-tones, and adding a bit more warmth—and suddenly, the photos looked like stills pulled straight out of the 2005 *Pride and Prejudice* movie.

"Thank you so much, Kate. That would've taken me at least an hour to figure out. They're going to absolutely love these." After a few more questions about an upcoming wedding shoot, she signed off, but not without leaving Kate's spirits more lifted than they'd been in days.

"Jane Austen had it right, Roma. What kind of affection would it create if Dani had to wait to find her happy ending, all because of me? One failed wedding shouldn't ruin it for all the Sullivans." She was bending to thread her fingers through the dense orange fur when a loud knock on the front door sent the animal streaking toward its tower.

Green-gold eyes watched from the shadows, as if the cat somehow knew about her prescribed medical leave and was silently judging her for taking on a new project.

"Don't look at me like that. This is what family does for one another. You know Dani would do the same for me." Sure, staying to photograph the island's flower festival in a few weeks wasn't the same as lying on a beach sipping umbrella drinks. But if anything would make her anxiety worse, it would be having nothing to do for an entire month. Dr. Weston might've been right about her needing a change after her most recent panic attack, but early retirement wasn't the answer.

She was fine. Really. Everyone got a little stressed now and again, right? Besides, she'd been finding ways to cope for years. This time would be no different.

A toothy yawn was Roma's only reply before Kate tugged open the door to the dimpled smile and designer haircut of her new brother-in-law.

"Who were you talking to?" Liam's chocolate eyes sparkled with mischief as he peered into the empty apartment. Crazy to think this tall man was her new brother-in-law, with his expertly styled brown hair and a watch that probably cost more than her monthly rent back in Petoskey. Yet he'd already fallen into the role of nosy younger brother with ease.

"Just Roma. She might not be the world's best conversationalist, but she's a decent listener once you get past the judgmental stares."

"Tell me about it. A year later and I'm still trying to convince her I'm not stealing Dani away from her." His chuckle was warm and relaxed. Shifting his weight, he cleared his throat, breaking the momentary silence. "Mind if I come in for a minute?"

"Yeah, of course."

Notes of garlic and freshly baked bread wafted from the pizzeria on the ground floor, reminding Kate she'd skipped lunch.

"Everything's still a bit of a mess, but we should have her all moved by tomorrow." That was, whenever her twin brother Oliver returned with the extra cardboard boxes. "Would you like some water or tea?"

Liam shook his head. "This won't take too long. I was actually hoping to ask you something. Although now that I'm here, I'm beginning to wonder if it's such a good idea."

"Oh?" She tried to soften his pensive expression with a smile. If it were Oliver, she'd have teased it right out of him. But she didn't know Liam well enough yet to know if he appreciated space or friendly prying.

"You know how we were planning a weekend honeymoon to Napa?"

Her sister had spoken of little else lately besides the wedding itself. "The Tuscany of America, right?" Short of the actual place, it sounded like the perfect trip for them. Dani had mentioned they were planning a longer one for later in the year, once her workload with all the upcoming festivals was over. A trip that was sure to impress with all of Liam's fancy hotel connections.

He nodded, but the sparkle had left his eyes. "That's what I told her. I wanted it to be a surprise when I gave her the real tickets this morning. For Rome."

"Italy?"

"One and the same."

"That's great, although I still don't see the problem."

His pinched lips said he had one. "The thing is, it's for a few more days than a long weekend."

"Like, a week?"

He winced and bobbed his head side to side. "Plus two more."

Wow, three whole weeks in her dream destination with the man of her dreams. Dani should be knocking down the door to tell Kate the news herself, and instead, Liam was standing there with his hands in his pockets. "What did she say when you told her?"

His flat expression and raised eyebrow seemed to say *You know Dani.*

"Just wait here a sec. I'm going to call her." Kate grabbed her phone from the charging station and punched in the number. Two steps into the bedroom, she heard Dani pick up.

"Hey Dani, this is Kate."

"Yeah, I kinda figured from the caller ID." The humor in her voice fell flat, replaced with a stubborn edge Kate knew well. A grunt, followed by the squeak of moving furniture, and then a moment of silence. "Is Liam over there?"

The crack of vulnerability broke Kate's heart. Only days into their marriage, and they were having their first fight. She reminded herself that it was nothing serious—not like a broken engagement. But the pain was still real, no matter how small the disagreement. A reminder for Kate to tread lightly.

"He is, and he's told me about the trip he's planned for you two. You've wanted to go to Italy forever, and now you're going. No ifs, ands, or buts about it."

Dani sniffed as if she'd been crying. Either that or she'd been wrestling with her own dust-encrusted boxes all afternoon. "What about the Apple Blossom Festival? I'm supposed to organize the vendors, not gallivant across Europe. Not to mention the interview with *American Wanderer*. And with Holly leaving soon for a wedding, we still don't have an event florist. I've called nearly every business in northern Michigan, and they're either too busy or not interested or haven't responded at all. This festival will set the tone for the entire year, which means if it doesn't work out and bring more tourists to the island, the hotel remodel will be for nothing."

Kate softened her voice. "You only get married once." God willing. "It's your right to be happy and make us all insanely jealous by going on an amazing trip."

Dani didn't respond right away, but neither did she argue, which had to be a good sign. For as much as Kate had loved getting reacquainted with her baby sister this past week, no amount of late-night ice-cream runs or family dinners could make up for the years they'd already lost. She wanted to be a good sister, and even more so, a friend. And if that meant seeing Dani off to the ferry herself, that's exactly what she'd do.

"What if I handle things here while you're gone?"

"Did you just volunteer to manage the festival? Don't you have a business to run?"

Which would have been a fair point if not for a stubborn doctor and Oliver's worried tone when Kate had called him from the urgent care clinic in Petoskey last month.

"That's exactly what I'm saying. And it won't be a problem." She coughed into her sleeve to loosen the tightness from her throat. Darn dust allergies.

She could almost hear Dani tapping her foot in thought until . . . "You'd do that, really?"

Success. Kate couldn't help but smile as Liam's gaze locked with hers, realization, then relief washing over his clean-shaven face. The hope in his expression made a different kind of lump form in her throat, one she worked to swallow down.

"What are sisters for? And if that's not enough to convince you, I'd owe you one for letting me take the lead with *American Wanderer*. A mention in a magazine like that could launch my photography business for life." And save her and Gabby from any lost business while Kate was away.

An excited squeal pierced Kate's ear, and she held the phone away.

"You're the best, Kate."

Chest swelling with satisfaction, she pasted on her best poker face before hanging up and rejoining Liam in the kitchen. But one look at his crooked grin had her slipping. "Pack your bags. You're going to Italy."

He jumped from the chair and caught her in a twirl. Giggling as her feet landed back on solid ground, Kate looked up at his sheepish grin. Little brother, indeed.

"Thank you, Kate. Dani's been so focused on everything but herself lately. First with the hotel and now the festivals. This is exactly what she needs."

"Consider it my wedding gift." This was far better than a gravy boat any day. "Just promise to take lots of pictures and eat your weight in pasta and gelato."

"I fully intend to." His warm chuckle filled the space, the weight from earlier visibly gone. He was halfway out the door, presumably to start packing, when he paused and turned. "Some guy's gonna be lucky to find you one of these days, Kate Sullivan." A wink and then he was gone.

The soft click echoed in his absence as surely as his parting comment.

Little did he know, finding a guy wasn't the problem. Lincoln St. James had found her five years ago and sealed their relationship with a promise. But that was before he'd walked out on her the night of their rehearsal dinner, shattering her visions of her own happily ever after.

At least one Sullivan sister would have hers. Kate would make sure of it.

All Dr. Weston had said was to take some time off from work. Which she had. But that didn't mean she couldn't call a few vendors and oversee a meeting or two in her free time until Dani got back.

Sparks rained down on Lincoln as flame and steel met in a ring above his head.

Form and function. Destruction and beauty.

He moved the blue flame across the red surface, touching the beaded wire solder to the final joint. Too little, and the entire frame could snap under the flowers' weight. Too much, and he'd be accused of shoddy craftsmanship.

"Not that a single member of Detroit society would be able to spot the flaw once tipsy on champagne and doing the cha-cha slide," he mumbled to himself.

But he'd know.

If you can't do something right, don't bother. His dad's words flowed uninvited, echoing as the hiss of the flame fell silent. He ripped his goggles off and set them and the torch aside.

The smell of hot metal mingled with roses, delphinium, Sumatra lilies, and the white Duchesse de Nemours peonies he'd ordered specially from a boutique farm near Edwardsburg. With no place for water in the live floral chandelier, he'd have to work fast. Silk flowers would have afforded him more time and flexibility, but they wouldn't catch the attention of the Great Lakes Bloomfest selection committee. They considered only the most exciting and innovative of florists for their yearly showcase.

Fortunately, Felicity had the delivery trucks and phones under control, allowing him to do what he did best.

Starting at the edges, he worked in circles as the halo of green began to take shape. The chocolate Queen Anne's lace came next, followed by hanging tendrils of burgundy amaranthus, as if heaven was extending its blessing over the happy couple. The rest of the flowers would have to wait until he had the floral chandelier suspended from the rafters of the Shinola Hotel's famous Birdy Room—a conservatory of vaulted glass and city views worth the six-figure price tag this wedding surely carried.

The distant chirp of a phone barely cut through the piano music from his Bluetooth speakers, followed by Felicity's melodic voice. His mother's oldest friend and the best assistant he could've ever asked for, Felicity could talk down the most flustered of brides while color-coding the entire year's calendar as if it was nothing more than a church picnic. The day she no longer needed this job was the day he'd close up shop. Just the thought of having to interview for a replacement made his skin itch.

"Mm-hmm, yes ma'am. Yours is the only wedding we have on today's schedule." Her blonde waves bobbed through the open door linking the studio to the back of the flower shop. "I have three thirty on my calendar, but I'll double-check."

Right as the piano piece was about to reach its climax, the volume plummeted. Felicity stood beside the now-silent speakers, her pink-and-lime-green kimono swishing around her knees as her blue eyes lifted from the workbench to the forest above. "My, doesn't that just take your breath away?"

Lincoln grunted his agreement.

An artist at heart, Felicity viewed everything as a miracle. A few more awestruck moments later and she finally spoke. "I have an anxious mother of the bride requesting an update about the arrangements."

"Tell her I'm almost finished here and should have everything loaded and ready to drive over to the hotel within the hour." He twisted another length of wire around a stem before climbing down from the stepladder.

She relayed as much before smiling and ending with enough overly profuse compliments to choke him. Hanging up, she returned her gentle smile to him and the flowers.

"How do you do that?"

"Do what, dear?" A quiet patience threaded her words. He'd have thought it impossible to appear so cheerful all the time had he not known the woman since before he could walk.

"How do you manage to turn every client into a friend? You and Mom always made it look so easy."

She twirled a single blue daisy that he'd set aside earlier between her fingertips, the creases of her forehead softening. "We all have our God-given talents. For some, it's hospitality, while others can make masterpieces out of nothing but fronds and florets."

She made him sound like some horticultural genius. "Mom was the real artist." Elaborate displays were one thing, but she'd had a gift for touching strangers' hearts with her bouquets. Lillian's Lilies had been a real-life Garden of Eden, the true inspiration behind his own flower business, Lily & Stone Floral Designs. If he could honor a sliver of her memory through his work, that would be enough.

"I miss her too. But she'd be so happy with what you've created." Felicity lifted the daisy and placed it in the palm of his scratched and calloused hand. A paltry remembrance of the woman who'd loved them. But a reminder, all the same.

The tiny brass bell dinged above the shop door, signaling an end to their conversation.

Felicity returned to her post inside the shop, taking her smiles and sunny disposition with her.

Lincoln reopened his music app and scrolled to a new playlist, then turned up the tropical lo-fi, the simple melody pushing back April's soggy cityscape as he got to work. He'd just swiped a pair of wire cutters from the bench when a pair of high heels stomped over the music.

He turned in time to see a smartly dressed woman barge in through the studio door with Felicity in hot pursuit.

"Mr. St. James. I need to speak to you immediately." She stopped short of the workbench, scrunching her upturned nose at the scattered mess.

"Mrs. Howard. How can I help you?"

Designer sunglasses perched like a crown on her short hair. Only snatches of sunlight had broken through the past week's drizzle, yet she was dressed like she was headed to a fancy garden party. "You can start by explaining what happened with the flowers for my daughter's engagement party. I specifically ordered apricot roses, not peach. Nora Carmichael already did peach last year for her daughter's wedding. I will not be accused of imitation. And don't get me started on those gaudy vases." She pronounced it *vahses*, casting a disdainful glare in Felicity's direction.

Lincoln felt as if he'd accidentally swallowed a stray spark, but he schooled his mouth into a straight line. "Yes, I remember the order. I had to call over a dozen vendors to find apricot roses in April." He'd done it without complaint, as the Howards were one of the most influential families in Detroit. But now he was beginning to think he should've listened to the rumors before taking her on as a client.

"Well? *Something* went wrong, didn't it?" The woman's burgundy lips dipped at the corners. "If you think I'm going to pay for these, you're mistaken. I expect you to rectify this by tomorrow and refund the money I've already wasted."

The spark grew to a small flame. He clenched his fist around the wire cutters to keep his anger under control despite the rushing in his ears. "Mrs. Howard, I'm sorry you're not satisfied with the arrangements we agreed on." Or had she already forgotten about their meeting last week? "But asking me to drop everything and redo a perfectly flawless order when I have other commitments is unreasonable." Not to mention it would cost him the biggest wedding of the season.

Her gasp was worthy of the stage at Fisher Theater, her mouth opening and closing like a kid playing with a snapdragon. "Of all the insolent, ill-mannered . . ." She huffed, as if remembering Felicity was still there. "Alistair was right. I should have gone with Nora's recommendation instead of taking a chance on some up-and-coming amateur. And don't think I won't be telling my friends to steer clear as well." Her gaze dropped to the table, nose scrunching as she sneered at the blue daisy beside the other exotic flowers. "Any florist who uses *weeds* isn't worth my time."

She turned on her heel and stormed out of the studio. The room fell silent except for the soft beat of the music and the jangle of the bell above the door.

Fire burned the back of his neck, his forceful inhale and exhale doing little to quench his temper.

This was why he didn't work directly with the clients. He couldn't be trusted not to lose his cool. Not only had Mrs. Howard walked away with a veritable steal of apricot roses, but she had the power and influence to make good on her threat.

"She still has the entire order," he said through slowly unclenching teeth.

"Let her keep it," said Felicity with a slight wave of her hand. "I doubt she'll be able to find another option with less than twenty-four hours. Besides, her daughter still deserves a happy day, no matter how difficult her mother might be."

"I sure hope the groom knows what he's getting himself in for," he said with a heavy sigh. An indentation of the wire cutter reddened his palm as he finally set the tool aside, looking up only to see Felicity's frown.

"Children aren't their parents." Her hand rested lightly against his arm. She meant it as reassurance, but all he could hear was his mother's voice making excuses for another of his father's drunken outbursts.

So maybe he wasn't his father, but he might as well be. After all, it was because of them that she was gone.

Acknowledgments

Lord, thank you for the gifts and talents you've given me. May my words honor and glorify you.

Patrick, Scott, and Mitchell—I love you forever. I wouldn't be where I am today without your love and support.

Susie May, thank you for helping me level-up my writing. Your friendship and mentorship are so deeply appreciated.

Thanks to the rest of the Sunrise Publishing team for bringing this book to publication.

Heart, home, and faith have always been important to **Lisa Jordan**, so writing stories with those elements comes naturally. Represented by Cynthia Ruchti of Books & Such Literary Management, Lisa Jordan is an award-winning, PW-bestselling author for Love Inspired and an author and line director for Sunrise Publishing's contemporary romance line, Hometown Hearts. She is also the operations manager for Novel Academy, an online writing academy powered by My Book Therapy. Happily married to her real-life hero for over thirty-five years, Lisa and her husband have two sons. When she isn't writing, Lisa enjoys quality family time, being creative with friends, or getting lost in a good book.

Learn more about her at lisajordanbooks.com.

Welcome to
Redemption, Alaska

Where broken hearts come to heal

PUBLISHERS WEEKLY BESTSELLING AUTHOR

Heidi McCahan

We solve the problem of what to read next.

YOU MAY ALSO LIKE...

When Noah Hebert inherits the struggling Blue Pirogue Inn, he must solve a puzzle left by his grandfather to save it from his family's nemesis, Isaac Bergeron. Teaming up with Elisa Bergeron, the café manager and his rival, they must navigate family feuds—and unexpected sparks—while racing against time.

Where I Found You **by Besty St. Amant**

Grace Howell leaves her life as a ballerina and returns to Heritage, Michigan, to heal. Teaching dance is just a temporary gig, until she finds herself unexpectedly charmed by small-town life and her growing attachment to Seth Warner, a man from her past with a troubled history of his own.

You're the Reason **by Tari Faris**

Dani Sullivan is determined to revive Jonathon Island's fading charm and reunite her fractured family. Her plan? Reopen the Grand Sullivan Hotel. But without the funds to restore the hotel, Dani's forced to accept help from Liam Stone—a big-city hotel developer whose sleek, modern vision is everything she's trying to avoid.

Meet Me at the Grand **by Lindsay Harrel**

We solve the problem of what to read next.

**WHERE EVERY STORY IS A FRIEND,
AND EVERY CHAPTER IS A NEW JOURNEY...**

Subscribe to our newsletter for the latest news, weekly giveaways, exclusive author interviews, and more!

Shop paperbacks, ebooks, audiobooks, and more at
SUNRISEPUBLISHING.MYSHOPIFY.COM